Also by Linnea March

Prevalent Notion Series

Faultless Notion

Treacherous Notion

Ruinous Notion

Seasons of Us

Wren's Winter

Villainous Summer

Second Chance Spring

Other Titles

Reckless Liar

The One You Chose

Second Chance Spring

LINNEA MARCH

To all my soft girls with
glasses and tattoos
and Rusty,
your sweatshirts always fit me
best.

Foreword

This book contains scenes that depict the effects of a fire and the victims of it.

Devin Haruki is a quarter Japanese. I took inspiration from my own niece and nephew who share the same heritage and to her call her grandparents by the nicknames of Baba (short for obaa-san for grandmother) and Jiji (short for ojii-san for grandfather) while this is not a universal experience for all, I have always loved their use of these nicknames.

One

Devin

WHEN THE YELLOW BUTTERFLY landed on my sedan wiper blade, I knew going back home would change me.

All my life, I had a talent of half premonition. While I never knew what would happen, for all the big events of my life, I knew when something was about to change.

At seven, I told my mom to be careful driving, and ten minutes later, she was rear-ended at the grocery store. Upon moving to Eagle Crest Lane, I knew the moment I met Cedar Eden, we would know each other for all our lives.

The night of the bonfire party, at a fresh eighteen, when Cedar sat beside me on the tailgate of his buddy's truck and offered me his ex-girlfriend's sweatshirt, I knew I would kiss him that night. My talent told me to give up dance and take up art, and when I was asked out my that cute guy in my physics class, it told me to stay far away from him.

The day my father died of a heart attack at the young age of forty-six, I was hit with a gut feeling. One moment, I was fixing my shirt to disguise a make-out session with Cedar in his car. The next moment, my mom is standing in the doorway, waiting for me with a shattered expression on her face.

I had seen my mom sternly talking down real estate agents, had seen her sad and angry and every way of happy before, but had never seen that bewildered look. My mother was many things—strong, funny, sometimes prone to cursing outbursts. The emotion she never showed in front of me was uncertainty.

I knew then, just as I always knew these things, that nothing would ever be the same.

And as I drove the dusty gravel road on the outskirts of town, a familiar twinge of heartache that something was being set in motion for me made itself known. Whether it was good or bad, my talent would never tell me. But as sure as the empty La Croix cans rattling around my backseat, I knew I would never be the same after this trip.

Listening to my instincts had become so second nature that disregarding them was making my skin feel too tight. Steering wheel in hand, I stretched my arms under my long-sleeved graphic tee emblazoned with a raccoon in an astronaut's helmet saying, *Houston, I have so many problems.* Along the fir-lined street, the mid-April rain broke through the branches to dot my windshield.

In the cupholder beside a clear cup of an opaque mixture of melted ice and coffee, my phone chimed with a message. Above the daily affirmation my friend Autumn sent, *My greatest strength comes from being my authentic self*, was a few words from Marigold.

My eyes taken off the familiar road, I shot a quick message back, letting Goldie know I'd be at her house in three minutes and that the car would make it through the pothole unscathed. As if I didn't know the way better than my right hand, having had lived in the house across the woods for fifteen years.

Down a winding gravel road on the outskirts of Ridgewood, two houses sat back from the street, a swath of dense forest between them. It was there I grew up with my parent's house on one side and Marigold Eden's on the other. I had spent many a summer night tromping through the thick brush and fighting against blackberry bushes to where our properties connected.

Turning right, I went over the small bridge Goldie's late husband had built over a salmon stream. Goldie liked to say there were only four good things "that mean son of a bitch gave her"—her two children, that bridge and him dying, and thus, leaving her the hell alone.

Just like every other time, driving over the rickety wood, I said a prayer to the powers that be to not let it give way under my tires and collapse into the sludgy stream.

Cedar's younger sister, Clover, told me once that, when the culvert was built, the county tried to go after Goldie for disrupting what they called a "potential salmon stream." Goldie dug in her heels, fought with the county ordinances, and the wonky bridge stayed where it was. Never in all the years I lived at the end of the road did I see a single fish.

Pulling up to the back of the little cabin, I took deep, reassuring breaths. The old growth Douglas firs surrounded the redwood shake-paneled home.

Someone, likely Goldie's new wife Edith, had painted the trim a vibrant green that clashed wonderfully with the siding of the two-story cabin. I always loved this house.

While my parent's home, through the trees an acre and a half away, was grander, with white paint and river rock-trimmed columns, the Eden house was a home. Yet it was always a bit disorganized, with the door changing color to Goldie's moods. She allowed her children to decorate their rooms, leading to the neon orange of Clover's.

Against an ancient pine, the bane of our northwest existence, Himalayan blackberry bushes, had tangled around the handlebars of an old scooter I recognized as Cedar's. It was comforting that, despite the upsets of my month, the blackberry bushes still swallowed up discarded toys at the Eden house.

It had been almost a year since being back. Staying away never made sense to others. My mom still lived here. My paternal grandparents still lorded over the town in their million-dollar waterfront home. Two of my three best friends lived in the area. Even though Seattle was a ferry ride away from Ridgewood, in recent years, I've successfully found many excuses on why I couldn't return to that gravel drive and this town—up until the previous few weeks, that was.

In a perfect storm of events, here I was. Back home. Or close enough.

I couldn't blame my roommate, Annie, for moving into a new apartment with her fiancé. Or even the sudden shuttering of the organic juice start-up I had accepted for less-than-fair wages in exchange for now-worthless shares.

There are only so many times you can ask your mom for rent money before it gets pathetic.

In a moment of ill-conceived lunacy, I went to my situationship, Dane's, to see if I could stay with him.

I found him lying half naked on his threadbare orange couch with his head between another woman's thighs.

He pulled his face off her shaved lips and tried to explain, but I left before that handlebar-mustached-mouth could form a coherent word.

Getting in my car, I waited for the tears over the loss of the closest thing to a boyfriend I had in years. Instead, I was filled with his audacity of going down on a girl.

He had always complained he didn't like blow jobs, so it was only fair he wasn't asked to reciprocate. The few times he had tried, it was shockingly bad. He liked to press my clit like it was a doorbell that would ring with unmoving pressure.

So, I sent up a small prayer for the safety of the woman's left labia.

I was all about supporting polyamory, but bad head is where I draw the line.

After a day of watching organizational TV shows on the couch with jalapeno chips and cheap Moscato, I woke up with a killer headache and the realization that I would probably move back in with my mom—or worse, my grandparents.

Not that either was a bad idea—they were kind and always kept a space for me. But I would always be a child in their homes. I waited until I was twenty-three to even drink in front of my Baba and Jiji. And my mom, she meant well, but after losing my father almost eight years before, our relationship shifted. I was an adult; she was an adult, and in our grief, we grew apart.

Salvation came in the form of Goldie and her partner Edith needing a house sitter while traveling to Northern Europe. When my mom first volunteered me for the job, I was annoyed with her. She believed heartily in helping one's neighbor, often to the detriment of us. That was how I ended up cleaning up the toilet paper out of my high school teacher, Mr. Miranda's, front yard. Or when she gave away all my My Little Ponies to her coworker's daughter. *You haven't played with them in weeks. Why would we keep them?*

In this case, her martyr complex worked out for me. I could spend the time to save my money for a deposit on a new apartment and use the seclusion to finish my newest commission of the custom illustrations I had sold through my website. My side hustle never made much money, but after losing my job, it was the only thing I had going.

I clambered to the front step, towing my oversized suitcase behind me. The wind was picking up, with leaves swirling around my feet and the trees swaying ominously overhead. A gray cloud covered the sky and threatened ever-present rain. A small pine branch whipped through the air and smacked me on the shoulder. The power was going to go out, a guarantee, not a guess.

I reached up above the door frame where Goldie kept her spare key behind the metal sign proclaiming *Welcome To Our Shit Show.*

Best to get settled before I lose power and have to rely on candles and flashlights.

The inside of the house still boasted the same wood plank walls and Georgia O'Keefe paintings. Cedar's senior picture. A picture of sophomore Clover in front of a sign for the University of Colorado Denver. A new photo of Goldie and Edith on their wedding day replaced the watercolor of downtown Ridgewood.

Everything looked almost the same as it did when I used to babysit Clover. While Cedar was busy with sports, clubs, and friends, Goldie would ask me to watch Clover, five years his junior. She was such an easy child it was a cakewalk.

She and I would spend hours in the loft above the kitchen, giggling over cute boys in magazines, listening to terrible music, and eating marshmallows melted onto wax paper with sticky, blistered fingers.

Sometimes, Cedar would come home early. Those were the hardest. It was a sad cliche, falling for the neighbor boy. Especially when he didn't know my name for years. When you're twelve and he's fifteen, why would he remember my name wasn't Dana?

When I mentioned my crush to my friends, they told me what I never wanted to hear: he wasn't worth wasting my time waiting. I had spent years pining for that boy, pictured him being my first kiss, my first boyfriend, my everything. But he hardly acknowledged me aside from a polite "hi" as he walked by.

I watched as he sauntered about campus, with his golden-brown hair growing long enough for his parade of girlfriends to run their fingers through, his easy smile. For everyone but me.

I had my friends, of course. The quiet Wren who moved into town. Autumn, the girl who was painfully sweet and even more painfully naïve but always saw the best in people, and her cousin, Summer, who was brash and loud and fun.

But never the boy with the golden hair and easy smile, Cedar, who always cracked a joke or could effortlessly defuse a situation. Prom King, star of the soccer team. The boy who gave his sister piggyback rides up the stairs every day when she broke her ankle by falling out of a tree.

Looking up at the loft, I rubbed the ache blooming in my chest. From all those nights up there, where I would stare down at him and his friends as they sat around the table talking and drinking stolen sodas from the fridge. From the jolt of recognition and shame, when Cedar would look up and catch me.

That was years ago. You are a different person now. It was a childish fantasy with him. He never cared.

Up until that party in the woods, I considered him one of my many misjudgments.

Before I lost my dad, I spent three glorious weeks with Cedar. After years of watching him from across the commons at school, of stumbling over my words when he would say hello as I tutored Clover at math every Wednesday, I finally got my chance.

Maybe if I hadn't been abandoned by my so-called date at that party in the woods. Maybe if he and Alivia hadn't been broken up at that moment. Maybe, maybe, maybe.

All I knew was he was there, offering me a sweatshirt, loading me into the passenger seat of his car. And I couldn't remember why I always got tongue-tied around him.

In the confines of his old green Blazer, I found the same Cedar I loved as a kid. We were together on the rain-soaked streets heading out of town, tires hissing as he drove.

So, when he leaned over and kissed me, I let him. And when his hands roamed under my shirt, I climbed over the center console, and there we were. Lips and teeth and hands.

It was supposed to be the light I was searching for. The love I was never allowed.

But for the first time, my instincts were completely wrong. Because, in the end, what I had with Cedar was a fleeting thing. It was a few weeks behind closed doors. As we started, it didn't mean the same thing to him as it did me. He was going back to his junior year of college in St. Louis, and I was heading to the University of Washington. It was a few stolen kisses; it was grappling over our clothes. I thought our shared history would be the start of a love story, just for it to mean nothing to him. It was me telling him far too much and him never telling me a single truth.

It was a weak, shameful part of me that fell for Cedar. From the first moment he poked his head into our tree house to accuse me of stealing his soccer ball, his blue eyes locked on mine, tanned face stretched in a lopsided grin, and I was done for.

If life had been taken another path, if I didn't lose my father, maybe things would have turned out differently.

In my grief, I lost days, then weeks, then a month. Time had no meaning after losing my father. A brain aneurysm sounds so made-up. He was healthy, spry even. He had just completed a hike on Mt. Walker a week before. And then he was gone.

I had Wren, Autumn, and Summer for support, but deep down, I wanted to walk the three acres between mine and the Eden house. But still, I stayed huddled in my room, bed-ridden, my phone on silent.

Four weeks later, I emerged to walk the distance, the woods as familiar as my favorite brushes, passed down from my Baba when I was twelve. As I stepped foot outside my door, a chill whispered over my skin.

I shouldn't go over there. Something is waiting at Cedar's, but I should stay.

But I ignored that voice.

Climbing over the fallen fir that was rotting into the ground and soft with thick moss. Past the treehouse the previous owners had built in the eighties. Ducking under the low-hanging alder branch and around the sword ferns that camouflaged an intricate root system.

Maybe it was my grief that stopped me from listening to the voice or raging hormones and the need to find comfort in the one person I thought understood me. Whatever it was that led me there, I could ignore the uneasy sensation until I reached his front door.

Long legs, a flat stomach, blonde hair, and thin wrists was Alivia Drummond, Cedar's ex-girlfriend and the original owner of the sweatshirt he had so tenderly pulled over my shoulders a month and half before. With the tables turning painfully, Alivia was wearing *my* shirt, an oversized Camp Twin Lakes shirt I left in his car. The one I tie-dyed myself.

She cocked her head and frowned. "Can I help you?"

"I—"

Words congealed on my tongue.

Told you so, told you so, the little voice echoed in my head.

"Who is it, Liv?" Cedar called out.

"Your little neighbor, Darcy."

"Devin," I rasped out, my mind whirring in every direction.

Cedar had never promised me a thing. He never said he loved me, and even in my grief, I knew I wasn't his girlfriend. But the sight of Alivia standing in his home, wearing the same threadbare shirt I had pulled over my head and tossed in his backseat after we swam in the bay had me undone.

Cedar emerged from the kitchen, wiping his hands on a towel. His hair was longer, shaggy, over his forehead.

"Devin?" His brows furrowed as he took me in, my greasy ponytail, three-day-old dress, and hollow circles under my eyes. "You, okay?"

And I knew.

Whatever it was I thought I had with Cedar was never and would never be real.

He stepped out onto the landing, closing in Alivia. "When I hadn't heard from you . . ." He sighed. "I heard about your dad, but I wasn't sure if you would want me to come over. I texted, but—"

A lump hardened in my throat. Dozens of things, from insults to pleas, piled up on my tongue, but nothing came out. Instead, my eyes welled with tears.

"Oh, hey, come here. I'm sorry for your loss. Let me—" He put his arms out and leaned forward.

But a hug from him would've been worse. I was splintering, and nothing could've held me together.

Stepping back, I put my hands up, voice shaky. "No, no. I—" Swallowing hard, I willed myself to get the words out. "Have fun at college. Tell Alivia hi."

As I walked back, my feet found the roots I swore I could mark in my dreams, my body moving but my heart cracking with each step I took leaving Cedar Eden. Vowing to never put myself in this position again.

Told you so, told you so.

And I kept that vow.

In the span of my dating experiences, the time Cedar and I spent together was a blip. Yet, here I was, almost a decade later, the hurt still blooming over my chest as the wound reopened. I was struck at how much it hurt. It shouldn't have been painful to see these opaque memories waiting to burst upon me.

Closing my eyes, I remembered the way Cedar had looked at me with such intensity before pressing his lips to mine. The short bristle of his hair against my fingers as I pulled him closer. The feel of his body against mine, the wall digging into my back deliciously.

In my freshman year of college, I went to a party with some friends. A cute boy with short light-brown hair and hazel eyes brought me lukewarm beer from a keg.

He leaned against me and complimented the shirt I was wearing, told me I sounded smart. When he leaned in to kiss me, my back against the doorframe of the kitchen, I let him.

His lips were all wrong, and he smelled of beer and cinnamon gum. His hands were too soft on my shoulder.

He wasn't Cedar.

I kissed him before making an excuse to leave. Afterward, I went back to my dorm that night and cried into my scratchy pillow case, distraught with the knowledge that what I felt with Cedar was precious. That I would always chase the feeling he gave me and that I would fall short each time.

After that, I dated guys who were the opposite. Pretty boys who wrote poetry and debated the integrity of Gabriel Garcia Marquez over cups of yerba maté. I dated boys with dark hair and dark eyes, boys who were precious, boys who could fit into my jeans, and boys who played acoustic guitar at open-mic nights. Boys I met in my art classes and who could make craft cocktails and pickleback shots. They would never be Cedar, and as hard as I tried, I couldn't commit to anything less.

Shaking the thoughts away, I glanced at the note hanging from the fridge instructing me to feed their irritable corgi, Emily Barkinson, affectionately known as Kinny, twice a day, along with other instructions, and to, most importantly, make myself at home.

I took that to mean I could use the largest bedroom with its jetted tub.

Kinny lifted her head from one of the four oversized dog beds around the house and narrowed her eyes at me, giving a low growl.

"I know you don't like me, but I'm all you got for the next few weeks."

Kinny glared at me, then lay her head down and closed her eyes.

After lugging my suitcase up the narrow stairwell past the room Clover claimed as a child, I found the door firmly shut.

I hadn't been over here since I was eighteen, when Clover no longer needed me as a babysitter. I wondered about her preteen room. Was the poster of the British boy band still hanging over her mirror? Would the air still smell of the teenage pop star perfume? That little burn mark on her mattress, a mistake from when she confided she tried to smoke a stolen spliff, came to mind. The orange-and-pink leopard bedspread and the scattered black eyeliners on her dresser.

Squinching my eyes shut, I backed away, colliding with the opposite door.

The green-and-yellow Supersonic stickers were still plastered all over the particleboard door of Cedar's room. Reflexively, I ran a hand over the corner of one, pushing against the door. It swung open, revealing the mess inside.

The bed was unmade, with an old backpack leaning against the wall. Clothes were piled on top of the dresser, and magazines dotted the floor. Posters of the Seahawks and scantily clad women splayed across sports cars had been plastered on the walls.

I shook my head as I pulled the door shut and continued down to the back bedroom.

Neither room held anything for me.

Lounging back in the tub, the bubbles up to my shoulders, I took a long sip of the wine I got from the grocery store for ten dollars a bottle. I was a firm believer in buying wine by the inventive labels and refused to spend over fifteen dollars a bottle on principle. This one had a label that looked like a tarot card and was $7.99 at the gas station.

My shoulders ached from hefting my supplies up the roughhewn ladder into the small loft. Goldie had mentioned I was free to make whatever mess I wanted in their small reading nook. So, I spent the afternoon rearranging the furniture and carrying up my canvases and paints.

Sitting in the warm water, I began to feel like this move was going to be a positive one. It could be my chance to regroup and plan my next steps. Maybe I was due for a fresh start somewhere else.

I had family in Arizona and could try my luck in Phoenix. There had to be jobs in graphic design down there, right?

In the years since college, I had visited my cousins a few times for long weekends. The area was fun, warm all year, and had a good nightlife. With the cheaper cost of living, I could stretch my meager savings further. As much as I would miss being away from my family and friends, a reset might be exactly what I needed.

I leaned back and closed my eyes, imagining myself poolside, with a fancy margarita in hand. The warm breeze over my body as I enjoyed happy hour with new friends on a rooftop bar. Chatting up the cute guy I met at the new agency I was hired at, our Bohemian wedding among the cacti. Christmas in Sedona, summer trip to Ridgewood to escape the heat of the desert. The jealousy of my classmates when I show up tan-brown and healthy with a hot Arizonan by my side.

A loud thump broke me out of my reverie. I bolted upright, holding my breath.

Silence for a moment.

Relax, Devin, it's probably just Kinny or the wind. They did forecast a bad wind storm tonight.

I leaned back again, settling into the warm water.

Another thump sounded, followed by a low curse. I stood to wrap a towel around my body, pausing again.

Scraping and mumbling.

Noises that could not be blamed on a twenty-five-pound corgi or the weather.

Creeping down the hallway, I was relieved that I left the light on so I didn't have to fumble in the dark.

When I peered down the staircase, the silhouette of a large man was moving around the kitchen, and I froze.

Oh God, it's a serial killer who has broken into the house to murder me and then burglarize the place. Or burglarize the place, then murder me. No one knows I'm here, and they'll find my body in two months after Kinny has eaten my face. This is how I go, drunk off gas station wine and covered in lavender-scented bubbles.

I tried to remember what you're supposed to do when someone breaks into your home. Do you stay still? Call the police?

Yes, call the police. Don't be that dumb girl from a horror movie.

Another thump sounded in the kitchen, followed by the click of the refrigerator opening.

I ran back to the bedroom to grab my phone off the bedside table. After dialing 911, I held my finger over the call button.

"Don't be a serial killer," I whispered as I crept down the stairs, holding the phone and my towel.

Halfway down, it occurred to me that throwing some clothes on would have been smart, but it would make too much noise.

I stepped on the second-to-last stair and heard its familiar creak.

I knew that creak—Clover and I were always careful to avoid it when we'd sneak down to watch horror movies.

The shadowy figure turned toward me, and I froze again, staring. He was tall and broad-shouldered. I urged my feet to backtrack and run upstairs. While I couldn't see his face in the shadows, I could feel his eyes on me.

He stepped forward, and I let out a bloodcurdling scream.

Two

Cedar

IT WAS ALWAYS MY plan to come home to Ridgewood. I hadn't expected to do it so soon, but between the long overdue dissolution of my relationship with Tainslee a month before—my decision—and the downsizing at the rehab facility—not my decision—I figured the best thing to do was go home.

The director of Ridgewood Physical Therapy, Dr. Foster, told me he would love to interview me when I came home. Crossing the state line, I wondered why I didn't make this move back sooner.

Tainslee was pissed, but there was no way we could work out. For the past six months, she had become way too controlling and jealous. She thought I wasn't living up to my full potential working at a nonprofit and would question how I knew any woman who said "hi" to me. When she started leaving her laptop open in front of me with pictures of diamond rings out of my price range, I knew I had to end it.

I made it to my mom's house just before the storm started to rage. While there are probably fiercer winds in a lot of other places, the dense trees and their proximity to power lines always led to a few issues. I just hoped I could make it home and catch the game before the power cut off.

Using the key I had, I let myself in the front door.

Kinny looked up at me from her large pillow and sniffed the air in contempt. We never did get along.

The lights were mostly out, and I set my bag on the floor next to where the lamp was supposed to be. Reaching for the light, I only caught air. Edith and Mom were always rearranging things.

I cursed under my breath and made my way across the small living room to turn on the light, hitting my shin on one of those plush footstools.

Kinny got up and stretched her stubby little legs before turning and plopping down.

"A fat lot of help you are," I mumbled as I rubbed my leg.

In my pocket, my phone vibrated. Tainslee was calling me. She must have heard the news that I actually made good on my promise and had left town. Silencing the call, I shoved the phone back in my pocket.

A sound above my head gave me pause. I could have sworn Mom said she and Edith left that morning for their vacation, but maybe I got the days wrong. I probably should have let her know I'd be in town early, but I didn't want her to feel like she had to postpone her vacation just because I was here. She always worried about me.

I didn't even know if I would get the job at Ridgewood Physical Therapy, and it was possible the converted barn house I was going to rent might fall through. My rental agent was slow to get back to me.

The only car I saw when I pulled in was a little green Toyota. I didn't recognize it, but I hadn't been home in a while. My hand was on the cord of the lamp when a creak made me turn toward the stairs. I caught sight of a curvy woman with dark hair piled on top of her hair and a towel wrapped around her body. The sight struck me mute.

All thoughts ravaged by the sight. My breath caught in my chest, expanding painfully. I was held taut by something I couldn't place.

I couldn't see her face, with the only light coming from the upstairs, but if her face matched what the towel was covering, I knew she'd be gorgeous. My hand dropped away from the lamp, and I stepped closer. My foot was barely on the ground before she let out the most horrific scream I had heard outside of a movie.

I stepped back and put my hands up in the air. "Whoa." Then scrambled for the lamp.

Warm light flooded the room, and I stood there, awestruck, as recognition came over both of us.

Our former neighbor, Devin Haruki, was staring back at me, her eyes growing large, and she lifted her hands to her face in shock. Black-framed glasses, slightly fogged up, slid down her nose, and as she used a finger to push them up, the towel she was holding up came tumbling down.

Her soft stomach flared to full hips. On each of her thighs was the bright ink of intricate tattoos I couldn't quite identify. Across her sternum was a large blue watercolor triangle of a cherry-pink blossom between heavy breasts.

I didn't have time to register what I was seeing as Devin caught the towel before it hit the floor and pulled it up.

Both hands clutching it against her breast, she sputtered. "Cedar?" She glanced around as if I was a ghost. "What, I don't under . . . What?"

As I listened to Devin moving around above my head, I dumped the remainder of the wine in the fridge into a coffee cup.

In all the situations I envisioned tonight, this was not it. The last time I had seen Devin was over five years ago at my cousin Rhodie's wedding. The whole night was hazy for me, with me starting the celebration early with cousins from out of town.

I remembered seeing Devin there. Her hair was shorter, with large streaks of red dispersed through her natural black. I recalled thinking her tits looked great in her dress, but at the time, I was preoccupied with trying to hit on Rhodie's new sister-in-law.

Devin and I had a little thing for a few weeks while I was home from college. As a rule, I don't live with regret. People make mistakes, and all we can do is to learn and grow. I could count on a single hand the number of times I had genuine regret, and number one would be the way I handled things with Devin when I got back with Alivia.

One day, we were making out, having fun together, and the next, she stopped responding to my texts. I assumed Devin wasn't interested anymore, so when Alivia showed up at The Skol House with a gaggle of girlfriends, I figured there was no harm in getting back with her. The next day, I found out about Ken Haruki's passing.

I tried texting a few more times, but nothing went through.

I was young and stupid. Devin wasn't my girlfriend or anything, but I liked her. The least I should have done was go over and paid my respects. But like a coward, I stayed in my little bubble with Alivia, telling myself it was no big deal.

And I believed that until the day Devin showed up on my front step, despondent, her big green eyes filling with tears behind her glasses. I told myself it was nothing more than a little crush, a passing attraction. But deep down, I knew I had fucked up.

I tried to message her a few more times, but my calls went straight to voicemail. After a few tries, I realized she wasn't getting back to me. And once again, in my youthful ignorance, I thought it might be okay.

So, I went back to finish my degree. I had a few girlfriends, and I had girls who I had fun with. I played soccer and partied. My grades were good enough to graduate. While working on my clinicals, I met Tainslee and had all but put Devin out of my mind until I saw her standing on the bottom step in nothing but a towel.

Thank God for little slippery towels.

Devin stepped down into the living room, looking from me at the kitchen counter to the front door. She wore black leggings and a *My anxiety is chronic, but this ass is iconic* tank top.

I stifled a laugh at the words.

Her hair was still wet in spots, clinging to her neck. Even though I couldn't tell how long it was, I assumed it had grown out in the past five years.

She looked good. Better than good. Incredible.

You cannot be fucking around right now. Yes, Devin looks great, but you just broke it off with Tainslee.

She was never what was considered a thin girl, but the confident way she held herself was a transformation from her past timidity. Before, she'd fold into herself if you looked at her too long. But she boldly stared at me with the same green eyes behind thick black frames.

Devin grabbed the empty bottle off the counter and shook it with narrowed eyes. "Thanks for drinking all my wine."

"Relax, Dev, I'll get you another bottle." I leaned back, smile widening. "What did it cost, seven dollars? Eight? I'll get you two bottles."

"What are you doing here, Cedar?" She cocked her head, pink-and-purple streaks framing her face as her hair tumbled over one shoulder.

A flash of what that hair felt like when I would wrap it around my fingers to pull her in for a kiss sparked behind my eyes.

I blinked away the thought. "I live here. This is my house."

"You don't live here. You live in California or Florida or Arizona or something." Her cheeks flared pink. "N-Not here. You live somewhere else. Marigold would have told—"

"I didn't want to tell Mom I was back. She'd just be on my case."

Devin's face softened. "Yeah. I know." Devin pursed her full lips. "Still doesn't explain why you're here, though." She crossed her arms and stuck out her chin.

I looked away so I didn't have to look at how, when she crossed her arms like that, it pushed her tits up. The careless way indicated she had no idea how attractive that stance made her.

"I have an interview at Ridgewood Physical Therapy tomorrow afternoon. I knew Mom and Edie were going to be gone, so I figured I'd stay here, watch the place while they're gone. Cheaper than a hotel."

Devin kept her narrowed gaze on me. "You can't 'watch the place.' I'm the one they asked to house-sit."

I shrugged. "Well, now you don't have to. You can run back to Seattle and have fun at your poetry slam and hookah parties—or whatever it is you do."

"My what? That's not even remotely a thing." She pursed her full lips. Had I forgotten how full they were? Had she always had such a sharp Cupid's bow? "I'm staying here. All my stuff is here. I drove from Seattle to be here and . . ." She paused as if considering whether to tell the truth. "I'm between apartments right now."

I tried not to let my reaction show.

"So, you're homeless." I walked over to the fridge to pull out a new bottle of wine, popped the cork, and filled our glasses.

"No, I said I'm between apartments. My roommate had to move out, and I haven't found the right apartment yet." She took the glass as if swallowing her irritation down with the wine.

"It's okay, I'm technically homeless too," I assured, smiling.

"I'm not homeless, just between jobs and apartments and, and, and . . ." She waved dismissively, looking away from me.

"Same for me. All of the above."

She rubbed her hands over her bare arms, glancing out the window where the branches scratched against the glass. "It's not the same."

I walked to the coatrack next to the door, grabbed the first thing I found, and threw it at her.

She caught it in the air, unfolding it. "Thanks." Devin pulled the oversized sweatshirt over her head.

Her shirt rode up to show off a swath of her soft stomach. I thought back to what her tits looked like when she dropped her towel. That was a sight I'd be thinking about for a long while.

She turned to me, and I stifled a laugh.

"That's my sweatshirt."

Devin glanced down at my stained Washington University St. Louis shirt and frowned. "Then, why was it on Goldie's coatrack?"

"I don't know. Maybe I left it here, maybe she stole it at some point. Still my shirt. I was wondering what happened to it."

She pushed the long sleeves up to her wrists, her hands looking dainty compared to the voluminous sleeves. "Well, I'm not taking it off. It's mine for now."

I waited for the familiar irritation of having her wear my shirt to bubble up the way it had with Tainslee, but it never did. "Whatever. It's fine. I'll just get it back tomorrow when you leave."

She shot me a glare. "I told you. I'm staying here. Goldie asked me. You're the one who is an interloper here, not me."

"Have you always been this stubborn? I seem to remember you being far more agreeable than this."

"I'd be shocked if you remembered a single thing about me."

"You'd be surprised, Dev." I leaned closer to her until our knees brushed against each other.

A sizzle shot up my leg and groin. My focus moved down to her lips before settling on her throat, where her breathing seemed to pick up.

The outlined tattoo of what could've been a leaf or a flower was peeking out behind her ear. How many tattoos did this woman have?

As I stared at the long column of her neck, I wondered what her skin would taste like. A powerful urge to pull the strands away from her skin and lick the spot between her throat and collarbone ripped through me.

"I remember all sorts of things about you."

The little sounds she made when I touched her flashed in my memory, a low throaty moan that, almost a decade later, still made me stiffen. Shifting on my stool, I adjusted myself.

Fuck, what was the matter with me? You'd think I had been celibate for years with the way my body was reacting.

Devin stilled as I leaned closer, my knee tucking between hers. I could smell the wine on her breath. Her body heat coming off in waves. The moment strung out between us like a tension bound strand. She leaned into me, and her tongue darted out to wet her lips.

She let out a shaky breath before pulling back, blinking several times. "That's sweet but still a lie."

"Why would I lie to you?" I asked, the corner of my mouth turning up as I took her in.

As a thick lock of purple hair curled soft against her collarbone, I imagined running my fingers through her hair, tracing her hairline at the base of her skull, the give of her silky strands through my fingers, the softness of her smooth skin. The way she would turn into my hand, allowing me more. I wondered what else I would do if given the chance.

"Why would you tell the truth?"

Her voice was softer.

Maybe it was the cheap wine that loosened my tongue. Or seeing her naked for a moment before getting a word out. Whatever it was that galvanized me, the words were out before I could second-guess them.

"Because you know me better than that." Lifting the tendril from her neck, I wrapped it around my finger, once, twice, three times.

"I thought I did. But that was a long time ago."

Her words were low, so quiet, I wasn't sure they were for me.

"I could have sworn it was just the other day when you took me up to the tree house. I bet you still make that little sound when I would kiss you right here."

With my finger, I brushed the spot on her neck where she had a small mole. I had somehow forgotten that little brown dot, but now that I could trace it with my finger, I never wanted to stop touching it.

Her eyes betrayed her, softening, as she recalled what we did all those years ago.

"I should go—bed—sleep, um . . ." She stood suddenly. "Go to bed, in my bed. Not your bed, obviously, not your bed. My bed or Goldie's bed, not yours. Um . . . yeah."

She picked up my mug of wine and drained it in a single gulp. I watched as her throat arched, mesmerized by the motion. I didn't move as she made her way upstairs, only the click of the lock releasing the tension in my body.

I had no idea what was happening to me, but a wave of fear coursed through me. If I stayed here with Devin, I'd be in grave trouble. I'd need to leave right after my interview, or I had a sneaking suspicion I'd do something we'd both regret.

Overhead, the track light flickered ominously as the wind outside picked up. This could be a long night.

Devin

THE WIND HOWLED OUTSIDE the window, and at least three times in the night, I woke to a branch smacking the glass. The fourth time, I sat bolt upright, the bright orange floral Vera Bradley comforter falling off me as I came to three unwelcome conclusions.

1. I need to brush up on my survival skills. If that had been a serial killer, I would have been dead before the towel had fallen on the ground.

2. I really should have shaved my legs while in the bath.

3. I was still absolutely one hundred percent attracted to Cedar.

Damn him for looking so much better than he did eight years before. His hair, once so artfully styled with gel, was longer, framing his sharp jawline better and curling slightly over his ears. He had a beard a few shades darker than his hair.

And once again, the urge to flee filled me. I stood little chance of holding back my feelings when Cedar was around. I had always been a fool for him. I had only a few days before my resolve would break, and I would have to leave once again. Even when I wanted to be here, this town was my home, too.

I loved Ridgewood, from the dense trees that surrounded my mom's home to the thin strait of Freedom Bay and the cobblestone pathways between the shops of downtown. The bakery, with its fresh krumkake and doughboy donuts in the shape of a person. I loved watching the boats pass in the bay.

What I didn't love was living across the acreage from the boy who would never want me the way I wanted him. Even then, if he had reciprocated my feelings, I would've lost myself. I would have followed him and fallen in love. I would have offered myself up to him to break a million times over.

When I was eighteen, I swore I would leave my feeling for Cedar Eden in the past. Cedar was my lesson, and for the past eight years, I've been telling myself I had learned it well.

Yet, here I was, twenty-six years old, mature, experienced, and still just as foolish around him as ever. For the first time in years, I felt like I was seventeen again, in glasses and a nerdy shirt, my hair an absolute mess, in a lopsided bun looking like a Bugle chip.

I wasn't the same girl I used to be. Before I was let go at the agency, I had a somewhat fulfilling career. While the last time I had an orgasm was with another person was four years prior, I did well enough on the dating scene. Although I wasn't looking to get married to the next man I saw, it would be nice to find someone of more substance. At least more than a thirty-five-year-old coffee artist with four roommates who hated the patriarchal labels of monogamy and, on several occasions, explained how to make okonomiyaki as if my father didn't make it every Saturday.

Despite the loss of my job and apartment, I was trying to look at this change as a new opportunity. But something about Cedar made me feel the same way, and just like my insecurities, all my lust came out, too. I found I was still getting turned on just by him sitting next to me.

And the way he looked at you. And then when he wrapped your hair around his finger and said . . .

I flopped on the bed, ignoring the creaking of the house being pelted with the raging squall.

It was dangerous to wonder what would have happened if I hadn't of scooted away. Would be have leaned in closer? Would his mouth still taste of cherries? Did he still like it when the hair on his nape was pulled? My hand trailed along my neck, picturing Cedar's fingers moving down the front of my body and tracing the waistband of my underwear.

A loud crash from somewhere outside stopped me. Bolting up in bed, I glanced blearily around the dark room. I squinted toward the alarm clock but only saw black, my hand patting around until I found my glasses and phone.

It was 3:33 in the morning. No other sound but the wind. A streak of lightning lit up the space before plunging it back into darkness.

I lay back on the pillow, closing my eyes.

Nothing more than a spring storm. Over the years, I had been witness to countless. The worst that would happen was losing power for a day or two.

Resting my hand on my soft stomach, I tapped out a rhythm, counting out the seconds between the thunder and lightning. Thirty, forty, forty-one.

A second crash shook the house, and a loud curse sounded from down the hall. That couldn't be good.

My robe slung over my shoulders, I headed out into the hallway. Framed in his bedroom door was the silhouette of Cedar, one hand gripping the edge. With a quick glance, I registered he was shirtless, wearing a pair of low-slung pajama pants. I filed that away for material to use later.

"Are you okay?" we asked each other at the same time.

He stepped closer to me, raising a hand, before settling it back down at his side. "What are you wearing?"

I glanced down to find I was still clad in my tank top and underwear, the robe hanging open in front.

"I could ask you the same thing." I waved a hand at his body. "Sorry, I didn't put on a party dress for this meeting in the middle of a storm."

A crack of lightning illuminated the sky, and fear crossed Cedar's face.

"A branch broke through the window." He motioned toward it.

I followed him as we peered into his room.

It was almost too dark to make out the thick branch resting over his dresser. The wind howled ferociously. His entire window was smashed out. Broken glass has sprayed in every direction, over his carpet, bed, and clothing. Sleet from outside came in sideways through the opening and soaked everything it touched.

"What do we do?" I asked, having to raise my voice over the howling wind. "Do we push it back out?"

Cedar glanced from me to the open window where the branch sawed against the sill. "I should probably cut it off."

"Do you know how to do that?" I yelled.

He shot me a look that I felt more than saw. "What kind of question is that? How hard can it be?"

When you're searching for a chainsaw in the pitch black of a raging storm, the answer is extremely. After some arguing that I should stay behind and me telling him I would do no such thing—and when did he start thinking a little rain was going to make me melt and then him conceding that it wasn't even that cold?—I followed Cedar out to the old shed behind the house.

Using a flashlight we found in a junk drawer as our beacon, we were able to dodge the storm-strewn branches dotting the backyard. From the look of the shed, it hadn't been maintained in a while.

After searching through various tools, sticking our hands in several spider webs, and almost stepping through a rotten piece of the flooring,

Cedar pulled out a chainsaw.

He stalked out of the shed, motioning for me to stand back.

Under protecting the roof, I watched as he held the chainsaw up and pulled the cord with a smooth motion. It made a low *blump, brump* before going silent. He yanked again, each time his muscles flexing.

I admired the way he looked as he worked, the rain-slick in his light-brown hair, the taut muscles in his forearms flexing.

He repeatedly tried to start the chainsaw, but after the sixth attempt, he set it down. "Must be out of gas."

"What do we do now?"

He glowered at me. "I don't know. You got any bright ideas?" Placing the chainsaw down where he found it, he glanced around the dark space.

I put my hands up. "Hey, don't be mad at me. I'm just pointing out the fact that you have a big ass tree branch in your room. If we don't get the window taped up, the carpet will get waterlogged."

"You think I don't know that? It came crashing into my room like a demon hell-bent on my balls." He scrubbed a hand over his day-old scruff.

"Well, we better figure something else out because the branch won't cut itself," I snapped. An itch started in my nose before I sneezed. "I wonder who's talking about me," I mumbled, wrinkling my nose to fight the tingle.

Another sneeze came out, followed by a third.

"What?" he asked, a brow furrowed.

"When you sneeze, that means someone is talking about you."

I didn't mention that my Jiji would say three meant someone will fall in love with you.

He blinked at me and shook his head. "I've never heard of that."

"Well, now you have."

Ignoring my comments, he grabbed a small hatchet off the wall and waved it around. "This will have to do." Without another word, he motioned for me to follow him back into the house.

With our clothes soaked to our skin, we searched until we found an oil lamp under the kitchen sink and, after a few tries with the childproof lighter, lit it.

I held the lamp as I followed him up the stairs to his room, the rain somehow intensifying the smell of soap on his skin. Taking a deep breath, I tried not to notice the way his Henley stretched across his broad shoulders and clung to his strong biceps. Those were the kind of arms that could carry a girl to bed before ravishing her.

He stopped before the threshold of his room. "You shouldn't come in here. The glass could cut you." He held his hand out.

I rolled my eyes as I pushed past him, glass crunching beneath my rain boots. "Don't be ridiculous. I'm not a child. I know how to avoid a little glass. Besides, you can't cut that branch by yourself with that little tiny ax."

He held up the tool, waving it around menacingly. "I could do it."

I tipped my head to the side, glaring. "But I'm here, and you don't have to do it alone. Come on, it will be faster if we do it together."

I cleaned off all the items on the top of his dresser, grabbed a pile of socks, and tossed it over my shoulder on his bed.

"Hey, what are you doing? You can't just come in here and start throwing my stuff around."

With another stack of clothes in my hands, I paused. "Oh, I'm sorry, did you want me to fold your underwear while it's raining inside the house?"

He took the stack from me and gently set it on the bed. "No, of course not. Just have a little respect for my system here."

I glowered at him. "Fine, you clean off the dresser. I'll knock the big pieces of glass out of the way."

He stilled. "I don't want you doing that. You could get cut."

"Then, give me something else to do." I put my hands on my hips. "You know, if you put your clothes inside your dresser, it might be a better system."

"I was getting to that." He pointed to the dresser. "just don't throw them, okay? Place it on my bed."

I picked up a stack of shirts on the edge of the dresser, and some glossy papers fell. I bent to pick them up—

"No, stop!"

After grabbing the item from the floor, he clutched them to his chest, his hands covering the front of what was obviously a magazine. Between his fingers, I could see a woman's areola.

I glanced from the magazine to his fear-ridden face and bit my lip to contain the laugh threatening to escape. "Relax, Cedar. I don't care if you have porn in here." Even in the low light of the oil lamp, I could see his cheeks getting pink. "It was your room when you were a teenager. What teen boy didn't have a couple of nudie mags? You think I didn't do the same?"

"You did? Wait, what? I don't . . . What?"

I turned away from him, feigning nonchalance as best I could, enjoying his discomfort a little too much. "Yeah, it's no big deal. Now, can you grab the other side so we can move it away from the window?"

He stared at me as if he had never seen me before.

Cedar was able to lift the dresser, while I did barely more than drag it across the carpet, the whine of the wind paired with crunching glass against the bottom of the wood.

Cedar started on the branch, swinging at the wood with measured strokes. The small ax made divots in the wood, but it wasn't giving way. I watched as Cedar swung the ax down, forcing the wood to crack. The way his muscular arms worked to break through, the shards of glass from the window tumbling onto the floor sparkling like jewels in the lamplight.

"Almost got it." He grunted as he gripped the branch, bending the piece down.

When he couldn't get it to break, he changed tactics, pulled the branch toward him, and leaned back with all his might.

A loud yelp sounded as the piece gave way. The branch fell to the floor, and he held his arm up, a shard of glass embedded into his forearm.

He grimaced as he cursed, blood dripping down his skin.

"Oh, my god, Cedar! Let me see," I ordered, sticking out my hand.

He hesitated before offering his arm.

I pushed up his shirt to see where the shard of glass had impaled him.

In college, I took a few first aid classes, so I had to think back what I learned from years before, the dummies we'd wrap with brown ace bandages as we giggled over their pliant rubber flesh.

Holding Cedar's arm, the blood blooming over my skin, I was awed by how different it was to see it firsthand.

With his muscles under my palm, I could count his pulse under my fingers.

"We need to leave the glass in until we can get you to the hospital." I grabbed a T-shirt from the bed and wrapped it around the wound, careful not to disturb the shard.

His arm was warm under my touch, his muscle flexing in pain.

Cedar shook his head, reached over, and moved the shirt. He clenched his jaw, gripping the edge of the glass, and pulled it out of the wound in a swift movement.

"Cedar! You're supposed to leave that in so you don't bleed out."

He scowled at me. "I'm not going to bleed out. It's a little cut." He tossed the glass on the floor, and it landed with a soft *plink*.

Frowning at him, I set a shirt against his wound, placing his good hand over the cut.

"Press down hard." I wrapped the shirt around a few times before tying it tight. I inspected my makeshift bandage in the lamplight, ensuring it would hold until we could get him treated. "Come on. That thing needs stitches. I'll drive."

"Devin, I'm fine. It doesn't need stitches. We're not going to the emergency room and wait around for seven hours just to have them put on some antibiotic gel and a butterfly bandage."

"It could get infected."

"Not if I wash it out. It's barely a thing. You are overreacting right now," he chided. "It's just a scratch. Who cares?"

"I care! I care if you get sepsis because your stupid ass won't get treatment. Your family will care. What would I tell your mom?" The words flew out of my mouth. I lowered my voice. "I care."

He stared at me, dumbstruck, his jaw flexing. He stepped closer, and he shook his head. "It's not a big deal."

"Cedar Eden, if you do not get in my car right now, I will call your sister and your mom and let them know you are here, bleeding all over the floor and refusing to get treated. Goldie will probably cancel her trip. Do you want that on your conscience?"

"Fine. But don't you dare tell me you're tired of waiting with me." Cedar glared at me before glancing back at the window. "We still need to cover the window."

"I'll do it. Sit down and keep pressure on that."

On the bed, Cedar grumbled as I haphazardly stapled a garbage bag over the open window.

Downstairs, I tried to help Cedar with his rain jacket, but he shrugged me off, placing the hood over his head and the shoulders in but leaving his arms out.

Kinny shot us an annoyed glance as we hustled out the door, no doubt because all our noise was interrupting her sleep.

I had to clear off the passenger seat of my car, grabbing handfuls of papers, two makeup bags, and a jacket to throw them in the backseat before Cedar could sit down. His left arm resting against his chest, he reached under the seat to push the bar, releasing the seat so his legs would fit.

I hadn't had someone so tall in my car in a long time. Dane was only five-seven, which worked fine since I inherited my mom's short stature. But Cedar had to be over six feet.

I backed up, fallen cedar boughs crunching under my tires. The wind still whipping through the trees, I drove down the long drive, my headlight illuminating the road.

I glanced over at Cedar. He was trying not to let me see it, but his jaw was clenched. Almost at the main road, I slammed on my brakes. Cedar and I stared, dumbstruck, at the sight.

Fallen across the bridge was the trunk of the massive fir that had flanked the entry to Goldie's home for hundreds of years.

There was no way out.

Four

Cedar

AFTER RETURNING TO THE house, I let Devin help me with my coat. I could do it myself, but something about having her helping me felt good, right even. I couldn't tell her the main reason I didn't want to go to the hospital was because I didn't have health insurance. The wound probably needed stitches. It wasn't too wide, but it was deep. It hurt like a son of a bitch, but I tried to keep it together when I was pulling the glass out.

She directed me to stand over the kitchen sink as she collected first aid supplies from the closet. As I held my hand out, she slowly unwound the shirt from my arm. I grimaced as she pulled the fabric from the wound. She cleaned the area with hydrogen peroxide, the sting stuttering through my body. When she wiped the area clean with dry gauze, I couldn't help but grit my teeth.

While she worked, she talked aimlessly about her life, filling me in on her job at the graphic arts agency she was working at in Seattle. How she was let go and had to move out in the same month. She shared how she was going to think about starting over in Arizona, where her college roommate lives, once Goldie and Edith would come home.

As she wrapped my arm with medical tape, I stared down at her. Her glasses were slipping down her nose. She bit her bottom lip, her white teeth against the plump berry of her skin. A tendril of hair fell into her face.

Using my right hand, I picked it up between my fingers, marveling at the softness, before tucking the piece behind her ear, where my fingers lingered.

She looked up at me, both hands pressing down on her makeshift bandage. I was so struck mute by the honesty in her green eyes I couldn't even feel the burn of my arm.

"Cedar . . ." she whispered.

I looked down at her lips, imagining what she would taste like.

Eight years ago, she chewed bubble mint gum. Even now, the scent would make me think of her for a flash.

Pulling away, my hand sizzled from the feeling of her skin.

Her cheeks flared pink and shoulders shuddered, and she took a step back as if trying to compose herself with steadying breaths.

"We should probably get a little sleep. It's been a long night, and we can't do anything about the fallen tree right now if we're half delirious."

I nodded at her briskly. Still reeling from the feel of her skin against mine. With my arm still held out at an odd angle in front of me, I watched as she cleaned up all the first aid supplies, throwing them haphazardly back into the box.

"I can put that away."

She nodded her agreement stiffly. Clutching her sweater to her chest, she walked up the stairs. I listened for the creak of the floorboards and click of the door lock before putting the kitchen right.

At the top of the stairs, I realized I couldn't sleep in my bed anymore. I assessed the staple job Devin had done over the window and determined it was as good as I could have done at four in the morning. I would work on fixing it in the light of day, but for the next few hours, it would hold.

I needed to figure out where to sleep. There was only one other free bed in the house. I considered the loveseat downstairs, then decided against it.

Annoyed, I lumbered into Clover's bedroom, climbing onto her daybed. My feet hung over the end of the bed as I tried to find a comfortable spot that didn't bump my arm. On the walls were the same soft-cheeked pop stars Clover loved to sing along with. Even though I never allowed someone else to control the music in my car, Clover found a way to play her songs.

Outside, the rain was dissipating, the wind dying to a low whine through the trees. Come morning, there would be a long list of projects to do to get things in order. Clean up all the glass in my bedroom.

Why is Devin's skin so soft? Does she use a special lotion?

I would need to replace that window as soon as possible so that Mom and Edith wouldn't see it. There had to be tutorials on how to replace a window somewhere, or maybe I'd have to hire someone? My savings were meager, but I could figure out a way.

Don't think about kissing Devin.

Hopefully, the power would come back on soon, or else the food would spoil. Maybe Mom had a generator somewhere. I'm sure she mentioned it once. Power outages are such a common occurrence around here.

God, when Devin's towel fell . . . Her tits are amazing. I bet they'd feel so good in my hands. And those tattoos. I've never been with someone with extensive tattoos before, but something about the ink across her skin is . . .

We'd need to do something about that fallen tree blocking the driveway. The closest gas station was a few miles down the road, but I could make it to get the chainsaw working again.

Devin is gorgeous. Has she always been that gorgeous? What was the matter with me that I didn't remember?

It had been so long ago I could hardly remember the moments we had together. It was only a few times. A make-out session here and there. Just having fun—or so I thought.

Thinking back, it was as if I was some other person at twenty-one, fooling around with Devin. I always thought she was cute. Sure, she didn't look like the other girls at school. She certainly didn't resemble any of the girls I dated, my on-again, off-again girlfriend Alivia. Tainslee, the girls in college. They had blonde hair and light eyes, tall and thin. Devin had dark hair and soft curves. Without heels, the top of her head only came up to my chin. She wore flowing skirts with big leather boots. Funny graphic tees and crazy colors in her hair. Her fingers were always stained with ink and paint.

She had those soft eyes in the shade of a dark forest, her wide smile, and a little scrunch of her nose. She was the same girl she had always been, but something in the way I saw her had changed. I couldn't pretend that she wasn't always this beautiful, that her skin wasn't always this soft, and that her lips weren't begging to be kissed.

As a teen and into my early twenties, I saw the way she looked at me. Sometimes, when she was tutoring Clover, I'd glance over and catch her watching me.

Back then, a lot of girls looked at me. I wouldn't say I was full of myself, but in our small town, I always had girls into me. I would never have called myself the best-looking guy out there, but with being tall, athletic, and having what I considered good hair, it was enough.

A few days into my break between junior and senior year of college, I was at a bonfire party with some of my buddies. Six months before, Alivia had dumped me because she was doing a semester abroad in Costa Rica and wanted to "explore her options."

I only shown up at the party because a few buddies talked me into it. A few beers deep, I had caught sight of Devin arriving with a guy I knew, Zack Rogers.

Surprised to see her, I watched her for a bit, the silver can of beer in her hand, the way her face would grimace with each sip.

Zack had left her alone the minute he got to the party. She wouldn't have had any friends there. This crowd was older, and while I couldn't remember who else she was friends with, I doubted they would be here in this backwoods clearing. In the reflection of her glasses, I could see the flames dancing around.

She rubbed her arms vigorously, warming herself, since she wasn't dressed for a bonfire party. I ran to my truck and grabbed a sweatshirt Alivia left there to bring it over to Devin. Holding the shirt out to her, she looked at me, and her breath caught.

In the bonfire's light, she looked tiny, smaller than I remembered her being. Alivia's sweatshirt was tight across her chest but hung over her hands. Devin pushed them up and smiled up at me.

Until that moment, I hadn't realized how full her mouth was.

We talked, conversation flowing easier than I expected. When I needed a new beer, I asked her to come with me. I got her one of those fruity drinks my buddy John's girlfriend brought. We sat on the back of my truck as we drank and talked. When people came over to chat, I was surprised to find that she could talk to everyone, making conversation about all sorts of topics. She had a deep, throaty laugh that bordered on infectious.

When Zack came over to ask her if she was ready to leave, I offered to drive her home. Even though I expected Zack would give me a hard time, he shrugged and then we were alone.

I told myself I was just protecting a childhood friend. That it was the decent thing to do.

We didn't end up going straight to her house, driving through the empty streets of Ridgewood. We ended up in some parking lot.

I don't know who reached for who. One moment, we were talking and then her lips were on mine, her hands on my shoulders, my hands on her hips and then moving up and over the sweatshirt. Our lips meeting and falling over each other's. At one point, she climbed over the middle console and straddled my lap. Her shapely body pressed against mine. I marveled at the weight of her breast in my hand, the way I couldn't fit the whole thing in my grip. It was a marvel I wasn't used to in all my years with girls made of sharp angles.

When I reached down under her stomach to unbutton her pants, she pulled back, looking down at me breathlessly. "We can't. Not here. Not like this."

Leaning forward, I pressed my lips to her throat, whispering to her skin, "I can make you feel good."

She clutched my head to her and moaned softly, "You already do. But I can't." She moved my head to place one more lingering kiss on my lips before climbing off me. "Can you take me home now?"

We had a few more times like that. They were hot and only lasted a little while. Being with Devin felt good. There was faith in the way she would give herself to me that was intoxicating. I felt powerful with her, worthy of the world. I took her kisses, and I used them.

Then Devin disappeared on me. And the big regret.

Alivia dumped me a few weeks into my senior year for the last time. A few years later, I saw her at the bar. She now has a husband and three sons, works in real estate, and has a completely normal life.

I was shocked to find I didn't care at all.

Down the hallway, Devin was sleeping. I wondered what she was wearing, what she was thinking of me. Did she want to kiss me the way I wanted to kiss her? How would she sigh as I would move down the column of her throat, her soft skin against my lips, as I would pull the shirt to the side? How would she melt into me? I knew all of this because I had it.

For a moment, without knowing what I was losing, I let her get away. I wanted it again. And this time, I would take all she offered me.

Devin

IT WAS AN EASY enough task to take stock of what items the storm ruined: the broken window, the wet floors, the shattered glass. What was far more treacherous was the way I spent the entire night with the memory of Cedar's skin under my fingers. Each time my eyes fluttered shut, I could feel his warmth upon my hands, smell his clean, rugged scent. The tremors of excitement betraying me every time my mind wandered.

Despite only getting a few hours of sleep, I woke at the same time my body always woke me, by 6:30. On an ordinary morning, I would get some of my commissions done. The light of the dawn was good for painting, and I enjoyed the time before the rest of the world was up and running around, where the air seemed still with the anticipation of what could be. I would get my cup of coffee with oat milk, then move into the airy loft where the morning sun filtered in strong.

As I set up my supplies, I considered the problems I could solve and came up with a few half solutions. I certainly couldn't chop up a fallen tree, so I'd have to look up the numbers of one of the local tree services. That seemed easy enough in theory.

There was little that could be done about Cedar's window, aside from the garbage bag cover. It would need to be cleaned, but I wasn't about to set foot in that room.

It was the afternoon in Oslo where Goldie and Edith would be on this leg of the trip. I sent her a quick email letting them know what happened the night before.

Turning back to the sketched-out canvas, I pondered which quadrant I wanted to start with. Typically, it was the bottom, with the client's face, so I could blend the flowers seamlessly. But something was urging me to start with the dahlias.

In the pocket of my leggings, my phone vibrated against my thigh. The message was from Goldie asking me to call Edith's nephew, Caleb, who owned his own tree service company. Despite the early hour when I called, Caleb picked up and, after I explained the situation, agreed to come out later that day.

It was past ten before I heard Cedar shuffling down the hall. From my spot above the kitchen, I could see him emerge from the stairway, his light hair in disarray around his head on one side and lying flat against his head on the other. The thin white shirt clung to his biceps as he moved into the kitchen and opened the refrigerator. Staring, he grabbed a jug of orange juice from the inside and drank it straight from the carton, his Adam's apple bobbing with each gulp. He set the carton back and wiped his arm across his mouth.

He seemed so beastly and uncivilized. Gray sweatpants hung low on his hips, and I could see a swath of his smooth back as his shirt rode up.

Under his breath, he sang a song off-key, the tune familiar enough to niggle at my brain but not enough to recognize it.

In college, we would draw the human form in classes. Gazing down at him from my perspective above, I envisioned the angles and shadows I would create if I had the chance to draw him. I hadn't worked with charcoal in a while, but something about the lithe way he moved inspired me.

"I can feel you looking at me," he called out.

Scrambling to appear as if I was busy, I turned my chair to face the window, focusing on the smudging the pink and purple of an aster together. "What's that?"

My voice was as innocent as I could muster.

"Don't play coy. You think I don't know what it feels like to have you staring at me from that loft?" With a large mug of coffee in hand, he settled onto one of the stools and gazed up at me.

From my angle, his eyes were rimmed dark from lack of sleep. If he still looked tired, I couldn't imagine how terrible I looked.

He rubbed his right hand over his face, with his left arm resting on the counter.

The bandage already looked dirty.

"That looks disgusting. You need to wash it. You should shower."

He took a long sip of his coffee, his bright blue eyes watching me over the rim. "Do you want to come down here and play nursemaid again?"

I pointed my brush at him. "You're a grown man. I'm sure you can shower by yourself."

"But what if I don't want to?"

His mouth quirked up and, damn, if my core didn't pulse slightly at that grin.

Not that he could know that.

"You have a working hand—I—you'll manage—" I paused and skated my gaze over him snidely. "Everything you need to get it done by yourself."

The sharp bark of a laugh was coupled with throwing his head back, the cords in his neck standing out as his shoulders shook. "Okay, point taken. Thanks, Nurse Haruki."

"That's *doctor* to you."

He grinned, that devilish smile that won me over from the start, one of his bottom teeth slightly crooked. A fluttering sensation started in my stomach, and I had to turn away to hide the flush of my cheeks. Now facing my canvas, I braced my hand over the painting and willed myself to get back to work. To not think about how the last time he smiled at me like that was over the middle console of his car as he dropped me off at my house, the sting of his kiss still lingering on my lips, and the hope of finally falling for my dream guy high in my head.

There was the scrape of the stool against the hardwood floor and then his feet padding up the stairs and into the bathroom. Thankful for the thin walls of the house, I listened for the door to click shut behind him.

Alone once again, I was able to look at my work. Recently, I started a new style of custom painting that seemed to be popular with a certain clientele. Part person, part plant, it had different flowers and foliage sprouting from their heads.

The mom seemed sweet over her emails, and I hoped word of mouth would lead to more personalized portraits from my site. She mentioned she was on the PTA at an elementary school that I researched and found to be in an affluent neighborhood across the country. I could use all the jobs I could get until I found a new agency.

From the window in the loft, the sun dipped behind the trees. Halfway through, I turned on the small Tiffany lamp in the corner. Natural light was optimal for painting, shadows cast from artificial light not lending itself to realistic shading.

Cedar's boots in the hallway echoed up to me.

Holding my breath, I listened for his hands on the ladder, his boots on the rungs, but the sound of him approaching never came. Instead, it was the banging of his feet going up and down the stairs, rattling heavy metal tools echoed through the house. The chime of the washing machine starting and then the stomping of his boots up the stairs, clomping with each step. The whine of a vacuum and then, minutes later, a series of low popping.

Staring down at my painting, I mixed the umber on my palate to add to my canvas. The flicks of my wrists to add the color to my vision, the movement of my arm to get the depth right. Sucking my lower lip into my mouth, I heard the sounds of Cedar moving around the house reaching the little loft. My fingers faltered on my brush as I worked the canvas.

One more brush stroke, one more hour, one more day. You can get through this.

Downstairs, my laptop was charged up, along with the long list of companies in Phoenix I could send my resume and portfolio to. When I returned from my walk, I checked my phone. Autumn's affirmation, *I am the only person responsible for my happiness,* sat under a long strand of texts from my college roommate who currently lived in Arizona, Becca. Several emojis and exclamations in a row set off her telling me to "totally crash on her couch as long as it would take" and that her boyfriend Chaz would dig out the air mattress if need be.

I had only met Chaz once, when he asked me why Becca couldn't have big boobs like me, but at least she had better legs. I added "finding my own apartment" at the top of my list.

My stomach growled, and I strained to listen for the thump of Cedar coming down the stairs, but the house was silent.

Walking to the edge of the loft, I peered down to see if Cedar was downstairs. Kinny sat on her bed beside the fireplace, Cedar's book open face down on the table, a blanket bunched up in the couch's corner.

Sucking in a breath, I listened for Cedar's footfalls. Above my head, water came whistling through the pipes as he showered.

Cedar in the shower. Naked. He was naked in the shower. Water dripping down his back and over his shoulders, cascading from his stomach and onto . . .

Stop it, Devin. You're going to work yourself up and jump him again if you keep imagining this.

The clatter of paintbrushes hitting the floor startled me out of my daydream, streaking rainbow underfoot. Cursing, I bent down to retrieve them and wipe up the mess before it dried.

I was a twenty-six-year-old woman. You'd think by the way I was reacting I hadn't been laid in forever. Granted, I hadn't had a good lay in years. Quite a few long years. But still, that's not to say I hadn't figured out how to take care of those needs independently.

I bet Cedar could take care of your needs.

"Argh! Not helping!" I muttered to the space.

Paint materials in one hand, I climbed down the ladder and landed with a bounce on my feet. *Focus, focus. It is only another week and a half, maybe two.*

After cleaning my brushes in the sink, I turned to the fridge to put things together for breakfast.

The power was still out, so I used up what I could. When I pulled up the outage map, the estimated restoration time was over thirty hours away, but years of experience told me that the area on the outside of town was the last to get the power trucks. I had no issue staying in the house without power, but I wasn't sure about Cedar.

Goldie's home was old-fashioned, with a wood-burning stove for heat, and luckily, the oven and stovetop used gas.

On the counter, my favorite playlist was playing on my cell phone. Thankfully, my previous job had forgotten I was still using their hot spot. They would figure it out, but that was an issue for future Devin. For now, I would blast my witchy-earth-girl pop as I pulled coconut milk, oil, sugar, and flour out to make pancakes.

Opening three cabinets, I searched for the spices on the top shelf. At a whopping five-foot-three, I wasn't what most would consider too short, yet I couldn't reach the cinnamon, while Cedar and Clover came from a tall family.

Glancing around the kitchen, I saw no footstool in sight. The night before, I had seen a ladder in the back shed. Would it be worth it to go out there for a simple spice? No. My eyes caught on the stools resting against the other side of the breakfast nook.

Pulling the tall stool under the cabinet, I adjusted the feet to be stable. First, one knee and then another, I climbed up. It swiveled with my movements. Taking a deep breath, I waited until it stopped moving, grabbing onto the edge of the cabinet.

Cedar called out from the stairwell, "I got good news and bad news."

"Oh?" On level with the right shelf, I tucked the spices in the crook of my arm.

"The good news is I am as clean as can be. The bad news is I used all the hot water, and until the power comes back on, I don't think you'll want to shower . . . What the hell?"

Pushing against the cabinet, I turned the swivel seat toward Cedar, who was standing a few feet away on the threshold of the kitchen. I swayed before grabbing onto the top of the fridge. His face was dark with worry.

"What the fuck do you think you're doing up there?"

"Getting some nutmeg?"

"On a swivel stool?" His jaw tensed as he approached me.

My feet steadier, I glared down at Cedar. "I'm fine. I was just getting some spices."

Stopping below me, he glowered. "You could have fallen!" He put his hands on each side of my legs as if to catch me.

In the years I would spy on him from the loft above, I was familiar enough with the top of his head, but I had never seen annoyance on his face.

I handed down the cinnamon, nutmeg, and allspice. "The only time I almost fell was when you yelled at me."

As he set the spices on the counter, he scowled. "You could've slipped and cracked your head open."

With one hand on the top of the fridge, I balanced my stance into a crouch. "You sound like my mother."

Cautiously, Cedar grabbed my hands, setting them on his shoulders. His right hand hesitated in the air before resting on my hip. "Use me to get down."

The heat of his hand on my hip scorched me through my thin T-shirt. His fingers dug into my back, and his thumb rested just to the side of my belly button.

"Use you?"

I intended for the statement to come out teasingly, but it came out breathy and low.

He nodded at me.

At the same level as him, I could see that he had a faint scar above his left brow that ran into his hairline. With his focus on me, I froze in his gaze.

His thumb jerked against my stomach, digging in deeper. In the movement, my shirt rode up, and his fingers brushed over my bare skin. My gaze drifted from his face down to his shoulders, where my hands rested. Slow enough to be accidental, I rubbed my fingers across his shoulders.

He gripped me tighter, his thumb tracing a small circle against my skin.

Taking a chance, I moved my hand to his throat, brushing his shirt out of the way.

The skin of his neck was softer than I expected. My hand traced the way up to his throat, the feel of his stubble against my fingertips. His blue eyes followed me as I ventured over his face. Delicately, my fingers moved across his jawline and up his cheek to trace his scar.

"I always wondered what happened here."

Voice hoarse, he moved his hand up my waist to rest on my ribs. "Clover pushed me into a brick wall when she was ten."

As our faces got closer, I could feel his warmth radiate and smell the coffee lingering on his breath.

"What a mean sister."

His lips were so close I could feel his words pushing against me.

"The worst."

I wanted to surge forward and press my lips against his, to taste him on my tongue. His eyes leveled me, a fusion of green and blue and gold and gray.

When we had our tryst, his kisses were needy, deceiving me into believing that he felt the same way I did. How he would push his body against mine, the feel of his hands on my hips, familiar and forbidden.

In one motion of his thumb against my skin, it brought me back to when I was eighteen. The beauty of his kisses and the destruction of losing them.

Ducking my head, I allowed him to hold me closer, his arms wrapping around my waist to help me down. My cheek skimmed his. When his lips brushed against my ear, I shivered.

"You smell so good," he murmured so softly that I didn't think he meant to say it aloud.

I considered turning, how easy it would be to move to him. To fall, I could catch his lips with mine. I could give in for just a moment, could risk myself and all I had built. His touch was taking me under, and I wanted to savor the shiver that ran up my spine. Really, I could do this, could give in and kiss him. No longer a lovesick teen but an adult. In my years of experience of kissing men, I would not be hurt by him again. It had been years.

As Cedar stepped back, he kept his grip tight around my waist. But the angle was all wrong. As I leaned forward, my weight caused him to tumble back. Stumbling on his feet, he staggered back into the dishwasher, and I slid down his body, landing crudely on my feet. My elbow jabbed his left arm with a muted thud. Cedar gasped, his face going white. He made a wheezing sound and then cursed.

"Oh, God! Did I hurt you, Cedar . . ." Grappling for words, I clasped onto the hurt arm, trying to soothe him. "I'm so sorry. Are you okay?"

His jaw clenched as he stared down at me.

"I'm fine." He gasped out as he stepped back, pushing my hand out from arm's length. He took a shallow breath.

I was sure my eyes were as large as saucers.

What's a person to do in this type of situation? Inspect the area? Cold compress, yes, cold compress.

"Right!"

Dashing to the freezer, I grabbed a bag of half-frozen broccoli and slapped it onto his bandaged arm.

He let me put the cold pack on, coughed, and put his right hand in front of his face. "I'm just going to . . . go." Turning toward the stairs, he pulled his arm closer to his body, cradling the pack of frozen vegetables. Grimacing, he nodded at me one last time. "I'll see you later."

Refusing to look at him as he left me, I plopped onto the same stool from earlier. "See ya." Sinking onto the empty stool, I cradled my face, pinching my jaw hard.

In the ever-growing spring light of the kitchen, I knew there was no denying my desire.

Still shaky from his touch, my legs quivered. If I closed my eyes, I could feel his body against mine, his fingers on my skin, his breath fanning across my face as he leaned in close. Even without him there, an ache thrummed through me, wanting more of his touch, to brush the hair from my face, to press his mouth to mine. The phantom of his kiss aching across my lips. I needed his hands on my breasts, on my ass, pulling me closer to him, to feel his excitement against my core.

Nothing about my attraction to Cedar had waned. I wanted him just as much as I did when I was eighteen. Over the years, my relationship had been more physical than emotional. If he was any other man, I would have no qualms about sleeping with him.

You're no longer eighteen. Yes, you want him, but it could just be sex.

The opportunity to finish what we started eight years before could be cathartic, closure I never had before. All I would need to do was safeguard myself against feelings.

In the past eight years, I never fell for anyone. I was a professional at keeping feelings and sex separate.

Falling for Cedar was a girl's game. I hadn't been that girl in a long time, and I wouldn't let him bring me down that road again.

Of course, he might want nothing to do with me after I fell on him. How could a moment, a beautiful almost-kiss, go so wrong?

Maybe I could listen to my instincts telling me to stay and make things right.

Cedar

As the pain in my arm subsided, I had a wholly new issue to contend with.

Despite my better judgment, knowing that Devin was leaving soon, I was edging closer to crossing a line. I flirted and taunted and got perilously close to kissing her.

Did I flirt with a lot of women? Sure, of course. But Devin wasn't just any woman but my former neighbor. My mother adored her, and my sister looked up to her. In no world could things between us be casual. Years before, I thought what we shared could be a simple hookup, but one look on her face when she found Alivia on my doorstep told me I was wrong.

Still, this time around with Devin felt different, more charged somehow. What was I doing holding Devin like that?

Clover had told me once I was too dependent on monogamy, and that's why I couldn't stand being alone. As much as I wanted to tell my twenty-one-year-old sister to shove it, I couldn't. While there were a few one-night stands here and there, the bulk of my dating history was long stretches with a girlfriend. Once I got out of a relationship, I was back in one again. This month-long break from Tainslee had been the first time in years I was single. Devin couldn't be long term; she had told me as much.

No matter how much I wanted Devin, I would need to keep it in my pants. I had a job interview in a few hours, a fallen tree over my only road out, and a plump corgi sleeping on top of my bag.

Kinny gave me a scathing look as I pushed her off and pulled out my phone to call Ridgewood PT.

Luckily, I still had reception and was able to reach Dr. Foster. After explaining that a storm knocked out the only road off the property, we debated whether we should reschedule or cancel, then settled on a video call.

Double-checking that my hot spot still worked without power, I pulled up my search engine, hesitated, then typed in *Devin Haruki.*

The first thing that popped up was a minimalist website of logos for different brands, some I recognized. On the bottom was a link to her shop. She sold custom paintings with a button that said *Inquire about pricing,* which always meant expensive.

Scrolling back to the image results, my eyes raked over the pictures, which were filled with mostly Haruki Murakami fan art and anime, I saw something that stopped me. In the photo, she was younger, her hair chin length, with streaks of blue and green. She stood between two oversized paintings on a gallery wall. One had three women, one with curly dark hair, one with sleek blonde, and another with auburn. Bright flowers bloomed around them as they laughed.

The other was of a woman embracing her lover. Her olive skin contrasted with his pale. The hunger in her green eyes as she gazed up. Ferns and moss growing from the edges and creeping onto their skin.

It wasn't the eroticism of the painting that made me stop scrolling but the tattoo behind the subject's ear, a triangle of a bird, rose, and leaf that matched Devin's. Long dark hair brushed over one shoulder, the same plump lips. At first, all I could see was her in this self-portrait. And then

I looked closer, and the man's face was clear.

I knew those blue eyes, the dimple on his chin, and that light scar from hairline to brow.

It was my face. My scar, which, only a few hours before, she tenderly traced from her perch above me.

Even from my unskilled eye, I could tell her craft had improved in the time since taking this picture. The examples on her website were more realistic, the lines sharper and more controlled. Yet it was unmistakably me. Me from eight years ago, with an eighteen-year-old Devin. This was the version of us in our youth before the pain of losing her father. The girl who was never hurt and the boy who was too foolish to see what was in front of him.

The date in the picture was from over five years before. Long enough that I couldn't take it as a sign she still cared about me. A possessive burn took up in my chest. It was my face she painted, my face she looked at for hours on end as she put what we shared on display. Maybe other men would be bothered by this, but I couldn't bring myself to feel anything but a sense of righteousness.

I had no rights to her, to her feelings, and to her memories. But all I wanted was to create a future when she could see me that way again.

Spirits lifted, I glanced out the window to see a man walking through the trees up to the house.

The familiar squeak of the front door opening echoed up the stairs. From my spot at an upstairs window, I saw Devin meet him in the front yard. She pulled her oversized white sweater over her blue graphic tee shirt. Her hair was still up in that messy bun I had begun to love. Tendrils of her hair whipped around her face as she talked to the guy. He looked slightly familiar, but I couldn't place him under his baseball cap.

Sweatshirt pulled over my head, I made my way out the front door and toward the duo. Halfway across the lawn, the guy looked up, and my step faltered.

Caleb Hardin, Edith's nephew, was a few years older than me in school. We spent some time together over the years at family functions. His family was more conservative than ours, so he didn't see his aunt aside from holidays. I never liked the way his family looked down on Edith and Mom's relationship. They had the strongest example of a healthy love I had growing up.

I had few memories of my father, as he was away, working a lot, but what I remembered was how quiet we had to be when he got home from work. Being with Edith, Mom laughed, told loud stories, and moved her hands around while in conversation.

And someone who looked down on my family was standing in the yard, smiling at my Devin.

No, not yours—you can't say that.

After approaching them, I stopped next to Devin, standing closer than I probably should have.

Caleb smiled at me. "Hey, man. What's up?" He put his hand out to shake.

His face was friendly, but in his gaze was disappointment from seeing me. I wondered how often he tried to pick up women using his business.

I took his hand, gripping it harder than normal.

Caleb squeezed mine hard, his grip calloused and strong. He won out as pain shot across my hand.

I fought the urge to shake my arm.

Devin frowned at our hands, then looked from Caleb to me, a wrinkle forming between her brows. "So, I was going to walk down to the bridge with Caleb so he can assess how much work it will take."

"I'll go with you." Stepping closer to Devin, I hovered my hand above her lower back.

She glanced up at me, her green eyes bigger behind her glasses, the line between her brows deepening. One corner of her mouth turned down before shaking her head slightly.

We trekked down the drive, leaves crunching under our shoes. On the way, I hummed under my breath, the lyrics for my favorite late nineties song playing in my head. Devin glanced up at me, her pink lips parted. Green eyes darted from mine to my lips and down to the brown-and-tan flannel I had thrown on.

"Your collar is—" She reached forward, her fingers brushing the side of my neck as she straightened the lapel. "There."

Stopping, I savored the feel of her soft fingers against my skin. It took all my restraint not to grab her hand—and do what, kiss it? Was I a hand kisser? What kind of man was this woman making me into?

A loud crack of a branch snapped us out of our staring contest, and Devin shook her head before stepping toward the fallen tree.

When we got to the fallen bridge, Caleb jumped onto the tree to get a better look.

As he inspected measurements and walked around, Devin leaned in closer to me. "I can handle this myself, you know."

"I know that."

Caleb jumped on the fallen tree, something that would have surely made me fall off, but he kept his balance. Asshole.

"Sooo—" She waved around between us, waiting for me to go on

I studied the top of her head.

How many times have I seen her in the years we knew each other? Something about that painting had stirred me. That was the Devin of the past, which meant she was always this beautiful, this charming, this talented. And I was an idiot. What had I been thinking all those years ago, when I overlooked her?

Caleb jumped down from the tree, landing in front of us as smoothly as a cat.

"Let's go up to the house to talk. I bet Aunt Edith still has those little chocolate-and-hazelnut cookies stashed somewhere. I love those things."

Devin glanced from me to Caleb, annoyance slipping off her face into a friendly smile. "Sure, I'll put the coffee on, too. It's chilly out here."

She walked ahead of us. I tried not to look at her ass in her black leggings. When I glanced over and saw Caleb was doing the same thing, irritation slithered in me.

"So, what's the deal with Devin?" Caleb asked, motioning with his chin. "She got a boyfriend?"

Irritation turned into red-hot anger, but I choked it down. "No, I don't think so."

"So, you two aren't, you know, together or anything?"

"No, we're not together. She's a family friend, nothing more."

"Just friends, all alone, together." His eyebrow ticked up. "Staying at Aunt Edith's house together."

"It was a mix-up with the house-sitting duties. That's all." Sensing where this conversation was leading and not liking it at all, I dug my hand in my pocket to keep it from shaking.

He nodded, a peculiar look across his face. "So, I'm free to ask her out?"

Dozens of protests and excuses rose, but I couldn't get them out. I had no right to stop him from asking her out.

"If you wanted to, but she's not sticking around here. She's moving away soon, to Arizona or something. She doesn't live here in Ridgewood or anything."

He shrugged, watching the house as it loomed. "That's okay. She seems like someone who would be fun—if you know what I mean—but not the girl to bring home to Mom and Dad, you know?" He laughed.

As I tightened my fist, the first thought ran through my head that it would only take a split second to punch him in his bearded face.

"No, I don't know. Why wouldn't you?"

"All those tattoos and the crazy hair?" He put his hands up in front of his chest and motioned juggling. "And that body? Come on."

"She's more than a body. Devin's the total package," I snapped. "She's smart and creative and beautiful and . . ."

"But you're not into her at all." He smirked. "If you don't want me to ask her out, just say so. We're almost family. So just say the word, and I'll back off."

She wasn't my girl, wasn't my anything. I didn't know what Devin wanted. Honestly, I didn't even know her outside of the girl she was eight years prior.

"Do what you want, man," I muttered. "Just don't hurt her. My mom would kill you."

He gave me a toothy smile, and my hand twitched from wanting to slap the smirk off his face.

"Goldie, yeah, right?"

Simmering on the couch, I watched Devin serve Caleb little cookies and a cup of coffee. He sat on *my stool*, eating cookies Mom always bought for me, taking all of Devin's attention. He set a cookie down on the counter next to his napkin, then wiped his hands on his pants, crumbs falling all over the floor. Such a dick.

"You have two options. If you just want me to clear it enough for you to be able to drive onto the road, it will be at least five hundred. If you want me to clean up the whole thing, chip it, and all that, it will run you about twelve," Caleb explained.

"Twelve?!" I sputtered. "Twelve hundred dollars to clean up a few twigs?"

Devin and Caleb looked over at me as if they just realized I was still around. Devin's brow furrowed at me, and Caleb grinned as he put his hands up.

"Hey, that's the fair going rate. You have a large downed fir tree out there that will take hours and experienced manpower to get rid of. I have a long list of people who need me to clean up at their homes. You guys aren't the only ones who had fallen trees because of the storm. I could go down to an even *1K* for a family discount."

"Bullshit, family discount," I muttered. I sat forward, my hand folded in my lap. "Dev, we could call around and find someone else."

Shooting me a look of warning, she hissed, "Stop it." She turned to Caleb with a serene smile. "I can manage five hundred. We could just have you clear it enough, if that still works."

Leaning back harder against the couch, I glowered at them.

He was such a punk, coming in here, drinking her coffee, eating my cookies, tracking dirt on the carpet, and getting smiles from Devin. He wasn't here last night when we were in the pouring rain, wasn't there getting all cut up on broken glass. A straight-up punk.

Caleb leaned forward, his fingers brushing the collar of her shirt. "What's this from?"

Devin looked down, pulling the cream tee from her body with the words *Hello Goodbye* written on two palms beside a black umbrella. "Oh, it's just from . . . um. A show. It's nothing."

Caleb didn't move his fingers. A heat rose in me, seeing his hand so close to her.

She leaned back, and his hand fell away, dropping to the space between them.

Caleb sat up on his stool. "I could knock it down a bit." He paused to give Devin a big grin, looking her up and down. "I could do, say, four hundred, if you agreed to get a drink with me. You know, when you're able to get your car out of here. Or I could pick you up at the end of the drive."

Devin's cheeks colored pink, her eyes darting to me.

The air stilled.

I had no claim to her. But I needed her to say no to him. A hot surge filled me as I imagined them together. The way she'd meet him on the street, how she would climb into his truck, the shy way she would look at him over the table at dinner. She would listen to him talk, and he'd put his hand on her back as they walk out of the restaurant, leaning in to whisper in her ear.

My hand clenched my mug.

Since I met Caleb, I knew girls liked him. If you like that country-boy thing he had going on, he was attractive enough. He had a good job, a good relationship with his parents. Caleb was a little shorter than me, but he was broader. He spent his time working up in trees and had the muscle mass to show it. For Ridgewood, I'm sure plenty of girls would want to date him. I just didn't want Devin to be one.

Having no idea how smart or creative she was, he just saw her as some hot girl and didn't know how caring she could be. How she was kind of weird in the best way.

There was no way a guy like that could appreciate her. He needed a girl who was more down to earth, who enjoyed riding in a truck and bonfire parties and would eat the venison he brought home. Devin was a vegetarian. How could that work?

As Devin hesitated, I knew the answer.

Pushing away from the table, I got up. "Whatever you want to do, Devin, it's your money."

My voice came out sharp.

I banged my mug on the counter between them, the liquid sloshing over the side and splashing onto Caleb's hand.

He yelped as if he was burned, even though the coffee was lukewarm at best. Behind me, Devin cooed and grabbed a towel, helping him wipe his hand.

I stomped up the stairs to my room. I couldn't handle hearing her tell him yes.

An hour into cleaning up the glassy rain mess, Devin arrived in my door-way. By that time, I had cleared away the large shards off the floor and filled two garbage bags with unnecessary items. My old shirts that didn't fit me, posters of half-naked girls, all going into the bag.

Tainslee had called my phone again, leaving a message that I needed to call her back as soon as possible, a plea about needing to tell me something important.

Ignoring the call, I considered if the Sounders T-shirt two sizes too small for me would be worth keeping.

Leaning against the door frame, Devin's arms crossed against her chest, she tilted her head. Frowning at me, she watched as I worked.

Her oversized white sweater fell off a shoulder, and she shrugged it back up, pulling the fabric closer with one hand. Her fingers rested against her collarbone, the same spot that smelled of soap and paint.

"You care to explain what that hostility toward Caleb was about?"

Focusing on the broom I was grasping, I frowned. "I don't like him."

She laughed. "Yeah, I can see that." Sitting at the edge of my bed beside a garbage bag, she tilted her head. "And that's not an answer."

"It's enough for me." I grabbed a Mariner's T-shirt a few sizes too small for me off the floor to stuff it in the bag, keeping my face away from Devin.

"No." She took the shirt from me and placed it in the laundry basket. "I have seen you be civil to all sorts of people you don't like. You are always friendly and kind."

Leaning the broom against the wall, I fought to keep my voice steady. "Are you going to do it?"

She pursed her lips, assessing me. Her silence dragged out, and I won-dered if she understood my question. She finally looked from her hands to me. "I told him I'd think about it."

"If you like him, go out with him. If you're into that hypermasculine macho-man thing, I guess."

Devin put her hand in front of her mouth, but I saw the crinkle of a smile around her eyes. After a few long moments, she brought her hand down, still struggling to contain her grin. "Of course, what woman could resist a guy so macho? That's exactly what I'm looking for in a man." She lay the back of her hand against her forehead and sighed. "Oh, macho man, take me away."

"Okay, okay." I waved dismissively. "Knock it off. I get it."

"Oh, Caleb, come chop down trees for me. That gets my blood pumping for you." She let out a throaty laugh, throwing her head back.

Her throat was exposed as her shoulders shook. Her whole face lit up with glee.

"I said I get it, Devin." I grabbed the bag, heaving it to the floor. Settling in next to her, I folded my hands in front of me. "It was just a question."

"Alright, I'm done. No more making fun of you." She pinched her lips together, the corners still turned up. "Though I'm not sure why it's bothering you so much. It's not like you're jealous of Caleb." She laughed again, softer this time. "I mean, you couldn't be."

"Why not?"

"Because, that … we … you." She looked away. "Because there is nothing to be jealous about. Even if I did go out with Caleb, and I'm not sure if I will . . . I shouldn't affect you. You don't care."

"Of course I care. I've always cared."

"Can you honestly say you've given me the slightest thought in the past eight years?"

Her question was valid. In the past few years, I had thought of Devin only in the most passing way. When I thought about Clover in middle school, Devin was around. But to say that my nights were lonely without her in my life is something I couldn't do.

I realized how royally I had screwed up when I was twenty-two. What level of short-sightedness had allowed me to overlook her when I first had my chance?

Not wanting to lie to her, I shook my head. She raised an eyebrow at me as she stood, and I grabbed her hand. "Just because I didn't think about you before doesn't mean I haven't been."

"I'm not your responsibility to take care of. I can say yes to Caleb if I want."

"I know that. It's not out of responsibility. Trust me, the thoughts going through my head are the farthest thing from responsible."

She sank down next to me, watching me closely. "Oh."

Her voice was soft.

I had said too much, gave up more than I should have. I needed a change of subject.

"And what was that thing about making you walk to the end of the drive to pick you up? It's like a half mile to the road. That's bullshit."

She raised an eyebrow. "Cedar, I am an able-bodied person perfectly capable of walking the less than hundred feet through the yard." She paused, leaning closer. "I did it today, didn't I?"

"That's different. If it's for a date, he should take care of you. Coming to the door. Not making you walk by yourself."

Devin laughed. "What's going to happen to me in the driveway?"

There were small lines around her eyes as she smiled at me. "Laugh lines," my mom would call them. My mom hated those kinds of lines on her face. As a child, I would catch her in the mirror, pulling her face in different directions, tightening against her skull.

Devin laughed with unabashed enthusiasm. I couldn't help but be warned, even if she was laughing at me.

Fighting not to get caught up in how pretty she looked, I kept a straight face. "It's not right."

"It's fine, Cedar. Really. I used to meet up with dates all the time in Seattle. I couldn't have them knowing where I lived on the first date, you know? They could be serial killers."

Wrinkling my brow, I asked, "Why would you date a guy who could be a serial killer?"

Devin put her hands up, her palms facing the ceiling. "You can't tell who's a serial killer by looking that at them. I assume everyone is a serial killer at first. It's just basic staying-safe-and-not-being-murdered protocol for women."

"Did you think I was a serial killer?" I joked.

"Oh, you mean when I was all alone in a house in the woods during a storm and then you broke in when I was in the bathtub?" she asked, scoffing.

When I nodded, she smirked at me. "I was eighty-seven percent sure you were a serial killer or at least a burglar."

We stared each other down.

"Seriously, though, are you going to go out with him?"

She bit her lip and turned away. "I think I probably should. It might be fun. He seems nice and all . . ."

"He's only into you because he thinks you'll have sex with him," I shot.

I couldn't believe my ears. Before I could stop it, the statement flew out of my mouth.

She cocked her head, assessing my words. When she finally spoke, it came out thin.

"Did he say that to you?"

I considered lying to her. As far as I could see it, he didn't need to say it explicitly—I knew him, his family, and his circle of friends. He was small-town, backward-thinking. There was no way he would be serious about a girl like her. But saying those words made me feel like an asshole.

She sighed. "I didn't think so." She studied her fingernails, short and smooth, with little paint specks on them. "Cedar. I've been dating for almost a decade. I have had my share of dating mishaps. Believe me when I say I am familiar with the type of guy who only wants sex. I can handle that type of guy, and I don't think that Caleb is like that."

A pain shot up my arm from my wound, and I realized I had been clenching my fist at the mention of Devin with other guys. She was an adult; I knew she had experiences in the world. I just wanted to know I was the best she had. I wanted to be the one who made her forget every single one of those kisses she had. To be the one to wash away the memory of another hand on her body.

"I'm trying really hard not to say the wrong thing here, but the truth is, there is no way he could have a serious relationship with someone like you."

"Good thing I'm not wanting serious with Caleb." She paused, and her eyes darted away from me. "Or with anyone. I'm hoping to move soon, remember?"

"How could I forget," I mumbled. "I'm just trying to protect you, looking out, that's all."

The idea of Devin leaving made my stomach clench. I liked having her around, having her close to me, liked her conversation and her jokes. The way she hummed as she painted. Caleb couldn't appreciate those things.

She laughed haughtily. "Protect me? From what? A few free drinks? Some flirting? A one-night stand?"

I flinched. "I don't want some guy taking advantage of you or using you."

"And you, in your gracious heart, are so above that?" She bit off a scornful laugh, darkness coloring her gaze. "That's rich coming from you."

"What does that mean?"

Lips pinched together, she inhaled deeply through her nose and shook her head, her gaze darting away from me. Her throat bobbed with a hard swallow, and when her eyes came back to rest on me, it was with a mask in place. "You think women can't enjoy a one-night stand or even want one?"

She stood, brushing off invisible dirt from her leggings, her sight everywhere but on me. The conversation was getting so far out of my control it careened down the tracks to destruction.

"I never said that."

My words came out choppy as I stumbled to find solid ground with her.

Putting her hand up to stop me, she shook her head. "Please, Cedar, stop, for the love of God. Just stop before you say something truly offensive."

Her hand on the knob of the front door, she whirled around to face me, her evergreen eyes hard. "For the record"—her words were sharply methodical—"if I go out with Caleb, he couldn't hurt me. I'd have to care about what the other person thinks of me." Her voice dropped and knuckles grew white. "I don't know who it is you think I am, but it's not me. As if I'm a fool who can be swayed over a few nice words and a smile. Like there's any chance I'd catch feelings for a guy like that."

"Is it so much to worry about you getting hurt, Dev?"

The door open, her dark ponytail over one shoulder, her morose gaze pinned me.

"You're eight years too late for that."

Seven

Devin

STORMING OFF INTO THE woods probably wasn't the smartest move I could have made. Him not wanting Caleb to take advantage of me was the most ridiculous idea. Even pissed off at his pseudo-chivalry, I knew there was no one in the world who could hurt me the way he did. No one I would ever care for to the same depths.

I had tried, over years and boyfriends and girlfriends and self-help books and late-night hookups. Away from Ridgewood, I was able to tell myself it was a passing infatuation. I was a child who thought they knew what it was to be a woman.

Resisting the urge to scream, I stepped along the familiar roots and trails and crossed the property line between my old house and the Edens'.

The trees around me, I came across the old tree house I used as a child. The nailed-in planks looked withered, and when I tested my weight on the bottom rung, it spun to the left on the nail. Wiggling the other rungs, I decided they were safe enough and made the climb up to the trapdoor.

I wasn't sure who owned the house and, with it, the tree house, but the lock was still on. A hot-pink-and-purple monstrosity I had used for years. I twisted the dial: one, six, eighteen, surprised when the combination, the golden ratio, allowed the lock to open with a scratchy pop.

Climbing through the door, I looked around the space. Cobwebs hung from each corner, a pile of leaves rotting in the middle of the floor nest, on top of which was a layer of dead bugs. I brushed the floor clear and settled in, tucking my knees up under my chin.

On a practical level, I'd need to accept Caleb's date because I couldn't afford not to. He was attractive in a rugged, country-boy way. Certainly, he looked different from most of my previous dates in the past few years. I hadn't intended a long visit, yet despite my feminist objections to Caleb's manipulation, the chance to avoid wasted hours was too good to miss.

Ask not what you can do for the patriarchy but what the patriarchy can do for you . . .

But more than anything, accepting Caleb's date request was more rooted in spite of Cedar's ugly comments.

He didn't know me any longer. I wasn't that girl who showed up on his front step in a three-day-old dress and grief-stricken eyes.

Cedar had no right to dictate who I dated. I couldn't be some girl waiting around for him. He had always been my exception. But there was no way I could let him know that. He held too much power over me, and to give him more would be dangerous.

Despite my libido having other ideas, I would need to rub one out later. This sexual tension was getting to be too much and might lead me to do something stupid.

Although Cedar would probably turn down that idea. Sure, I was ready to kiss him in the kitchen earlier. But when it got ruined by me falling, it was a clear sign I needed to slow my roll.

I wouldn't force myself on him again. After flashing him, falling on top of him, and storming away from him, I had reached my limit of embarrassing moments with one guy in a single year.

At least ones who I care about. Caleb, on the other hand, might be perfect. I needed an escape and to get Cedar out of my system.

Pulling my phone out of my sweater pocket, I dialed Caleb's number.

After feeding the chickens and trying to collect eggs, I walked in the door and was stopped short at the sight of Cedar in a pale green button-down and a forest-green tie. With his laptop in front of him, he talked to the screen.

His sight flashed to mine, holding me still. The shirt made his eyes appear brighter than normal. A rush of pink colored his cheeks.

Someone on the computer said, "Mr. Eden, besides your knowledge of the field, what would you say is your greatest strength?"

Cedar's gaze broke from mine, back down to the computer. Clearing his throat, he shifted in his seat. "I think connection. Patients just want someone to empathize with them, to respect them. There can be no healing without first understanding."

In the years since I last saw Cedar, I had known he got his degree in physical therapy. Dumbstruck by the sensitive and thoughtful response he gave, I reckoned with who this man was.

The idea of who Cedar was at eighteen would be easy to let go of whenever this thing we had between us was done. But the grown man in front of me, talking about mutual respect and throwing out words like "pathology," "LOA," and "ROM" was new to me.

I was staring at him like a fool, so I shook my head, trying to disperse my racing thoughts as I mouthed *Sorry* and went up the stairs.

Through the open door of his old bedroom, I could see carpet clean of the glass, with vacuum lines and a small trash bag sitting next to his dresser. A bright blue tarp stapled along the edge of the window blocked out the midafternoon light. His bed was cleared off, the bedding stripped. After walking over to the bare dresser, I pulled open a drawer to find all his old clothes folded inside. The edge of a shirt soft under my fingers, I rubbed the fabric. He had worn this shirt to school the day he was nominated for the homecoming court.

Sitting in the back of my freshman English class, the crackling loudspeaker boomed as our ASB president listed off names: Zoya Porter, Ronan Pryce, Cedar Eden, Alivia Caffey, Matthew Bellamy—those bright students with shiny hair and winning smiles.

Cedar and Alivia were in the lunchroom that day, Cedar sitting on the table, his legs stretched out on a chair, his arm tight around Alivia's waist. Alivia's long blonde hair braided over a shoulder and her too-tight graphic tee showing off a swath of a smooth, pale stomach.

Her focus narrowed as I stood on the doorstep that day so long ago.

Flopping down on the bed, I stared up at the ceiling. What was I doing? I was here to work on my last commissions, to make a plan to move out of town and start fresh.

What I wasn't here to do was ogle my former neighbor, no matter how hot he looked in his button-down shirt that made his eyes seem so much greener. I wasn't going to daydream about running my hand down the front of his shirt, popping each button free, letting my fingers wander over bare skin.

This would not do. I had a plan, had a schedule—or something like a schedule, a concept of a plan. Something like that.

Cedar Eden did not factor into this at all.

As I wiped my hands on my pants, the grime from the fort skid across my palms. Glancing up at the mirror, I saw I was a mess in every single meaning of the word.

Yet, in the quiet of the bedroom, Cedar's voice rang in my ears. The earnestness of his words struck me. In my years of dating, I had met men who hated their jobs, boys who worked dead-end ones they couldn't conjure the energy to even describe. I had dated a financial planner for a while who loved talking about his career. Some used their work for money, some for clout.

Not a single one had the joy like Cedar. I wasn't sure if I even liked my job that much. Creating was fun sometimes. But drawing corporate logos for accounting firms was not what I had in mind when I was sitting up in my room, doodling.

Flopping my suitcase onto the bed, I frowned.

The contents did not inspire confidence. Nothing I packed would make me appear sexier or even cuter. I packed for the function of being the only one in a house for days on end while I worked on my painting commissions. Leggings and oversized shirts. I didn't even pack a pair of sexy underwear.

Briefly, I wondered if Clover left anything from high school in her closet but decided against it. The idea of dressing up in Clover's old clothes for Cedar seemed problematic.

Not that I'm doing this for Cedar. I am not getting dressed for him. I'm just covered in dead leaves and dirt and need new clothes.

I couldn't even get that lie past myself.

Shaking my head, I grabbed a slouchy sweatshirt and leggings.

Fresh from a cold shower, I came downstairs to find only Kinny sleeping on her bed. A book in hand, I settled into a squishy armchair and waited for Cedar to reappear. Between reading sentences about Viscount Rodolphe and his lover, Beatrice, I listened for any sign of him.

The slate wall of clouds darkened as dusk fell. In my book, Beatrice had confronted the Viscount for eavesdropping on the terrace. Upstairs, there was a scratching and thuds of someone cleaning. Surely, at some point, Cedar would come down for dinner or a drink. For something, anything.

In the end, it didn't matter if I wore my prettiest underwear or the cotton multi-pack. He wouldn't see them because he didn't want to see me.

As darkness fell over the house, I snuffed out the candles and lanterns and made my way upstairs alone.

As I closed the door to Goldie and Edith's room, another door down the hall opened, and the soft padding of footsteps down the stairs echoed.

It was late in the morning before I caught sight of Cedar. Once again, I watched him from my perch in the loft, but unlike the morning before, he just filled a travel cup with coffee before leaving the house.

As the red-and-gray flannel stretched over his shoulders, he leaned down to pick at something on the ground, then placed it in the small bowl in his other hand. I recognized the metal bowl as one from the counter where Marigold put food scraps. After unlatching the wire gate, he scattered lettuce and what looked like yellow flowers over the feed. The multicolored birds came down from their coop, surrounding him. He hopped around them, dumping thee last of the scraps while the largest one, Barbara, was pecking at his shoe.

Covering the smile on my face, I watched as he dodged the chickens and nudged them with his feet to make his escape.

The Rhode Island Red, Phoebe, slipped out the gate before Cedar could close it, so he stepped away and shook a finger at the errant chicken. With his free arm, he scooped Phoebe up, who squirmed and flapped her wings indignantly until Cedar stuck her back in the coop. As he was about to pull his hand free, the rooster, Josh, rushed him.

He must have pecked him because he stuck the side of his finger in his mouth and sucked on it before shaking it out. His back was tense, and he shook his head at the rooster. My gaze followed him until he walked to the other side of the yard and out of my eyeline.

Paintbrush in my left hand, I twirled it between my forefinger and middle, the familiar catch of the metal ferrule and wooden handle against my callouses.

The early afternoon sky was a greige wall, socking us in with a fog that wisped around the top of the trees. When I first got up to the loft, the morning chill soaked in through my thick wool socks, and I had to pull a sweater over my gecko in a cowboy hat shirt with the words *You just yee'd your last haw* written in rope lettering.

My gaze still on the window, I swiped at my canvas. The gray streak in the wrong area bloomed across the cheek of my subject, and I cursed. From the living room, Kinny barked at the interruption of her sixteen-hour nap.

Taking my mistake as a sign I needed a reset, I fixed it before it had time to dry, then grabbed my used brushes. That day's landing was more graceful from the day before, and I went to the sink. As the water ran, I rinsed out the bristles, then shaped them to dry upside down by their holder.

With the power still out, the only heat in the house was still the old wood-burning stove in the corner. Kinny was sleeping contently on her oversized pillow beside it. The window in the front flickered flames, and I slowly registered Cedar had restocked it before he left me alone.

Ignoring the funny twist in my stomach, I opened the fridge to find tepid air greeting me and the slightly sweet odor of rotting food. It was quick work to remove the items that wouldn't last another few hours without keeping cold.

Double-bagging up the stuff that had already spoiled, I put them to the side to take out in a few minutes. The power company website said the restoration time was a few more hours away, but I wouldn't hold my breath.

On the counter beside an oversized mug that read *My tummy hurts, and I'm mad at the government* was a single-serve instant coffee pack. The teapot on the stove was still warm. With that simple gesture, my stomach clenched. It was such an intimate thing to do.

Every morning before my father left for work, he would leave out my mother's favorite mug and her favorite creamer. There was no way Cedar could have known this little habit between them. It was so small, and when he was alive, the gesture had felt insignificant. But the sight of the same offered for me caused a lump to form in my throat.

My hands shaking, I traced the edge of the mug. It was a silly gesture. Nothing meant by it, yet in that moment, it held so much.

That was when Cedar walked back in, crisp air on his skin and rosy cheeks.

He startled at seeing me, pausing in the open doorway. "You taking a break?"

I took him in, the stretch of his faded flannel over his shoulders, the flush of his cheeks from the spring wind. The careless tousle of his hair and that damn scar on his hairline.

When I didn't respond, he furrowed a brow. "Look, about what I said yesterday. I was out of line." His jaw tensed, and he glanced away, his words coming out choked. "You can date whoever you want."

Until he mentioned it, I had half-forgotten the argument, so caught up in the way those blue eyes bore into me. I certainly hadn't thought about Caleb and our upcoming date.

My hands wrapped around the lukewarm mug, I studied the black liquid, at a small spot of coffee grinds clinging to the edge in a teardrop of sludge. If only I had creamer to dull away this bitterness.

The urge to forgive him was rising in me. I swallowed a gulp of cooling coffee, trying to come up with the right thing to say.

"Are you going to go with him?"

His voice was soft, and a pang of regret churned in me.

"Yeah, I kind of have to, don't I? We have to get out of here at some point, and I need to save my money."

"I'll pay for it. I don't want you to go out with him to save money."

Sucking my bottom lip into my mouth, I shook my head. "No, I already told him we'd go out. And I keep my word. Besides, your mom will pay me back."

His jaw tight, he swallowed hard, first to look away. Settling at the counter, he pulled his laptop toward him and booted it up.

His sleeves rolled up to reveal muscular forearms. Firm tendons ran from his elbow to his wrist, little blond hairs spattered over his skin, almost invisible in the light. I imagined how strong they'd feel braced against my back as he'd pull me to him. The rush of his breath against my neck as he'd lean in close. Did men realize what a set of strong forearms did to women? They looked like the arms that should be braced on either side of a girl's head as he pushed inside her.

Cedar's voice cut through my daydream.

I blinked a few times, focusing on his face. "What?"

He frowned. "Last night, sorry about taking over the whole downstairs. The Wi-Fi doesn't work as well in Clover's room."

His words took a minute to sink in.

"Oh, that's fine. I was taking a walk, anyway. I hope I wasn't too loud when I came in during your interview."

As I leaned my butt against the counter, my sweater fell off my shoulder, and I caught Cedar glancing at my bare skin.

I pulled the shirt back up. "How'd it go?"

His eyes popped back up to mine. "Fine, good. I had already done a preliminary interview. This was more a formality for the board."

I offered a reassuring smile. "I heard a little of the interview. They'd be fools not to hire you."

Cedar ducked, smiling down at his hands, his cheeks pink. "I hope so."

His humility was surprising. I leaned over the kitchen counter, placing my hand over his. "I mean it. I'm sure you are a great physical therapist, and they'd be lucky to have you on their staff."

Underneath my palm, I could feel the veins on the back of his hand, the callouses of his knuckles. His thumb lifted, brushing against the side of my hand. I didn't move away, his thumb rubbing circles on my wrist. I wondered if he could feel my heart beating faster at his contact.

His hand slowly turned until his palm met mine. Lacing our fingers together, I was struck by how well they fit. There were small cuts between his fingers from the tree incident. I was entranced by the way his hand felt in mine, centering me.

Outside the window, the sun was getting low, casting shadows over the lawn.

Slowly, Cedar pulled his hand out from beneath mine.

I trained my face still, the pang of wanting something reverberating through me.

"You hungry? I was thinking I'd throw something together."

Smiling, I jerked my head toward upstairs. "Did you even have dinner last night? Seems like you didn't even leave your room."

"Clover's room." He shook his head. "I had some crackers and the last of the salami from the fridge. Not a balanced meal, but it was fine. The harder part of last night was sleeping. Clover's bed is painfully small. I don't know how she can sleep on it."

An idea popped into my head, one I knew was terrible, but I offered nonetheless. "You know, Goldie and Edie's bed is a California King. It's massive. The is more than enough room for both of us in it if you wanted to just crash in there tonight?"

"Are you sure? You wouldn't feel weird about it?"

"Of course not. We're friends, right?" I let out a hollow laugh that didn't sound the least bit convincing to my ears. "I promise not to accost you in the night."

He chuckled. "Pinky swear?" He reached out his good hand, extending a pinky.

We joined pinkies as we smiled at each other. Neither of us let the other go, our fingers entwined. A warmth spread down my arm, into my chest. I wanted desperately to pull him closer.

A thud outside shattered our staring contest. The branch that had hit the side of the house waved in the wind. Kinny barked from her pile of pillows on the floor.

We both jumped back from each other, the moment shattering. Cedar hushed Kinny, who narrowed her beady eyes at us before turning around twice on her bed and plopping back down.

He then wiped his hands on his pant legs. "Right. Well, now that my virtue has been protected, what do you say about dinner? I can't make much, but we have everything for a pasta dish."

"That sounds great, as long as it's . . ."

"Vegetarian, I know. I remember."

Studying him, I tried to recall when I told him.

While I had stopped eating meat in my sophomore year of high school, I still had family who saw me multiple times a year who would try to serve me tonkatsu and beef udon. Not to mention my mom's uncle, who insisted I tried his "famous" lutefisk, which, even if I ate meat, jellied cod was a no-go.

He turned away, beginning to pull out pots and pans. He was limited on what he could make with the power still off, but luckily, the stove still worked.

Once the dishes from our simple pasta dish were cleared to the side, Cedar refilled my third glass of wine.

A second bottle pulled out from its spot above the microwave. A red blend, the brand the same as the one I had the first night I was here. The label was designed like a tarot card, a couple embracing each other. The Lovers.

As he pulled the cork out of a second bottle, I watched as his muscles flexed, and I had a flash of what those arms felt like under my fingers, the ripple of strength as I held on to him the day before.

For over an hour, we were able to keep the conversation light, about his previous job and then mine. I told him about my terrible roommate from college who would bring her boyfriend over to have sex while I was two feet away, and he shared that he'd sold knives door to door and once locked him out of their room when he was having a sales party.

As the sky became dark outside, we scavenged for candles and lanterns. The open-concept pace between the kitchen and the living room became warm with flickers and shadows.

Cedar had just finished telling me a story about the first time he went snowboarding and how he somehow ended up in the bowl where the experienced snowboarders do their aerial tricks.

"I really thought I was going to get decapitated by a Shaun White wannabe." He laughed. "I had to take off my board and run to the tree line. My friends thought it was hilarious."

"Your friends sound like dicks," I teased.

"Nah." He shook his head. "I would have given them a hard time if it happened to one of them, too. Luckily, I got better. It wouldn't endanger my life if I got stuck there now."

"I tried skiing once with Autumn, but I never got the hang of it. I just didn't have the stamina or something. It's just not my idea of fun, I guess. Too cold. Too physical, too . . . ugh . . . whatever it is. Give me a nice warm room and a sketch pad any day. A big mug of tea and a roaring fire. No wet, cold, sticky stuff stinging my face while hurling myself down a cliff."

"I wish I could have seen you out there." He laughed.

I looked away.

He was there. That whole winter season, we rode the same bus chartered to take us to Steven's Pass. Autumn and I sat a few rows ahead of him. He just didn't remember. The sting of invisibility twinged.

"Um, well . . ."

There was no reason he should have remembered, and if I hadn't already drunk three quarters of a bottle of merlot, I would have schooled my face better.

I downed the rest of my glass to hide the flaming of my cheeks. Better to blame the flush on the wine and not the way I had obsessed over Cedar as a teenager.

He watched me, awareness dawning on his face. "Oh shit. Were we on the same ski bus?" He scrubbed his hand over his face. "I was such a jerk back then."

I pulled it away from his cheek. "No, you weren't a jerk. You just weren't interested in hanging out with younger kids."

"I was such an idiot." He turned his palm to lace his fingers with mine. "I can't believe it. Look at you now. You were right there. You were always there."

His words were so low I wondered if he meant to say them out loud.

Pulling my hand away, I straightened up, grabbing the bottle to replenish my glass.

I couldn't want this.

"In the kitchen yesterday morning? I wanted to kiss you," he blurted.

My hand froze on the wine bottle as I slowly raised my face to his.

Cedar

THE WORDS CAME OUT before I could stop them.

Devin's cheeks burned pink. "What? No, you didn't."

Fighting the urge to rub my finger over them, I turned away.

It was my turn to smirk. Now that the words were out there, I refused to take them back.

"I did—it's okay. You wanted to kiss me, too."

The heat between our gazes collided.

"You did?" she asked softly.

I leaned in and stroked a finger over her cheek. "Of course I did." Edging closer to her and moving my hand to her chin, I held her in place.

The candles flickered, casting shadows across her skin. My fingers on one side disappeared into the darkness, and the illuminated part of her face flushed at my words.

Her breath washed over me, laced with wine and something sweeter. I wanted to breathe her in and keep her. A flash of Caleb came through my mind. Of Caleb kissing her, holding her the way I was.

Stomach clenching, I swallowed hard. I didn't like it. It had been years since I had seen Devin, yet in a day, I was feeling annoyed at another man for touching her.

"Why didn't you kiss me, then?" she asked softly.

"Because you assaulted me a second later," I joked.

"I did not!" As if she had been pushed, she reared back, my hand falling away. "It was an accident. I didn't mean to fall on you like that."

"It's really okay. It doesn't hurt anymore." I laughed.

She laid a hand on my arm. Her fingers were long and elegant against the coarse blonde hair on my skin. Multicolored paint flecks clinging to her short nails. I put my hand over hers, reveling in the warmth of our touch. "It's just so embarrassing. I am sorrier than I can tell you."

"It's fine." Rubbing a circle on the back of her hand, she softened.

"No, it's not fine. If I hadn't done that, we would have . . ." She bit her lower lip, and I wanted to soothe the score she created on her pink mouth. "Do you still want to kiss me?"

Leaning forward, I wrapped a tendril of her hair around my finger, studying the silk of it. "I do." I dropped the strand, pulling back. "But I don't think it would be a good idea if you're still thinking about going out with Caleb."

"What?" she sputtered. "What kind of chauvinistic bullshit is that?"

"Because if I kiss you, I won't stop. I want to consume you, and there won't be enough of you for any other man."

My words were barbaric; if my second-wave feminist mother heard me saying them, she would have reamed me a new one. I didn't care.

"Oh." Her cheeks colored a lovely pink. "Well, that has to be the most misogynistic and romantic thing I can imagine."

"I aim to please."

Devin grabbed the wineglass in front of her, realized it was empty, and reached in front of me for mine. "That's not the word I'd use." Our gazes locked as she took a long sip of my wine, the red liquid settling on the soft space where her lips met. Setting the glass down, she turned to me, leaning forward. "Tell me more. Offend me with your romanticism. Tell me what you'd do."

I took my glass back and drank, my gaze not leaving hers. Her eyes were the color of a forest on the darkest of cloudy days. "You couldn't handle it."

She smirked. "You have no idea what I can handle." She stretched her arms over her head, her shirt riding up to show a delicious swath of her soft stomach.

The move pushed her breasts out as she arched her back. Her shirt fell off one shoulder. Did she have any shirts that stayed on her?

"Would you kiss me softly, your lips pressing lightly against mine, or would your kiss be hard, your tongue in my mouth and taking my breath away?" she murmured. "Would I feel you on my lips for hours later?"

The bluster faded out of me. The intensity of her unraveling all my composure. I stammered out some indiscernible sound as she talked.

"Would your hands be in my hair, pulling my lips to yours? Or would they trace down my arm, down to my hips and over my ass? Would you pull me close, pressing against you?"

As she talked, her fingers traced her chin, down her neck, and across her collarbone. Her thumbnail scored her skin, leaving a pink line. "Would your lips kiss me here and here and here . . ." She dipped her fingers into the neckline of her shirt, her touch disappearing.

My breath hitched as I watched her touch herself, hands itching to feel her.

As she straightened up, her hands fell at her sides. "But maybe you're right. Maybe one of us is all talk."

She stood, a wine glass in each hand. I reached forward, grabbing onto her hip, and pulled her to face me. Then I took the glasses and set them on the table.

Standing over me, she stared into my eyes.

My left hand still on her hip, I pulled her closer until she was between my open legs.

"I'm tired of talk."

We closed the gap, our lips brushing. Hers were feather soft against mine, barely touching.

I leaned closer, deepening the kiss. One hand was in her hair, and I marveled at the softness. It was so much longer than when we were kids. My other hand rested against her waist. Her arms wrapped around my neck, pulling me closer, soft curves pressing against mine. My tongue traced the seam of her lips, and she opened for me. Blood rushed to my head, and I could feel my heart beating harder.

I scrambled to hold her closer, wanting more and more. My lips left hers, tracing to the corner of her mouth and her jaw, teeth dragging against the tattoos she had beneath her ear, and as she tilted her chin up, my lips moved against her throat.

"You taste better than I imagined."

My words were soft against her skin.

She groaned and pressed her body closer to me. "Have you been thinking about this?" she asked, breathless.

"All day and night." Nothing but the truth could come out. My fingers traced up her back, discovering her skin. "What you'd feel like, your taste. It's been nonstop, taking over my every thought."

"Since I saw you," she whispered.

I slipped her loose shirt off her shoulder, letting it fall down her arm, and ran my finger under the thin strap of her bra on her shoulder, bringing it down to the side with her shirt. My fingers traced the column of her neck, my thumb branding her collarbone. Her skin was silk, flushed and warm.

"Since that first . . . Oh . . ."

Her gasp thrummed through me, shooting heat down my body.

I nipped at her bare shoulder. "Definitely when I saw you naked." She yelped—whether it was from the bite or my comment I didn't know—as I sucked her skin into my mouth.

Melting into me, her body became pliant in my arms. Her fingers were in my hair, scraping my scalp.

She pushed me away, leaning back to grab the hem of her shirt. After pulling it over her head, she tossed it to the floor, where it landed in a crumpled mess.

When we were fooling around in high school, I never truly saw Devin without a shirt. The glimpse of her body when I surprised her, when I first arrived, played on a constant loop in my head. Seeing her in the light, the way her smooth skin would look, the heft of her breasts, the curve of her stomach. I had thought I would be prepared for the sight of her body. How wrong I was.

Her bra was a sheer black thing that looked like it would tear with the smallest pressure. Her breasts were full, just a little more than a handful. Above the lace edge, she had a small freckle begging to be licked. The triangle tattoo on her sternum was made of bright colors. On the inside of each of her arms were a multitude of inked objects: a rune covered ax, a flight of birds, two plump red cherries, something that looked like a misshapen heart.

Not that I hadn't been with a woman with tattoos before, but the kind I normally slept with had dainty ones, hearts on their hip bones, or tiny flowers. Devin's were big, art across her skin.

"Now you." Devin motioned to my shirt. I snagged the back of it and pulled over my head in one motion. Offering me a devious smile, Devin ran a hand over my chest. "God, I love when guys do that."

The idea of how many men had pulled their shirts off for her gave me a quick flash of anger.

By sitting on the stool and her standing between my legs, I didn't have to angle much to grab her head and pull it to me, my mouth urgent on hers.

She parted her lips, tongue touching mine.

I pulled her closer, my lips on her neck. "Guys? Or me?"

She tilted her head back to give me access to her, murmuring, "It's sexy."

Bringing my mouth to her skin, I sucked hard, wanting to mark her.

She tasted of salt and sex. Her hands caressed my bare shoulders, warming me with each pass of her fingertips. I wrapped my arms around her body, bringing her chest to mine, playing up the bumps of her spine until I got to the edge of her bra.

Running a finger under the seam to touch the indented skin, she pushed her chest into me. I nudged the strap off her shoulder, kissing a line down her chest until I reached the top of her breasts. My teeth scraped against her smooth skin. Everywhere, my mouth touched, flushed from my unshaven face.

"How are you doing this to me?"

My words fell against her skin.

Taking one finger, I pushed the cup of her bra down to expose a perfect tawny nipple.

Devin shuddered above me, a gasp escaping as my finger circled the peak.

I tweaked it lightly, the tips hardening under my fingers.

"You like that."

My words were rough.

She nodded, breaths shaky.

Leaning forward, I pulled her into my mouth, my tongue laving the sensitive nub.

Devin dug her fingers in my hair, her back bowing out as I scraped my teeth against the sensitive flesh.

With my other hand, I grasped at her other breast, pulling the cup down. Moving to the other, I licked her, the wetness shiny in the light. My eyes moved up to her face, seeing the way her lips were trembling.

She stared down at me, her top teeth biting into her bottom lip.

Not moving my gaze from hers, I blew lightly on her nipples, feeling the peaks stiffen with the cooler air.

She reached between us, her hand against my lower stomach, then palmed me through my pants.

I hissed through my teeth at the contact, thrusting up into her hand.

"I need this so bad." Under my touch, I felt Devin freeze, her body stiffening.

My words were rough as I reached around her back to release the clasp of her bra.

"Wait." She stepped back, pulling her bra up quickly. "We need to . . . wait . . . stop . . . um . . ." Devin's wrapped her arms around her chest, covering her naked torso. Her face turning away from me frantically.

"What's the matter?" I asked, my hands reaching out to rest on her hip.

She stepped back out of my grip, giving me a smile that didn't reach her eyes. "Nothing, I just think we should cool it. We had a lot of wine—or I did. And I don't think we should do something we'd both regret." Dropping into a crouch, she retrieved the shirts off the ground.

Talking to the top of her head, I try to reason with her. "I wouldn't regret it."

My shirt hit me square in the chest.

"It's getting late, Cedar." Straightening up farther away from me, she pulled the shirt over her head. "I'm going to bed. We both should. We have more stuff to do tomorrow if we want to get the house together before Goldie and Edith come home."

Before I could refute her, she turned on her heels, leaving me downstairs with nothing but dirty dishes, endless questions, and a painfully hard cock.

I've never been the domestic type. My sister valued cleanliness over most things and could never go to bed until every item was put back in its place.

I was never this way, as I'm a wash-the-dishes-when-you-run-out-of-spoons type guy. At any other time, the idea of having to hand-wash a pile of dishes would have annoyed me, but after that tailspin, I was relieved to focus on a menial task.

Scrape off the food scraps into the compost bin.

Fill the sink with hot, soapy water.

Scrub the plate, rinse the soapy water off, stack the plate to dry. Repeat. Repeat.

What wasn't as simple was the mess in my mind. Her body against mine had lit a fire in me like nothing I had ever experienced. No other woman had me feeling more out of my mind than Devin.

I was with Tainslee for years. We had a good enough sex life, but I never craved her touch the way I did Devin. I never experienced wanting as terrible as when Devin walked away from me. Maybe it had been too long since I last had sex.

You're just horny. Devin is a gorgeous girl, and there is nothing else going on. You've known her forever; you've made out with her before. It's nothing.

Even in my own mind, the lie rang hollow.

Flashlight in hand, I trudged up the stairs and opened the door to the bedroom, hoping sleep would snap me out of whatever this mind fuck was. Somehow, Clover's bed seemed even smaller than it did the night before. Devin had offered for me to stay in Mom and Edie's bed with her.

But that was before something scared her off. I didn't want to talk myself out of it. It was just sleeping. If Devin didn't want to do anything, she didn't have to.

As I pushed open the door, Devin stirred under the covers. "Dev?" I whispered.

It was silent for so long I wondered if she had fallen asleep. If she did, would she be pissed if I just climbed into bed? She had offered, but that was before we kissed. After she seemed to change her mind in the middle of our kiss, her body didn't seem to move once I entered the room.

Taking a step closer, I studied her shoulders. I didn't want to wake her up, but it seemed rude to show up without warning.

One of her feet were sticking out on the bed. Reaching down, I touched a finger to her ankle. She twitched and pulled her foot under the covers. Her voice was dramatically thick with sleep, as if she were faking. "What do you want, Cedar?"

"You said I could sleep in here." In the flashlight's beam, the creamy set of her shoulder peaked over the multicolored quilt.

Flinging an arm above her head, she turned to look at me. "Fine, yes, whatever."

Her eyes were closed, but judging by the stiff way she held her body, I sensed she forgot about the invitation.

Resting on the edge of the bed, I considered if I should take off my shirt. I normally only slept in my boxers, but I didn't want Devin to be uncomfortable.

"All I ask is to take your socks off if you're going to be sleeping in here."

Furrowing my brow, I glanced over my shoulder at her. She was still facing away from me, and in the low light of the candles, the contrast of her dark hair against her skin was mesmerizing. Small dark lettering stood out from her nape.

The corners of my mouth turned down.

"No, that's bad luck."

"What?" I narrowed my eyes, one corner of my mouth ticking up in a confused grin. "To wear socks to bed?"

"Yeah, it speeds up your death." She paused, shaking her head. "Obviously."

I was already pushing my luck by asking to sleep here, to question whatever superstition she had felt like was too much.

A small tea light flickered on the bedside table. It was irresponsible of her to leave that burning. Walking to the table, I picked it up to blow out the flame.

"It's fake, Cedar," she mumbled, turning to me. "It's a battery-operated light. Goldie had a bunch under the bathroom sink. Probably for taking baths in that big tub. I'm not so scatterbrained I'd leave a candle burning."

Sitting on the edge of the bed, I set the light down. "I never said you were."

"You didn't have to say it. I could see it."

Her voice was low and sleepy.

While I was pulling my socks off, Devin stuck a long pillow in the center of the bed.

"You read minds?"

I meant for it to be a joke, but my voice pitched.

Stretching out on my side, I faced Devin with my hand resting against my head.

Watching me from her side of the bed, she smoothed the quilt under her hand. "I don't need to read your mind to understand you, Cedar."

There was something behind her words that chilled me. Even in the dark, I could feel her gaze.

Sinking into the bed, I lay my head on my pillow. Her words ricocheting in my thoughts. The sense that she understood me, possibly more than so many others I had spent years with, was jarring. I hadn't seen her in almost half a decade, yet something about us together opened me up.

She said she could understand me, but how could she when I wasn't even sure what I wanted from her? Yes, I wanted to feel her body under mine, wanted to hear her laugh, wanted to discover the shape of her skin, and wanted to watch her paint.

She was leaving soon. This pull I had toward her needed to be ignored.

I wasn't interested in a relationship. There couldn't be anything emotional between us. We were too connected by the past, by my family, by this town. To go down that path would be dangerous for us both.

"I don't know why we kissed," she whispered.

The large body pillow was a thick barrier between us, but Devin had squished the top down so we could see each other's faces.

I turned to face her. "I wanted to."

Devin burrowed deeper into her pillow, her face half hidden. A thick lock of dark hair fell over her cheek. She swatted it away with a furrowed brow. "Is that all you're going to say?"

"You wanted to kiss me, too," I supplied.

Maybe what she was asking of me was more than just a kiss. I didn't know how to answer. She said she understood me, but in the dark with nothing but moonlight and battery-operated candles around to light the room, I knew nothing at all.

In the dim of the moonlight, her eyes were closed, hands tucked together under her cheek. Her voice was so low I wondered if she was answering or talking to herself.

"I know I did."

Nine

Devin

WARMTH SURROUNDED ME FROM all sides. The thin quilt tangled around my legs as I pointed my toes. Bitterness coated my thick, dry tongue. My head was pounding, and my neck twinged from the odd angle. Blearily, I opened my eyes to find Cedar on my side, his face wedged between my bare shoulder and the mattress.

A heavy weight across my stomach stopped me as I tried to shift my body. Cedar's arm was slung across my middle, his hand resting on my bare hip bone, his middle finger tucked into my pajama pants up to his top knuckle.

My headache and full bladder were begging me to get up, but I couldn't move. The first rose gold strands of dawn were edging into the room.

Cedar's hair was mussed, one section sticking straight up, while another was flattened to his pale scalp. Creases from the pillow etched pink lines onto his cheek. Since we were out of hot water, he hadn't shaved since his first shower. His stubble was growing in shades of burnished gold and brown except for a patch growing in lighter, a perfect circle of white blonde hair on the far side of his face where his jawbone and ear met. It was a small patch so faint I wouldn't have seen it if the sun wasn't illuminating the spot perfectly.

With tingling fingers, I raised my hand to touch that spot, then curled them into a fist. I couldn't.

Our kiss from the night still burned on my lips. The feel of his mouth on my throat and the rasp of his stubble against my breasts. His hands roaming over my body, lighting flames of pleasure.

It was consuming to be in his arms like that. I was ready for him to take me. Out of my mind with desire, I would have done whatever he wanted if he hadn't said those words.

I need this so bad.

I need this . . .

This.

Not me but *this*. Sex. He just wanted sex. If he was almost any other person, it wouldn't be an issue. If he was Dane, a random guy at a bar, or a vacation time fling, if any other man made me feel the level of desire Cedar incited in me, I would have slept with him in a moment.

But he wasn't just any guy. He was Cedar. My Cedar, the first boy I loved.

The boy I stared at from the loft, his name the one I had penciled into my middle school diary. The one who kissed me as a gawky teenager and made me feel beautiful for a shining moment. The one who could never feel the level of affection for me. The man who had broken my heart.

This pulse under my skin would never be casual. There was too much history. My desire wasn't safe. Not when it was just me and him inside this big house. Not when there was no escape if things went sideways.

Beside me, he grumbled in his sleep, scratching his nose on the mattress, before flipping over to his other side, taking the blankets with him. One of his legs slung over the top of mine, and he burrowed deeper into the bed, his breath evening out.

Slowly, I shimmied out from under his leg until my feet were on the cold wood floor. As I grabbed my robe off the chair, he didn't move.

An early morning chill swirled around my bare ankles as I roamed the kitchen to make coffee. Unplugging my cell from the battery charger Cedar had found in the back of his car with an odd assortment of camping gear, I scrolled from today's affirmation from Autumn, *I choose to let go of fear and embrace courage in all aspects of my life*, to check my emails while drinking my first coffee. A few emails popped up about small commissions from my online shop and promotional information about an old gym membership.

I would need to get to the post office in the next few days if I was going to get the child's portrait mailed off in time. I had already wrapped it up and addressed it and set it by the front door for when I could escape the house.

In case it would be longer than I planned, I drafted an email to the PTA mom to let her know that shipping may be a few days late, as I was in the middle of a storm and offered her a discount for her next order. It would be a drop in my bank account, but I'd rather have a repeat customer than lose out on more commissions down the line.

In the night, the wood stove had burned low. The embers of the fire from the night before glowed orange beneath a pile of ash. I shoved the last two logs into the flames and hoped they'd catch.

I was never very good at fire making. Cedar had taken over that task when he arrived, and I wasn't too proud to allow him to do that more masculine job.

When the logs didn't catch, I frowned at the dry wood. Glancing around the room, I saw a pile of old newspapers in a basket, then balled them up and tossed them on top. Nothing.

Settling back on my haunches, I considered the cold space.

I could do this. I am an independent woman. If Cedar hadn't shown up, I would have needed to figure this out, anyway.

After a few tries with more paper, a lighter, and a tea light I had snagged off the coffee table, I saw the first flickers of a fire catching.

With my second cup of coffee, I climbed the slanted ladder to the loft to work.

The wide single-pane window allowed cold air to seep into the small room. I hoped the warmth of the fire would follow me, but it was fuzzy slippers and my oversized robe to keep me warm.

Picking up my paintbrush, I studied the canvas. My bestselling work was a watercolor of a ranunculus bouquet. I had done these types of painting so often I could finish a few in a day if I worked hard. It was muscle memory, the movement across the canvas, the mixing of the colors, and the shading of the flowers. Losing myself in the motions, I let my imagination bloom vividly across the black space. Art had always been my safe place. The one area I could create, allowing myself to feel with my brush strokes, letting the emotions go until the once-stark white was a tumult of colors.

Resolutely, I flicked my brush, making a warm gold swish, the same color of his stubble in the early morning sun.

Not helping yourself, Devin.

The blue I used was the color of his shirt the day before, the pink the shade of his lips after drinking wine.

This is impossible.

I had to get it together because I wouldn't be some dopey girl mooning over a guy who didn't care about her. I was too smart for that, had come too far. Never could I allow Cedar to ruin my progress on my life just because he had beautiful blue eyes or strong hands or melodious laugh. Or—

I would take a cue from him. If he wanted to talk about the night before, we could, but I wouldn't bring it up. If he wanted to kiss me again, well, we'd figure that out as we talked.

He would likely act like the night before, with its mind-blowing kiss and scorching touches, didn't happen.

I could do that. I'd tuck it in the back of my brain to break out when it was just me and the vibrator. He didn't have to know that it was the best kiss I had ever had or that, with the slightest touch, he made my body feel like it was on fire. Nope, he didn't need to know any of that.

It was none of his business.

Because he wanted *it*.

Not me. But it.

Both hands wrapped around a mug with the words *Male Tears* printed in gold script, I climbed down the ladder.

At the counter, he was watching me, where, only hours before we had dinner, wine, and the best make-out session of my life, but I was trying to forget that.

Neither of us spoke, daring the other to go first. Lifting the cup up to his mouth, he glanced at me over the brim.

Silently, I reached for the French press to make myself another cup. My nerves were frayed from the two cups I had already drank, but I had to do something with my hands, or I might have done something stupid.

Like grab Cedar by his face and kiss him. Or rip my top off and ask him to take me right there on the counter.

Nope, can't have that. Play it cool, Dev.

Jumping at the sudden sound of the trill of his phone, I dropped the cup, cursing, as scalding coffee splashed over my hand. Before I could register his movements, he was out of his seat, grabbing my hand and pushing it under a stream of cold water. The sting of the hot coffee had soothed, but a new sensation of scorching was building where his fingers wrapped around my wrist. His brows furrowed as he turned my hand over to inspect.

"It's fine, Cedar. It was just a little burn. I was more surprised by your phone than the hot coffee." I pulled my pink hand out of the water and away from his grip. Wrapping my hand up in the kitchen towel, I kept my eyes away from his. "Was that the clinic?"

Studying me for a long moment, he finally looked away to grab his phone. The edges of his mouth tensed as he clenched his teeth. It was so minute that if I hadn't been obsessively categorizing his every expression for years, I would have missed it.

"It was no one. Spam call." He set the phone face down on the counter and looked to me. "Are you sure you're okay?"

I barked out a laugh, the sound harsh to my ears. "I'm fine. It was nothing, really. It's not like I impaled myself with a dagger of glass."

A small smile flickered on the corner of his lips.

"I think calling it a dagger is a misrepresentation of what was a two-inch shard."

Frowning, I tucked my throbbing hand closer to my chest. "When it was embedded in your arm, it looked like it was two feet long."

"And for me, it looked like you just dripped boiling liquid on your hand."

"Lukewarm coffee."

"Sliver of glass."

While I was trying to keep stern, Cedar tipped his head back and laughed. His whole face brightened when he smiled like that, the corners of his eyes crinkling and straight teeth on display.

This wasn't the laugh he used in public. In my years of watching Cedar, I watched as he talked with friends, who were joking and laughing. His head never tipped back, eyes never squinted, and he had never put his hand on his stomach. This was a new laugh, a just-for-me laugh. I yearned for more. To make him laugh like that again, to be the one who he joked with, the one he could trust with this guffaw.

But I wasn't. I was leaving, and he didn't want me like that. I shouldn't hope for things I couldn't have.

"Well, I'm going to get ready for the day." I edged my voice so that it would sound as brisk as possible. "While I'm getting ready, can you call the power company and see when we can expect the power to return? I'd like to not freeze to death here with you."

Leaving him standing in the kitchen, I hurried upstairs.

I wouldn't allow myself to fall into the same pattern that brought me pain years before. I couldn't fault him for saying what he did. He didn't owe me anything more than friendship. He was perfectly within his rights to expect that I would be casual about our kiss the night before. Just as I was in my rights to never kiss him again.

The thwack of an ax hitting wood sounded outside. From my perch in the loft, I could see the woodshed and Cedar's back as he balanced a log on a flared splitting block. Both hands gripping the ax handle, he brought it down on the log, breaking the wood in half. He picked up the two pieces and tossed them to the side in a pile. His plaid flannel stretched across his back. He had pushed the sleeves up, his corded forearms flexing with each swing of the ax.

Having dated men who more likely pick up David Foster Wallace than a tool, I was shocked by the tingles running down my body at the sight of Cedar. It was giving me lumberjack man vibes I certainly appreciated. Who knew I had this kink?

Mesmerized by the sight, I set my brushes down to devote my time to Cedar-watching. From my angle, there was no way he would know I had a direct shot for my daydreaming pleasures. My hand crept up to my neck, holding my throat, remembering how his lips felt on my skin. The sight of him working was giving me all sorts of ideas. Dirty ideas of Cedar picking me up, holding my ass in each hand, my legs wrapped around his hips. Of him driving himself against me while we kissed. Of him holding me up against the wall while he sucked on my breasts.

The pile of split wood was knee high to him. He walked to the shed, opening the door to hang up the ax. Reaching down, he gathered up the logs, stacking them over his bandaged arm. Once the pile was up to his chin, he turned toward the house.

His face immediately looked up, right into the window, where I was standing like a fool. His free hand came up in a casual wave.

I cursed under my breath.

My face flamed red, the heat of my fantasies coming out across my skin.

Dumbly, I raised my hand in a half-hearted wave before turning away.

God, I could never face him again.

The stomp of his boots came as he brought in a dull thud as the logs were stacked into a pile next to the wood stove.

"You want to help me with the rest of the wood?" he called up to me.

No, I want to crawl in a hole and contemplate all the wrong turns I made before getting to this moment of horny humiliation.

"Sure, I'll be right down. Let me grab my boots," I called down, my voice much calmer than I expected.

With the last load in our arms, Cedar stopped, cursing.

"What?" I rushed around him to check his injured arm.

No visible change. It wasn't until I looked up at his face that I saw the culprit. A white streak was running down the side of his face and into his ear.

Pursing my lips together, I fought back the laugh bubbling up.

"Don't say a thing," he warned, swiping at the mess with his free hand and looking up at the evildoer in the sky.

"It's good luck to have a bird poop on you."

"In no world is that true?" He glowered at me.

"It is! It's a sign you'll soon have more money. My Jiji always said so."

"Well, if your grandfather said it's okay," he grumbled, walking past me and into the living room, where he set the last logs down.

Once inside, he arranged and then rearranged the logs in an orderly pile beside the fireplace. When I attempted to help him stack, he waved me away, creating his own system that didn't seem to have any order but was intent on finishing.

The bandage on his arm was looking even more worn and brown, tinged with dirt.

"You need to get that cut cleaned again. Put a new bandage on it."

Cedar stood, wiping his hands on his jeans. The corners of his mouth turned up. "Aw, look at you, acting like you're my nurse. Acting like you care."

Warmth bloomed across my face. His words were soft and not unkind. Frowning, I mirrored him, wiping my hands on my black leggings. "Of course I care." Turning away, I motioned for him to follow me. "Come on, I'll get you the stuff to clean it up."

After laying out all the items on the counter, I turned to leave him in the bathroom.

Cedar sat on the edge of the bathtub, his long legs stretched out in front of him. "You won't try to heal me?"

"Are you not capable of cleaning up? What was it you said? 'A small poke' or something like that?"

"Something like that." He shot me a mischievous grin. "So, will you help me?"

"Are you just asking me because I'm a girl and that girls should know how to do these things?" I countered, refusing to break a smile in his presence.

"No, it's because it's on my arm and cleaning a wound one handed is tough."

Narrowing my eyes, I assessed him. "Only because you're one handed."

"You are nothing if not charitable."

He didn't move his legs to the side, so I had to step between them to get closer to his arm. The heat from his body radiated out to me. It was a bad idea to be so close to him in this little room, where I could practically count each freckle across his nose.

Working quickly, I unwrapped the gauze, throwing the soiled fabric to the side. The wound was smaller than I remembered. When I squirted the cleaning solution over the wound, Cedar let out an inhumane sound of pain and tried to rip his arm away.

I held tight as he struggled. "Hold still so I can finish."

"You don't need to burn my arm off with chemicals."

"It's just a little hydrogen peroxide. You obviously haven't been taken very good care of this thing, or it wouldn't be as dirty as it is. I should let you get sepsis for all the whining you're doing."

"Some sweet nurse you are." As I pressed a new piece of gauze down on his arm, Cedar grimaced.

"I never said I was sweet or a nurse. You get what you get, buddy." Wrapping up his wound, I tied it in the best knot I could. In Girl Scouts, I was terrible at tying knots, and that hadn't changed in the years since I struggled to earn merit badges. Inspecting my own handiwork, I deemed it as good as it could be. "Alright, that will have to do for now until you can go to the doctor."

"I'm not going to the doctor for this, Dev." He glanced to me, and his face broke out in the smile that I loved, big and wide, his eyes crinkling at the corners and teeth flashing in the moonlight.

Cedar was a positive, smiley person by default. He smiled when he opened doors for little old ladies at the store, smiled at the female teachers in high school, and smiled and joked and laughed with everyone. But something about his smile this time felt different, his gaze centering on me.

I had never seen him keep eye contact as he smiled. A tenderness in his gaze caught me off guard.

Shaking my head, I gathered up the cleaning supplies, placing each item in its designated spot. Stepping away from Cedar, I was able to take deeper breaths without his scent distracting me. I shoved the med kit under the sink and rose to leave the bathroom.

With his good hand, Cedar reached out, touching my elbow. "Hey, I have a question for you."

Turning to face him, I planted my feet, determined not to move closer.

"Can you tell me what happened last night?" he asked. "One minute, we're talking and then we're kissing and then more than kissing and then you just . . ."

"I was tired."

My voice was thin even to my own ears.

"Tired?"

His brow rose as he studied me.

I lifted my hands in an uncertain gesture. "Yeah, that's what I said."

"I don't think you were tired."

"Oh, so now you know how I feel? Are you the mind reader today?" Snapping, I turned to the door, storming out.

His words were against my back as he followed me into the kitchen.

"No, but I know what I felt, and you felt the same way. I could feel it in your body. Don't deny it."

Cedar caught up with me, his hand shooting out to grab my wrist.

I stared at his fingers.

I wanted his hand to travel higher. For him to gather me up in his arms and kiss me senseless again. I. Simply. *Wanted.*

My breath caught at his contact, at his questions.

"Last night you said, 'I need this so bad.' Did you want me or did you want sex?" I spoke down toward his hand, not trusting myself to meet his eyes.

He dropped my wrist, and I stepped back, bumping into the refrigerator.

Furrowing his brow, he scratched his chin with his thumb. "I mean, both?" He shrugged. At the words, an ache formed in my chest, sharp and unbidden. "It's been a while since I've—well . . ."

"Right. Of course," I murmured. Gulping down the lump in my throat, I set my jaw. "I think the best thing we can do for the time being is to pretend that this never happened."

I savored the look of shock on his face as he took in my words. "You want to act like nothing happened between us? That we didn't kiss?"

"I think it's for the best, don't you?" Wanting my words to sound stronger than I felt, I stuck my chin out.

Crossing his arms, he surveyed me. "Best for who? Best for you? For me?"

I waved flippantly. "Both of us. It was a onetime, drunken thing. We don't want to do anything we'd regret."

He approached slowly. His height filling up the space around me and heat soaking into me. As his hand lifted toward my face, his fingers brushed slow against my cheek.

Flickering from my gaze down to my lips, I glanced at the callouses on his thumb grazing my jaw.

His palm was rough, but his touch was featherlight against my skin. His fingers grasped a lock of hair. The rasp of his hand against my face as he wrapped the hair around his finger held me in place.

"I told you last night I wouldn't regret anything."

Yes, but once you're gone, I'll regret everything.

I sent a silent plea to my feet to move to the side, to step away. My legs worked with my heart. My brain was not to be obeyed when Cedar was in front of me.

"Please," I whispered.

Whether it was a *please stop* or a *please keep going*, I didn't know.

Cedar bent down, his lips inches from mine, his breath a whisper of warmth.

Devin

"We shouldn't be doing this," I murmured against his mouth.

"I want to."

"You don't want me, not like this."

My words gave me the strength to turn away from him. With my back to him, I gripped the handle of the fridge to steady myself.

Cedar's body slammed into mine, pinning me against the door. The cold metal felt delicious against my skin as his arms bracketed me to the spot.

I could feel all of him, his flat stomach against my back. His shirt sleeve pushed up, revealing muscular forearms, muscles tensing. I should've ducked under his arm to give myself space, but I reached up behind me, my hand cupping the back of his neck.

He leaned forward, his nose skimming the shell of my ear. His unshaven cheek bristled against my bare shoulder. Tremors of desire jolted down my body . . .

I leaned farther back, closing the infinitesimal distance between our bodies.

Rough, his hand grabbed on to my hips, pulling me into him, and his hard length pressed against my lower back. "Don't say I don't want you."

His words rasped against my ear. "All I can think of is you, this skin, those lips." His hand came up inside my shirt, dancing over my rib cage. "You're so soft."

My shirt was pushed up above my breasts. If I were in another mindset, I would have been embarrassing by the state of the old cotton fabric. If I had known it was going to show anyone, I would have worn something far sexier that my old discount superstore bra.

He pushed the cups down, my breasts popping free. Between his fingers, my nipples puckered in the cold. "I've been dreaming about these since I saw them the other day. The shape of them, the beautiful shade they'd get, how they'd weigh as I held them. How perfect they'd look in my hands. They're even better than I thought they'd be."

His filthy words sent sparks of pleasure through me, lighting me up.

I pushed my ass even harder against him, grinding on his thick erection. When he pinched my nipple, I let out a groan as the fire burned down to my center. His hands were rougher, his fingers gliding down my ribs and over my stomach.

He dipped one finger inside the front of my pants. His teeth nipped against my throat, and I let out a low moan.

"God, you taste so good."

We needed to stop.

We needed to go further

I shifted my hips back, allowing him more access. His finger traced my underwear. Brushing against my clit, he rubbed lightly with the tip of his finger. I shuddered at the contact. Wetness flooded my core as he moved against me.

"You like that."

His warm breath grazed my shoulder.

I nodded.

"Tell me you like that."

My voice breathy, I ground out, "I like that."

His finger brushed my center again, skimming my clit before he pushed my soaked thong to the side.

Flesh on flesh, he circled my entrance. "God, you're drenched."

I gasped at the contact.

"I'm going to give you so much more."

My breath hitched as he slid the tip of one finger inside me.

"Do you want more?"

I leaned forward, resting my head against the cold steel fridge as he moved deeper inside me.

As his pace quickened, I moaned with the movement. "I want you so bad." He nipped at my shoulder as his fingers plunged in and out, hitting the spot where I ached.

"I . . . I . . ." Gasping, I tried to form the words. " I want . . . I want."

Reaching behind me, I tangled his hair around my fingers. Tilting my head up, my lips met his. It was tongues and teeth clashing.

Then he pulled his finger from inside me, and before I could protest, his hands were on my hips, and I was being twisted to face him, my back against the icy surface.

Our eyes locked, and he brought his finger up to my mouth. "You taste that?" Slick with my wetness, he traced the seam of my lips.

I pulled his finger deeper in my mouth, swirling my tongue over the tip, and then hollowing my cheeks.

His gaze flashed with dark satisfaction.

"That's how much you want me." He smirked before bringing his fingers to his own mouth, licking the last of me off him.

I reached behind to steady myself as to not melt into the floor.

"You taste better than I could have imagined." Taking my hand, he pulled me away from the fridge.

I followed on weak legs, a pulse thrumming at my core.

He pointed to the couch. "Lie down."

I followed, my body humming in anticipation. I was edging closer to the line where I could not turn away, but my body was reacting to his touches in a way I could not control. Lying back on the couch, I watched him kneel on the floor in front of me.

Tongue against mine, he grabbed my pants and pulled them down, the slide against my legs and cool air hitting my center. Fingertips traced up my leg and over my thighs until they were inside me.

"I can't wait to feel you on my tongue."

He climbed on top of me, his mouth taking mine. One hand roamed down my body, the other holding his body up.

With both hands, I grabbed for his ass, grinding his erection against my aching core. His lips moved from mine and down my throat. I grasped the edge of my shirt, wiggling to get it free and over my head.

He trailed kisses down my naked torso, nipping at sections with his teeth. His face at my belly button, licking a circle. One hand squeezed my breast, teasing my nipple between two fingers. His other hand rested against my center, and the tip of his finger pushed on my clit, sending me closer. My hips bucked as he moved down my body.

When he got between my legs, he glanced up at me, his blue eyes locking on mine. "Is this what you want?"

I nodded at him, our focus not wavering from each other.

He leaned forward, blowing a stream of cool air against my heat. "Say it, Devin."

"I want it," I shuddered out as his fingers moved, tracing my clit.

His eyes flashed with thirst at my words, a devilish smile on his face. He dipped down, and his mouth was on me. His tongue licked up and down my center, sending shock waves through my body.

His fingers worked me over, words at my core. "You're the best thing on my tongue."

I thrust into his face, my head thrown back as he licked and sucked and teased me. The waves peaked as he worked me over. My hands came up to pull at my hair, my back arching. His lips fastened around my clit, and his fingers curled inside me. He sucked my pearl into his mouth, and I felt myself on the verge.

"I'm . . . I'm . . ." I shouted, and he sucked harder, his tongue grazing my most delicate place.

He was relentless, sucking my clit and plunging his fingers in my center, until I began to break.

Waves crested, and behind my eyes, colors exploded. I clenched around his fingers. My scream of pleasure shaking through me. My body shuddering as I came down. His fingers still inside me, he rested his head on my pubic bone. My whole body warm from the orgasm. His lips pressed against my hip. My eyes opened slowly to look up at the wood paneled ceiling.

Reality slowly ebbed into my brain when a loud click and then a buzz startled us. The refrigerator turned back on, and the beeping of different electronic devices pinged through the house. In the small space of the kitchen, the lights were blinding bright.

Coming down from my high, I realized the truth of what we had just done was stark.

I scrambled up into a seated position as I gathered my shirt from its place on the floor. "That was a mistake," I blurted out.

"Why?" Cedar asked. Slowly, he rolled over to sit up on the other side of the couch.

His bare chest was paler than his arms, a smattering of freckles and a dusting of golden hair covering it.

"Why what?" I asked, searching the ground for my underwear.

I couldn't look at him yet could see all I desired.

"Why was it a mistake?"

"Can you put your shirt back on?" I ordered.

He rolled his eyes but grabbed his shirt off the floor, pulling it over his head in a smooth motion.

"Happy now?"

No. Yes. That was the most amazing experience I've ever had. I hate you.

"Yes, thank you."

My tone clipped, I averted my eyes.

"Why was that a mistake?"

In the afterglow of the interlude, I couldn't form the words.

"I don't know. It just was." My underwear was still inside my leggings, inside out on the floor. I scooped them up and held them to my chest. "Now that the power is back on, I'm going to track down my laptop and write a few emails."

If I looked at Cedar, I couldn't trust myself to do the right thing. The way he touched me, the way he knew exactly what parts of my body to tease and lick. The speed he brought me to the most bone-shaking orgasm of my life. If I looked back at him for a moment, I would fall apart.

"Do you want to take a walk with me?" Cedar asked to my back.

I didn't turn to look at him, but I stopped walking long enough to let him know I was listening.

"When you're done with your emails. Please?"

His voice was low.

I nodded slowly. "Okay, sure."

Following him, I wove between trees and over roots, our boots squishing the mossy forest floor. Shoving my hands into my jacket, I considered his back as we walked.

Every moment I spent with Cedar, the more I wanted him. It would hurt when he left. When this all fell apart between us, could I handle the pain? I couldn't lie to myself anymore and think that I could only be physical with him—it could never be just physical with Cedar. With him, a part of me would always be eighteen, would always be more vulnerable.

The last trace of innocence and faith in another person was given to him in these very woods. I was a smart, strong, and capable woman in every other situation, but with Cedar, I was a teenager again.

Even though I hated this, I couldn't stay away from him and couldn't help stepping closer when he stood next to me, couldn't help but watch him. Couldn't help but want.

It would be another day or two days until the log was cleared off the bridge and until one of us could leave. I just had to hold on and not get myself into the position I was in an hour before. It shouldn't be too hard to not have sex with Cedar. It would be easy to do that.

He glanced back at me as we walked, and my steps faltered.

Okay, I could try to do that. I might be able to resist.

Holding his palm out to me, I stared at the proffered hand, the one that had brought me to the heights just a short time before. I laced my fingers with his as he led me deeper.

Stopping at the base of the tree house, he motioned up to the ladder. "My sister and I used to come here as kids."

I glanced up at the little wooden structure I had spent time in the day before. How my mind had been so confused, how I was still confused.

"I remember."

I didn't want to betray how long I spent out here, mooning over him, as he'd likely run the other way and sleep in the woods.

Cedar climbed up the ladder to the top and grasped the padlock, confusion crossing his face. "I forgot you put a lock on it."

I climbed up to of the rungs to look up at him. "It's a silly thing. It's not as if someone was going to break in. Only me and Clover went in it."

"You never know," he murmured with humor.

"Yeah, I do. You pretty much ignored me the whole time we were growing up."

Placing a hand over his heart, he gasped. "I am shocked by your hurtful words, Devin. I am a very observant person."

Tilting my head and shaking it twice, I motioned for him to come down. "You weren't the one that statement was hurting. Here, move out of the way. I'll open it."

Instead of climbing down, he moved over, with one foot on the ladder and the rest of his body to the side, one hand grasping a branch for balance. "No, I think I remember the combo. You told me. The golden ratio, right?"

I blinked at him, confusion clouding my head. "You remember that?"

He smirked. "I told you I remember all sorts of things, including what we did up in the tree house."

With the nearness of him heating me, I fought to regain control of the situation. "Maybe this is a new lock?"

"Why would you replace it? Do you not trust me?"

"Do you deserve my trust?"

My words were meant to be playful, but an understanding crackled as we gazed at each other.

He was first to look away. "I don't know." His finger turned the dial: one, six, eighteen.

The lock popped open with a low scrape, and with his gaze on me, he threaded it off the clasp.

With one strong push, the wooden trap door swung up.

Glancing at me, he gave me a joking smile. "Now that I know the combination, I can sneak in and spy on your sleepovers."

Forcing a laugh, I climbed into the tree house.

He came in behind me and sat on the other side of the wood floor.

"It's smaller than I remembered."

"I imagine so. It must have been over a decade."

As he peered around, a small smile played on the edge of his lips. "I had my first kiss in here, actually." When I didn't ask, he kept talking.

"Susie Carter. Do you remember her? She only lived here for a year or two. Military family."

Even though they were a few years older, I remembered her. Susie was a big deal when she moved here. Petite, with a spray of perfectly round freckles across her small nose, big blue eyes, and curly blonde hair. She felt like everything that was the opposite of me. Outgoing and giggly. She arrived with a southern accent that fascinated all the students. It made sense Cedar dated her.

"Uh, yeah, I think I remember her."

"We snuck out here during a party. Climbed up here, and she just planted one on me." He laughed. "If the door hadn't been closed, I could have fallen through it from the shock."

"Were you sad when she moved away?"

He shook his head. "Nah, not really. I was going out with someone else by then. Uh . . ." He cocked his head as he thought about it. "I can't remember who."

I knew. I could name every one of his girlfriends in school. From the girl he held hands with for a few days to the seriousness of Alivia.

Best not to mention that.

His legs stretching out in front of him, he looked over at me. The space was so small his feet were at my knees. "Who was your first kiss?"

"Brant Lawson," I struggled out.

"Wait, the guy who always wore a suit to school? That guy?" Cedar laughed.

"It's not funny." Smacking his foot, I put on my best offended face.

"Isn't he gay?" Cedar asked between chuckles. "No judgment, just curious."

"Yes, he is. I'm pretty sure I am the first and last girl he kissed."

Admitting it wasn't fun. The brief interlude we had was while preparing for the school's rendition of Brigadoon, where I made sets and Brant played

Jeff Douglas. It was a few dates hanging out with the actors in basements with chips and soda and one very sloppy kiss during a game of seven minutes in heaven. Brant came out the sophomore year of school, a few months after our "relationship." I tried not to think too much about it.

"There's my ego boost for the day."

Cedar leaned forward, his palms face down on his outstretched knees. "I would have kissed you."

I rolled my eyes. "Yeah, secretly. Like that little thing we had." Trying to keep my tone light, I glanced away.

It wouldn't help for him to know how much it hurt when he got back with Alivia. I couldn't let him know how much hope I had when I was fresh and eighteen.

"Besides, I was a mess at fifteen. Didn't know how to do my hair, still had braces. I was too scared to wear makeup."

He considered me, his face softening. "I remember what you looked like, Dev."

A lump formed in my throat. I couldn't let him rewrite history like this. It was inexcusable for him to act like he noticed me the way I did him. We both knew I didn't fit in with him and that his words were hollow.

"Who really cares about a first kiss? They're always disappointing, aren't they? Never once living up to the hype. I was one of the last of my friends to have a first kiss. My friend Wren went on and on about her first kiss and how amazing it was and how she was so in love—blah, blah, blah. I think I just wanted to get it over with. Move on to whatever the next step was."

"What, virginity?" Cedar asked with a smile.

I leaned my head back to stare at the wavy clear roofing panel, moss, and dead pine needles resting in the low spots. "You don't actually want to talk about losing your virginity."

"I can if you want to."

I lowered my head to stare him down. "Losing your virginity is a million times more disappointing than a first kiss. Plus, I'm sure you lost yours to Alivia. You two were together for all of high school."

"Almost all of high school."

The mention of when they broke up, all that occurred between me and him during that time.

"It's a boring story, no matter how you paint it. Whether it's your high school sweetheart or some random guy in your college dorm your freshman year."

"Is that how you lost your virginity? In your dorm, to some random guy?"

His voice was tight.

A spark of satisfaction lit inside me at his bothered tone.

"My point is, the first time of anything is terrible. It can never be as good as it is in your head. Putting too much faith into an experience just because it's the first is an arbitrary concept. No matter with whom or how I had these experiences, they aren't who I am, they didn't shape me as a person. It's all just lips and tongues and boners and boobs."

"Great visual."

"I mean it. Yes, I lost my virginity to someone I didn't love because I just didn't want to be a virgin anymore, although the concept of virginity as something you are or are not is ridiculous. What makes a virgin, even? What if you're a lesbian? Why does a penis inside a vagina have so much . . ."

"Stop before you make me horny," Cedar quipped.

Frowning at him, I went on. "All I'm saying is that, sometimes, we have too much hope in doing something that will inevitably let us down. Maybe it would have been better if we're told to lower expectations at least the first few times."

Cedar's face softened. "Is that how you felt about our first kiss? Was it disappointing?"

The grain of the wood rasped against my fingers as I drew circles in the dust. Cedar stared at me until I spoke, the silence pierced by bird calls.

"Today? No, it was the farthest thing from disappointing."

"What about when we were kids?"

"When we were kids—" Through the small window, I could see the wind's effect on the branches, where smooth green boughs swayed against the rough bark. "We were—or I was—"

Closing my eyes, I could see the look on Cedar's face the first time he saw me after he and Alivia got back together. The tensing of his jaw, the furtive glances between Alivia and me. Something sharp slicing through my chest as I froze in place on his doorstep. The sound of the gravel under my feet as I turned to walk away, the sun shining so brightly on my back.

"It was good. It was a good kiss. I don't think I have to tell you that you're a good kisser, Cedar."

"I think I'm good at kissing you." He nudged my thigh with his foot. "I'm sure there are plenty of women who don't think I'm a good kisser."

I doubt that.

He grabbed my ankle and squeezed it. "There is a lot more to kissing than just tongues and lips." His hand drifted up my leg until it rested just below my knee. "There's attraction, there's chemistry."

"Yes."

There's love. There's the ever-present way I can't stop wanting you no matter how I try.

"I think we have both." He tilted his head, adding to his statement, "I know I'm attracted to you. I think we have chemistry."

Nodding along, I didn't trust my words. How much honesty he could take from me.

"So, if we have attraction, and we have chemistry"—he hesitated—"what was going on with you when we started?" He moved his hands in front of him in a vague gesture.

With a brow raised, I stared him down. "When we started what, Cedar? Are you unable to say the words now? You were vocal earlier."

His cheeks tinted pink, a sight I hadn't seen very often. His voice stronger now he straightened up. "Why was today a mistake, and why did you stop me the other night? And none of that 'I was tired' stuff."

"I was tired," I offered. He gave me an incredulous look. "I was!"

"No, really, tell me. Because I thought the kiss was great. You were into it—I could tell. I wasn't pushing you too far, was I? If you didn't want to do anything more, I would have understood that."

I shook my head. "No, it's nothing like that. I know you wouldn't try to make me do something I didn't want to do."

This was true. Even as kids, when we would fool around, he never pushed me too far. He always checked in with me to make sure I wanted what was happening, getting my acceptance before he put his hand up my shirt.

"Then, what was it? I thought you were pretty into it."

I debated telling him the truth—that if we slept together again, I would become attached. That we hadn't even had full sex yet, and it had irrevocably worsened my feelings. I was already in danger of being hurt when we parted ways. That I knew he didn't feel the same way about me, and I was only trying to protect myself.

With every man after him, it could only be sex, and with him, it could never be.

"It's just complicated with us," I offered.

"It doesn't have to be," he replied.

"You and I were friends for so long and then we weren't and then . . ."

He leaned closer. "We were more."

The pang of his words stung my chest. I rubbed my fingers against my collarbone. For those brief weeks, how I felt wasn't just more but everything. For years, I had been chasing the feel of his lips against mine, the scrape of his freshly cut hair on my fingers as I pulled him closer, and his body pressing into me. The sensation of everything being exactly right for the first time ever and the knowledge that no man would ever measure up.

Could I do this? Could I allow myself to sleep with Cedar feeling the way I did?

If I let him know how I felt, I would ruin everything.

"Our moms are friends."

It was a hollow excuse.

He smirked. "That's a risk I'm willing to take."

"Cedar, I'm being serious."

"So am I. Screw my mom. She doesn't get any say in my sex life."

"Don't say that. It could get weird if they found out."

"And we are adults. We don't have to tell anyone. It can be our secret."

A secret. Just like in high school. Something he couldn't admit to. Shameful and dark. Something that was to be locked away and never revealed.

With steelier words than I felt, I told him, "Cedar, I don't want to be your secret."

His tone conciliatory, he put up his hands. "I didn't mean it like that. I won't to ask you to hide in the closet when she came home."

"Good, because I wouldn't do that." Asserting myself, I leaned forward to pull the door open.

"Are you leaving?"

Maneuvering through his legs to the open door, I set my feet on the rungs of the ladder, my upper body still inside the tree house. "I don't think there's any more to say about this, Cedar."

"All I'm saying is we don't need to tell her. You're moving away soon. I'm staying here as long as I get that job. It doesn't have to be a big thing. We can just have fun together," he called down the ladder as I stepped onto the soft moss ground.

Fun. Is that what he was feeling? Is that what this was for him? I had never told him differently.

As I looked up at his face in the trapdoor entrance, pangs ricocheted through my chest. I was the one talking about leaving. He was putting down roots here in Ridgewood, and I was trying to escape. How could he think any differently? It wasn't his fault I could never feel casual about him.

As I moved through the woods, his footsteps clambered down the ladder behind me.

"I'm heading back to the house." Without waiting, I walked away, the heat of his stare on my back.

He could catch up with me if he wanted to. And I could never let him know how much I wanted him to.

Eleven

Cedar

THE SUN DIPPED BELOW the trees before I made my way back to the house. From my view outside, I could see a lamp on in the loft area and the outline of Devin's arms sweeping as she painted.

She seemed to put herself into her art, the way her body moved as she worked, the emotions playing across her face as she touched the brush to the canvas.

Her moods were confusing me. One minute, we're kissing in the kitchen, I'm going down on her on the couch, and the next second, she's running away from me. I had never been the best at reading other people, but I could tell she was attracted to me. She asked me to keep going earlier. But why she kept stopping us was a mystery to me. Her excuse about my mom didn't add up.

What we had in this little cabin was much more temporary than messing around in high school, and she didn't stop me then. She said she was moving to Arizona, so I didn't have to consider whether this could go anywhere; she was the one leaving.

Trying to be quiet, I receded to my old bedroom to survey the damages. With the power back on, I was able to get someone to replace the window.

Wanting to distract myself from the whirl of emotions Devin was creating in me, I set to work. Tools were brought up the stairs, garbage picked up, and the bedding needed to be washed.

Holding the sodden sheets, I wondered if Devin would let me sleep next to her. Should I not wash the sheets as an excuse? I could pretend the mattress was still wet, though Devin could check that. After debating, I wadded them up and trekked downstairs to start a load. I'd be embarrassed if they turned moldy just for some action.

Going through my piles of clothes, I folded each item, placing them back on my dresser. Half of the clothes wouldn't fit me anymore, but I didn't have the heart to get rid of the items from high school. The blue button-down I wore to my college tour, the shorts I practiced soccer in, the sweatshirt I wore to bonfire parties. The adult magazines ended up in the garbage bag. They were too soggy to enjoy, and everything was online, anyway.

Hours later, the room looked halfway decent.

Vacuum lines on the carpet, and the top of the dresser was clear of debris. The tarp on the window was a little crooked, but it was going to be fixed soon enough. Through all my physical labor, I still hadn't figured out what to do about Devin. I had come to a few conclusions, none of which gave me any solace.

I really wanted us to spend more time together. She was leaving in a few weeks to another state, so I wanted to have sex with her. Things between us were complicated. I wanted to spend more time with her, having sex.

Retreating to the kitchen, I started with the fridge and grabbed a large garbage bag but was surprised to see the fridge was empty.

"I already threw everything away, including my favorite hazelnut creamer I bought special for this trip."

When I went into the kitchen, Devin was in the loft, still painting. Yet she was standing behind me, her arms crossed, a crease on her forehead as she frowned. Her hair was wet, and she was wearing a different outfit.

"Nah." I pulled out a block of cheese still in its packaging. "Not everything."

"I must have missed that." A brow raised, she pointed at the cheese. "You're going to give yourself food poisoning if you eat it. We've been out of power for days. The only thing in that fridge that would still be okay is the wine."

Grumbling, I threw the cheese in the bag and turned my back to her, diving back into the fridge. "I'm hungry and want food. I've been cleaning all day, and there must be something I can eat in here."

Behind me, Devin turned on the faucet, her words drowned out by the water running to wash her brushes.

I heard only every few words. "Pasta—eggs still—sorry—"

I pulled my head out of the fridge. "What?"

Flipping the faucet off with an irritated flick, she looked down at me. "I said have some pasta or eggs if you're so hangry, then."

"Oh, so eggs are okay? How is cheese dangerous but eggs are fine?" I snagged a tub of cottage cheese out from the back and threw it in the garbage at my feet.

I didn't need to sniff test that one.

"They don't need to be refrigerated unless they're washed. These eggs came from Phoebe and Barbara." When I glanced at her with a bewildered look, she shook her head. "The chickens? You don't even know the name of your mom's chickens?"

"I know Josh."

"Great, so the asshole rooster, you know. The one male." She paused, a smile playing at her soft pink lips. "The dog's name is Emily Barkinson, and the cat is Fluffy."

"They don't have a cat. Edith is allergic."

I considered a jar of pickles. *Shouldn't the vinegar keep them safe?*

"Glad you know that, at least."

"I know a lot more than you're giving me credit for—I just didn't remember the ridiculous names my mom gave her chickens." Sitting back on my haunches, I looked up at her.

She had taken off her sweater and was wearing paint-splattered leggings and fuzzy gray socks along with an oversized graphic tee with the words *The horrors persist and so do I* in a flowery font. Her hair was up in a messy bunch on the top of her head, purple streaks standing out against the black. A smudge of black was under one eye, but no other makeup was visible. Her cheeks were pink and shiny, her lips bare.

I wanted to kiss them.

When I was with Tainslee, I had seen her without makeup only a handful of times. She was a gorgeous girl no matter what, but if I was coming over, she told me to give her some time to "get her face on"—a phrase my own mother used.

Looking up at Devin, I wanted to run my hands up those legs and under her shirt to her soft stomach. She was so close all it would take was for me to reach out.

Turning back to the empty fridge, I closed the door, straightening up to stand over Devin. She pulled her lower lip into her mouth, running her teeth over the soft flesh.

"I'm sure that your mom would take offense to you saying their names are ridiculous." Her voice lost the steel it had when she was standing over me. "What's up with the rooster's name, though?"

"That was Clover's doing. She said, *not every Josh is an asshole, but everyone knows an asshole named Josh.*"

Devin rubbed her hands over her arms, warming herself. Her hair was still drying, little tendrils curling on her hairline.

"You want me to make a fire?" I asked, bending down in front of the old wood stove. A small round metal cup sat under a partially burned log. I pulled it out, inspecting it. "Do you know what this metal thing is doing in here?"

Devin blushed and looked away. "Oh, um, I don't know."

I raised a brow at her reaction but didn't press on. As I was arranging the kindling, a phone rang on the counter. For a moment, I thought it was my own, as Tainslee had been calling more often. Even though I should have blocked her number, I couldn't bring myself to do that just yet.

Instead, Devin answered, her voice high and bright. Focusing on creating the perfect fire to keep Devin warm, I tried not to eavesdrop on her conversation.

". . . Sounds great, I'll see you in twenty."

Who was she talking to? Was it Caleb? Were they planning their date?

The wood in my hand snapped as I envisioned them together. Would he know how she liked to be kissed? Or the little sound she made when you scraped your teeth over her neck?

The fire finally catching, I closed the door and stared at the red-and-orange flames licking at the log.

Behind me, Devin stepped on the squeaky step, the sound echoing in the house.

"Are you going somewhere?" I asked, trying—and failing—to keep my tone casual.

She turned to face me, her brow furrowed. "Yeah, I am."

Wiping my hands on my jeans, I swallowed down the barrage of questions, focusing on the only one that mattered. "With . . ."

Fuck, I can't even say his name.

Lips pursed, she studied me. "No, that's tomorrow night. Are you okay?"

No, obviously, I'm freaking out for no reason.

"Fine," I choked out.

Her frown deepened, but she didn't push me.

When she came back downstairs ten minutes later, she was wearing a skirt and thick tights. An oversized black sweater pulled over her shirt, and her hair was up in two woven braids on top of her head. I wanted to peel those tights down her legs and feast between her thighs.

"What does that mean?" I motioned to her shirt.

She glanced down and blanched at the words *Good Girl* in black letters with a bunch of smaller letters in script over them.

"Oh, um, I can't remember."

Her cheeks blazed pink.

I arched a brow. "Really? Then, why are you blushing?"

Raising a hand to her cheek, she averted her eyes. "I'm not. It's just hot in here with the stove."

Shaking my head, I leaned in closer. "Is it a pun or something?"

"Nooooo." She scratched behind her ear with her index finger. "Not a pun."

"Tell me."

Throwing her hands up, she shook her head. "Cedar, you don't want to hear it. It's an acronym from some books."

"Oh, like a spicy book? You're getting redder, I bet it is. Tell me."

"Shut the fuck up and take my dick like a good girl," she blurted, then looked like she wished she could immediately take it back.

My mouth fell open, and I blinked slowly at her. I wasn't sure if I was even breathing.

"Cedar, are you okay?"

"I—" My lips pursed together as I struggled to form words. "Well—"

Visions of Devin on her knees for me and her plump lips wrapped around my cock invaded my mind. Her, on the bed, her legs wrapped around my waist as I thrust into her.

I coughed, twisting my body to the side to not have her notice the growing bulge in my pants. A few calming breaths and a rehashing of the last filling I had at the dentist got me to calm down enough to turn back to her.

My living room companion, Kinny, shot me a disdainful look, then waddled over to Devin before sticking her paws on her knees and lolling her tongue out. Since when did she like anyone but Edith? One hand scratching behind the corgi's ear, Devin said, "Well, I'll be off. See you later."

"Where, who . . ." I swallowed down the questions.

I had no right to an answer. Yeah, we shared a few wonderful kisses and a little more, but she wasn't my girlfriend.

With a simple purse slung across her body, she tilted her head to study me, her green eyes bright. "I'm going to dinner and then the Skol House for a drink or two."

I opened my mouth to ask the follow-up question but stopped myself. Thankfully, Devin put me out of my misery. "With Summer and Autumn. Autumn doesn't drink, so she's driving us."

Relief flooded through me at the women's names . "So, it's not a date."

"No, it's not."

My breathing returned to normal, and I didn't fight the smile creeping over my face. Beside the door, she kicked at the ground with her scuffed, dirty black boots.

"When will they be here?"

She glanced at the clock on the stove. "Fifteen minutes."

"Sit down." I motioned to the couch.

"Why?" She crooked a brow.

"Just sit. Trust me."

Perched on the edge, Devin watched as I returned to the room, a wooden box in hand.

Kneeling at her feet, I opened the box, pulling out the polish, brush, and rag.

"Cedar, what are—"

"It will take five minutes, and I can have your boots looking like new."

"You're shining my shoes for me?" She blinked a few times, her gaze traveling between my face and the contents of the box. "You know how to shine shoes?"

"The kit was my dad's. He didn't leave me much, but I remember watching him as he cleaned his shoes every Sunday night before the work week." Taking her right foot, I set it on the footrest, the heel wedged into the notch. "It's one of the few good things I remember about him."

Devin's eyes softened. "You never talk about your dad."

Scooping the polish onto the hard brush, I focused on the toe of her boot, working it into the leather.

She was right—I don't talk about him. My memories of Edward Eden were of long, bitter silences over the dinner table and my mother's hushed reassurances that I had done nothing wrong. He was never a cruel man, but he was also never kind. I was thankful Clover couldn't remember him at all.

"There's not much to tell. I don't have a lot of memories of him."

"But he was your father."

Devin had a wonderful father, kind and smart and always made time for her.

"The truth is, my father wasn't a nice guy. But that's okay. I had my mom and, later, Edith. I'm not some neglected orphan or something."

Her hand soft on my shoulder, she stopped my brushing. "It's alright to want more. You don't have to act like everything is okay all the time."

Staring up into her deep forest eyes, a fissure inside me opened. There always was a little part of me that was missing. I told everyone else it didn't matter, and I never allowed my mom to see it, but there were days when I would watch boys with their fathers. Riding bikes, playing soccer, working alongside one another, and it would hurt to know I never would have that experience. That, even if he had lived longer, I likely wouldn't have.

"You can't want what you never had, right?" I quirked a careless smile.

"Of course you can, Cedar. It doesn't make you less than to want to be loved."

Her gaze was on the dense trees surrounding the house in shades of green and brown, sturdy and beautiful. I could get lost in those eyes. Lost in her. A shocking question crept into my mouth, one I could never ask.

Could you love me?

I swallowed the impertinent question down. I had no right to it. But the idea implanted in my mind, and I couldn't shake it. Alivia, Tainslee, all those girls before—I may have told myself I could fall for them, but there was always something holding me back. A sense that what we had wasn't right.

But with Devin, everything was different. Only a few days in her presence, and the things about myself I never wanted to face were being exposed. She made me want to be better.

Is this what falling in love feels like?

Devin's somber evergreen eyes studied me, and I had to look away, afraid my thoughts were written all over my face. Moving to the heel, I brushed the polish deeper into the leather, covering the scuffs and dry spots. Content with the right foot, I picked up her left, placed it on the block, and polished.

I started on the last step of buffing with a soft rag. As I moved to the inside of the mid-calf, I had to place a hand on her knee to keep her leg steady. The heat of her body rolled off her, soaking through her tights and onto my hand.

I allowed myself a single glance at her face. Her breaths were coming out low and staggered, her tongue darting out to wet her lips. Sheer tights stretched over her thick thighs. Thighs you can palm tight as you lean into her, thighs pillow soft enough around your waist as you drive yourself home between them.

Staring at my hand on her knee, she slowly parted her legs. My thumb traced a line up her inner thigh. The little gasp she let out was my motivation. Coming up on my knees, my face inches from hers, it was like a string pulling us together.

"Cedar, I—"

Her gaze flickered from my eyes to my mouth, and at her sides, her hands were fisted into the cushions. My palm slipped higher, to the apex of her thighs, to the sweet spot I craved so much. As I pressed my thumb against the center of her, her lashes fluttered shut, and she let out shaky air. One hand raised, she ran her fingers over the back of my head and to my nape, pulling me closer. Her short paint-flecked nails scraped my scalp.

A projectile of fur launched itself at the side of her leg, knocking her foot off the block and onto the floor.

Kinny sat between where I was kneeling at her feet and Devin, her tongue lolling out and a devious look on her caramel face.

Cock-blocking corgi.

Both boots on the ground, Devin blinked at me. Her knees fell shut, and her hands pressed against the couch on each side of her thighs. "Well, um." She swallowed hard. "My boots look great, so shiny, like new. My friends are probably waiting on me, and I should—" She got up.

As it opened, I jumped to my feet. "Let me walk you to the road."

She frowned. "Cedar, it's not that far."

"Let me have some peace of mind."

With a wave, she gestured *get on with it, then.*

Beneath our feet, the soggy ground squelched with every step.

As we approached the blocked bridge, Devin stopped. Her gaze darted to her heeled boots and back to the large fir obstacle in her path. "I didn't think this through."

Walking to the edge of the ditch, I assessed the depth of the running water and deemed it good enough. Leaning down, I started tucking my pant legs into my rain boots.

"What are you doing?"

The little spot between her brows furrowed, and her green eyes creased.

"The way I see it, you can climb over this tree here, or you can hop on." Pants somewhat secure in my boots, I crouched in front of her and motioned for her to climb onto my back.

"You'll get all muddy, though." She took one step forward, teeth pulling on her lower lip.

"Better me than you, right? I worked so hard at shining those shoes. You can't have them get dirty that quickly. You're going to fall a million times if you try to get through this in those heels." Grabbing her hand, I put them on my shoulders. "I have nowhere to be tonight, and you look too beautiful to get muck all over."

She opened her mouth to say something, a smirk playing on her lips, then shook her head, deciding against it. Arms wrapping around my neck, I hitched the back of her legs tight until her body was flush with my back. As I stood, her thighs tightened around me.

"I'm not light," she reminded me.

"You're not."

She slapped my chest with one hand. "Hey!"

"You're an adult, Devin. A woman. Don't you worry about me. I can handle exactly what you are."

A shiver ran down my spine at my words. It was going against my instinct to walk her away from the house, away from a bed, and onto the street, where she would be whisked away.

My hand covering her upper leg, I rubbed my thumb over her inner thigh. Her tights were too thick to feel her skin, but the warmth of her seeped through. Her arms grew loose around my neck, and she leaned her face against the crook of my shoulder, her breath warm on my skin.

It was hard to focus on my steps when her thick thighs were clenching my hips, breasts pressing against my back. The flow of the creek was rapid but one I had walked countless times as a child. I knew how many steps it took to cross onto the street side and up the slope to the road.

Once I got us safely across, it was time to put her down, but once I did, she would leave.

It had only been a few days of being stuck in that house together, but an expanding sensation was forming in my chest. Once she left, I would be alone. I couldn't ask her to stay here with me, could I? It was only a few hours with her friends.

And she's leaving, anyway.

In a week, Devin would be gone for good. Off to her next adventure, which had nothing to do with me.

Crouching, I released my grip on her legs, allowing her feet to touch the blacktop.

Safely on the ground, she stepped beside me, rubbing her arms vigorously.

A scowl crossed my face, and I pulled off my old college sweatshirt. "You're shivering. Who knows how long you'll be waiting for your friends, and I can't have you getting sick."

Her green-eyed gaze flickered from my lips back to my eyes and then away. As she took the sweatshirt from me, her gaze narrowed. "That whole cold-outside-getting-sick thing isn't true, you know."

"Says the women who believes bird poop is good luck."

Her arms pushed into the sleeves of the shirt, but she didn't pull it over her head. "That's true. You wait, and soon, you'll get everything you ever wanted, and you'll look back on this moment and know I was right."

What I wanted was to pull her close to me, kiss her senseless, have her wrap her legs around my waist, and carry her back through that creek and onto the couch where we would finish what we started.

When my expression caught hers, I didn't hide the direction my thoughts were going in. Her inhale was shaky as she stared up at me, her tongue wetting her lips. My fingers found her cheek, and I cupped the soft skin of her face. As I traced the outline of her lower lip, her mouth parted.

My gaze flickered between her mouth and that little spot on her collarbone as I reach for her arm to pull her closer. Headlights from a large truck flare over the darkening cul-de-sac, and Devin jumped back from my outstretched hands.

As the truck slowed, Devin grasped at the sweatshirt, scrambling to get it off. Pushing it at my chest, I held on to the warm cotton with one hand, the other still tingling from the warmth of her cheek.

The truck stopped beside us, an auburn-haired woman in the driver's seat beside a blonde. The driver shot us a wide grin, but the blonde was staring me down with narrowed eyes.

"Hey, Devvie! Who's your friend?"

"Cedar, Autumn, and Summer. And so on," Devin quickly blurted, the back door to the truck already open and one foot in.

Autumn leaned over Summer, who squished her body into the seat and grimaced. "Cedar, are you coming, too?"

"No," Devin blurted. She fake-coughed into her hand before clearing her throat. "No, it's just us girls, right?"

The blonde in the front seat raised an imperious brow and snorted at Devin. "Yeah, that's the plan. I told Van he's only allowed to send me two dirty messages. That's how important this girl's night is."

I raised my hands in defeat. "I couldn't possibly intrude. You ladies have fun." One hand on the door, I watched as Devin buckled up.

From this angle, the blue light from the dashboard reflected off her glasses, and her cheeks were flushed in a way that has nothing to do with the chilly spring air.

Leaning down so low only she can hear me, I whisper, "Call me when you return so I can carry you back."

She laughed. "Absolutely not, but thanks." She pulled the door closed, barely missing my fingers, a blush stealing into her hairline.

Across the creek, Kinny barked.

Twelve

Devin

MY FRIENDS WERE POLITE enough to allow me two drinks and a portion of avocado fries before they started on the questions. I was able to dodge them effectively by changing the subject.

Until we got to the Skol House.

Taking the last chipped particle board table in the corner, Autumn insisted on getting us the drinks.

Recently hired at a local spot, at Freedom Bay Brewery, Autumn was making Summer and me try the beers and give our opinions. How a woman got hired at a brewery who had never tasted anything stronger than kombucha was a mystery to me, but I wouldn't complain.

My phone buzzed on the table, and I glanced down to see a picture from Cedar. Clad in navy-blue sweatpants and a long-sleeved tee, he sat on the couch, Kinny lying on his lap.

Cedar: someone is missing you

I responded quickly.

Devin: someone, huh?

All night, I replayed those moments when he was shining my shoes. The way his shirt stretched over his shoulders as he worked. The sensation of sitting above him and him at my feet in such a position of submission. I had never had a man literally at my feet before.

And the way he looked up at me with those piercing blue eyes. Maybe it was a trick of the light, maybe my own horny thoughts clouding everything up, but I felt something pass between us. More than attraction, more than friendship.

For so long, I told myself I was okay not having Cedar in my life. But no one made me feel the way he did, with a simple hand on my thigh. Who knew shoe shining could be sexy?

Studying the picture, I noticed the golden stubble on his jaw and the way his biceps stretched the fabric. Little dots lit up the screen as across the table Summer said something.

Taking in the view for one last moment, I mumbled, "Huh?"

"Is that him?"

My gaze snapped from the screen to my friend. Heat rose in my cheeks, and I set the phone face down on the table.

Arms cross, Summer sat back on the bright orange vinyl chair and narrowed her eyes. "Autumn says I need to stop bugging you. That you've made your boundaries clear or some shit like that."

Arriving back at the table with three drinks, Autumn set two beers and a Roy Rogers down before taking her seat. Summer ignored her cousin, her clear blue eyes set on me.

"I said that if Devin wanted to share with us, she will in her own time."

It was amazing how much Summer and Autumn looked alike, apart from their hair color. Same blue eyes, same wide smile, though Summer was wearing her default frown.

"Make time, Dev. What's going on between you and Cedar?—and don't say nothing. I saw that guilty blush on your face. Nothing doesn't climb over a tree trunk and through a river."

"It was a barely flowing creek, and there really isn't anything going on. You don't need to be all up in my ass about a 'nothing' situation."

"You've always been a terrible liar."

"I think I'm a great liar." The beer Autumn grabbed for me was too hoppy, and I gagged into the dark auburn liquid.

"How's that one? What do you think?" Autumn motioned to my beer.

"Subtle hints of sweat socks and pine needles." I turned back to Summer. "You worry, and I appreciate it, but . . ."

"I remember how it was last time, Dev. You lost your dad, and that asshole cheated on you."

"He didn't cheat. We weren't really together . . ."

Summer kept talking as if I didn't interrupt. Years of friendship told me to let her rant until she ran out of steam. I pushed the IPA in front of her and took the other beer, a German Gose. Every word was one I've thought to myself, and despite her fervor, I smirked at her loyalty.

"Don't grin at me. I'm serious," Summer snapped, grabbing the IPA, then swallowing down a third of it, as if raving about asshole men made her thirsty—which, knowing her, was more than likely.

"You're so cute when you're protective." I push out my lower lip in mock sincerity.

Beside her, Autumn snorted into her soda.

The pint glass made an audible clink as it hit the fake wood table, and Summer cocked her head to assess me. "Tell me you're being careful."

"What, like condoms? I don't need the safe-sex speech, Sum."

"That's not what I'm saying, and you know it."

Autumn bit the corner of her thumbnail. "She had a point. You were really sad the last time."

"My dad had just died. Of course I was."

"It wasn't just that, and you know it. We're here for you, whatever you do, but I can't sit by and not tell you that getting involved with the guy who devastated you is a bad idea. I mean, you pined after him for years . . ."

"I didn't pine—"

"And then you go AWOL on us for a few weeks because you're making out with him at the lake or whatever and then he has a new girlfriend. We know you, Dev. Don't act like what happened wasn't a big deal—because we were there."

The sour beer coated my tongue, and I swallowed down the hard lump forming. This is the problem in getting together with your friends when you're in crisis—they know you too well to see through bullshit.

Something about my face let her know her point was made because she pushed the beer into the middle of the table. "Autumn, I can't drink this. It tastes like a citrus ash tray and unbrushed teeth."

Few things Autumn took personally, so she grabbed the half drunk beer and approached a group of men standing by the bar. Within a minute, she handed the drink off to a man in a vintage Mariner's cap and a graphic tee.

"Did you know him?" Summer asked, her laser vision on the man.

When the man glanced over, his smile faded, and Summer raised a taunting brow.

He averted his gaze.

"No, I just walked up and said, 'Does anyone like IPAs?' And he did, so he took it."

"From a stranger?" Summer narrowed her gaze. "That's suspicious."

"Everything's suspicious to you," Autumn argued.

"I call it being protective from skeezy men who want to take advantage."

"Pretty sure he's gay but okay." Autumn snorted.

"How could you know that?"

Hooking my thumb over my shoulder, I motioned toward the man. "His shirt says *Washington State Fairies.*" The man shifted, showing us the rainbow and ferry motif against a black background. "It's cute. I wonder where he got it."

Summer grabbed the Gose out of my hand, finishing it. "You're changing the subject."

"Which was?"

The empty glass on the table, Summer ran a finger over the edge. "Cedar Eden broke your heart. Don't deny it. You two didn't work out in the first place, and it's a bad idea to go back there with him."

"I'm not eighteen anymore. I can make my own choices."

Summer crinkled her nose at me. "Can you?"

"Ouch, harsh. Take that back," I snapped.

She didn't mean it, but Summer needed to be called out when she got on a roll.

Summer tilted her head back, her hands in surrender, and let out a big huff of air. "Fine, you can. Just don't let him break your heart again—because I will get violent, and I've already had one brush with the cops this year."

I loved Summer, but when she got righteous, she could be frustrating. "Just because what I have looks different than yours doesn't mean it's not as good. We can't all find hulking engineers who own their own boats, who plan special trivia nights, and who won't call the cops when we commit larceny."

"I didn't steal anything," she pouted.

"Who happen to be besties with *my grandfather.*"

"You forgot he gives me mind-blowing orgasms." Her face softened. "That's important."

"Not helping." I glowered at her. "You can't protect us all. I'm not eight years old and getting bullied for having the wrong backpack. No matter how much you'd like to, you can't push every guy who is mean to us into a river."

"Watch me," Summer mumbled.

"What?" I leaned in closer.

Summer rolled her eyes. "Fine, I'll let you make your own choices, and if he hurts you, I won't hire a private eye to blast all his embarrassing secrets."

"Aren't you the mature one?"

"I'm grabbing another round. Play nice, Summer," Autumn chimed in.

"I'm always nice," Summer snapped at her cousin, who only raised a brow and smirked. Summer crossed her arms against her chest and glared at Autumn as she walked away.

"I know your heart is in the right place," I assured her. "But you don't need to worry about anything. Whatever I do or don't do with Cedar, I'll be okay."

Autumn returned with another round of drinks, and before Summer could take one, I grabbed the red one. "I get huckleberry since you're being a snot tonight."

Taking the pear cider, Summer scowled at me. "Fine, okay. I'll stop for good."

"Or at least the rest of tonight," Autumn corrected. "That'll suffice."

It had been a while since I had stumbled through the woods after a few drinks. Busy sidewalks, sure. The middle of the streets and through the Seattle Center at one in the morning, absolutely. But the woods? No.

I had forgotten how many roots suddenly appeared when you're drunk, little hazards meant to trip you. Not to mention the creek Cedar so effortlessly traversed to with me on his back. It was a bit more challenging in the dark after a few too many ciders and in heeled boots.

The house was dark as I walked back in, and I was reminded of the late nights where I would sneak through the back door and hope my parents were already asleep.

I toed off my sopping boots—they would likely be ruined from my trip across the creek—and set them by the front door. So much for the polishing job.

As I tiptoed into the foyer, the floorboard creaked beneath my feet. The frame of a plush ottoman connected with my shin as I reached for the lamp to my right. I cursed as I tried to keep my balance and then the kitchen lights came on, Cedar on the stairwell in nothing but his boxers, a look of annoyance on his face.

"Could you make any more noise?"

Straightening, I pushed my glasses farther up my nose. "Possibly."

No point in pretending I was sneaking back in from the bar as I glided past him and into the kitchen, where I opened a cabinet door for a glass to find it was full of spices. I glared at the turmeric and cumin.

Soft footfalls sounded behind me, the opening and closing of a cabinet, then the sound of water. Cedar set the full glass down in front of me.

"You were supposed to call me. I was going to walk you back up."

"I was fine."

"How was the Skol House?"

"As disgusting as ever. I think I was hit on by at least three Navy guys. Might have been a record for me." I gulped the cold water, ignoring the way his muscles flexed deliciously as he crossed them over his bare chest.

"Did you—" He swallowed, "Never mind. It's not my business."

After draining the water, I set the glass to the side.

Cedar's brows pulled together, shoulders tensed.

"Did I what? Ask me, Cedar. Give one my number? Flirt shamelessly, reach over, and touch his arm? Did I kiss him? Or were you sitting here, imagining so much worse?"

"I wasn't imagining any—"

While Summer's line of questions was irritating, she wasn't wrong.

Cedar hurt me. Maybe it was the brisk air I walked through, maybe the courage of my friend telling me I deserved better. It was likely the drinks, but also, a vicious part in me wanted to see the same longing in him I carried around for years. Whatever it was, I spoke low and strong.

"Maybe I let him take me down the boardwalk? Does he know what my mouth tastes like? Maybe he slid his hand under my shirt? Maybe his fingers—"

"Stop. I don't want to hear it." Hands scrubbing his face, Cedar stepped back.

His dark lashes fluttered on his cheeks as he inhaled through his nose.

"Why? I had to imagine you like that. Remember? One minute, I'm grieving the loss of my father, but I think I still have you to lean on. The next, I see her in your house wearing my shirt and nothing else."

"Alivia?" His brows rose quickly before he gave a small shake of his head. "That was so long ago. I'm not that boy anymore."

I pursed my lips. "And I'm not the same girl who trekked through the woods for a glimpse of you."

"Yeah, obviously."

"So, if I want to take some random dude home from the bar, I can do that, and you can't say a damn thing. Because I don't owe you anything."

He blinked at me slowly as if seeing me for the first time. "Is that really what you want?"

Of course it wasn't. I wanted him. I've always wanted him, but I couldn't give that part of me up again.

Channeling Summer, I straightened my shoulders and stared him down. "Maybe I don't owe you an explanation, and you don't need to give me anything. We are practically strangers now."

"That's not true. I know you. We've known each other since we were kids."

"And I'm not a kid anymore, Cedar. So, let's put aside this childish infatuation and move on."

"Move on to what?" He stepped closer, and I stumbled back. "You think I'm going to move on from this? Do you think I haven't been picturing you all night, wishing I kept you here?"

"I'm not yours to keep," I whispered.

"Aren't you?"

"I haven't been for a long time. I've grown up. For the past almost decade, I've had plenty of men who made me forg—"

As soon as the words came out, I wanted to take them back. They gave away too much, told him the power he had over me.

My lies stopped in my throat as Cedar stepped to me, his hand coming up to cover my mouth, a fierce fire in his gaze.

"Stop talking about other men, or I'll—"

His jaw ticked, and he stared down at me. My back hit the pantry door, and his thighs brushed against mine. The muscles in his forearms tensed as he caged me in.

"You'll what?"

I meant for the words to come out haughtily, but the climbing lust in me coated them, made them lower.

Sucking air in through his teeth, he shook his head at me, warning me.

I thrust out my hips, grinding myself against his hard cock. He hissed at the contact, gaze blazing dangerously.

Then he was pinning me to the door, his lips on mine. His mouth was demanding as his tongue traced the edge of my lips, and I opened for him. Grabbing my hands, he pulled my arms over my head, holding my wrist with one hand while the other wrapped around my waist to pull me closer.

This was dangerous. I needed to stop, pull away. I would regret this in the morning. All these thoughts were beaten back by the ache building fast between my thighs.

Punishing kisses moved from my lips to my jaw to my neck as he ground himself against me. His hand moved from my waist, over my ass, then under my skirt. Cool air hit my bare skin as he pulled my thick tights down. They got stuck on my knees, and no matter how much I shimmied, they wouldn't budge.

Pulling away, a small smile quirked up at the corner of his lips. "Stay still."

Before I could react, he dropped to his knees, gripping my tights and pulling them from my right leg. When he touched my left knee, he gazed up at me. "Keep your hands up and don't move."

Obeying, I watched as he pulled the left leg free, but instead of placing my foot back on the ground, he hitched my knee over his shoulder.

A strangled gasp escaped my mouth as he swiped over my entrance with a long finger. "You're so fucking wet for me."

My breaths came out shaking as his tongue parted me, his eyes boring dark into mine.

I screamed at the sensation, and he tightened his grip on my ass, bringing me deeper into his mouth. Sucking onto my clit, his fingers plunged in and out of my pussy, hitting that spot that drew me to the edge.

With one hand, I covered my mouth to muffle the cries, and Cedar stopped. "I told you. Keep your hands up. I want to hear your screams."

Not wanting him to stop, I raised my arms over my head again, gripping the doorframe for support.

Between his tongue and his fingers, I was cresting, light and sensation flooding through me, and no hand over my mouth could have stopped my echoing cries.

Vaguely, I felt my foot hit the ground and my skirt being pulled back down over my upper thighs.

As I sagged against the door, Cedar caught me, his arms wrapping around my waist and pulling me tight against his body.

As my breathing slowed, I opened my eyes to him, grinning at me. "Come on, we're just getting started."

On shaking legs, we made our way up the stairs, his warm hand guiding me. Hitting the switch with his elbow, the room filled with a yellowy glow from the multicolored Tiffany style light on the ceiling.

I reached for the switch, but he stopped me, his head shaking. "No, I get to see you. I need to."

A slow kindle started in my chest at the words. This kiss was slower, tentative, in the room's quiet. Our shadows cast against the floral-patterned walls as his hand cupped my cheek, pulling me to him. My lips parted, blood pounding in my ears as he deepened our kiss. His bare chest was firm under my hand as I ran my fingers from his shoulders to his flat stomach. The groan he gave was fuel, and my fingers strayed lower, cupping his hard length.

With a strength that surprised me, he scooped me up. My feet were crossed around his waist, and he let go of his grip on my ass to pull my shirt over my head.

He stumbled forward, to the edge of the bed. His mouth found mine again, and we were kissing as I ground my core against him, the vibration of his erection against my clit sending a shock wave down my body. I never had orgasms back-to-back before, but the simple rub of his hard erection through his pants was getting me halfway there already. As he pinched the clasp of my bra, unhooking it with a single hand, I moaned into his mouth.

Clad in only my skirt, him in his low-hanging boxers, we fell onto the bed, and I brought my hips up to rub against him. The low groan he let out sent sparks to my core.

Taking my hand, he pushed it against his bulging erection. "Do you feel this? Do you feel how much I need to be inside you? I don't want—I *need* you. I need to fill you up, fuck you until you scream my name."

My hand brushed down his length. "You're so hard." My voice low, I glanced down to inspect what I had created in him.

"You do this to me." Squeezing him slightly, he twitched in my hand.

"Fuck." His head rested on my shoulder as he scraped my skin with his teeth. "Fuck, Devin. Only you."

I knew this could only be a lie, as there was nothing for us past this night, this moment, but I was too far gone to care. I would deal with the heartache in the morning.

Deftly, he pulled my skirt down my legs and tossed it on the floor. His fingers traced up my thigh, over my hips, until he reached my breasts. His hand splayed over my sternum tattoo, the top of his palm pressing into my chest to hold me down.

With a whisper of a touch, he traced over the triangle of color etched on my skin. "From the first moment I saw this, all I wanted was to taste it."

His fingers moved to my bare nipples, circling until he reached the buds. He dipped down, taking one into his mouth, his tongue swirling over the aching peak. With his other hand, he pinched the other, rolling it.

His mouth on me, his fingers, his skin. It was better than I remembered from when I was a teen. All the years I had told myself he couldn't be this good, that we couldn't fit together this well, I was wrong. It was better, more.

Then his finger was moving over my skin, skimming my sensitive flesh. One hand holding me in place, he parted my folds, plunging a large finger inside me. I broke off our kiss, groaning loudly. He curled a finger up, hitting me exactly where I needed to be touched.

"You like that. Don't you?" His fingers moved against me, rubbing my clit with slow, deliberate swipes. "You want me to make you come again, right here, don't you?"

"Ye . . . yes." I gasped out.

He dipped his head low, trailing fervent kisses down my throat. "I'm going to give you so much pleasure that, for days later, you'll be feeling me. You'll know what I do to you and that nothing will make you feel as good as I do."

"Nothing between us. I need to feel you." Hooking my fingers into the waistband of his boxers, I pushed them down.

He was bigger than I imagined.

Propping himself up on one elbow, he reached between us to grip the base of his hard cock. Stroking it slowly, his eyes were steady on me. "You want this?"

I nodded, unable to form the words.

"Tell me you want this. Say the words."

"I want it."

"What do you want, Devin? Tell me you want my cock. Tell me you want me to fuck you."

"I want your cock."

His eyes flashed with desire at my words, but he didn't move closer. His finger moved in and out of me, rocking against my clit, shooting sparks down my legs.

I gripped his shoulders, writhing on the bed.

"Say it all."

"Fuck me . . . Fuck me hard, Cedar. Fuck—"

He slammed into me, filling me up. His strokes were frantic, hitting the spot inside I needed. A wave rose inside me as my release built up. His hands on my tits, he pinched my nipple, rolling it again.

"Don't go yet," he warned. "Come with me."

"I can't . . ." I panted, moving with him, the crest of my pleasure reaching its peak. I threw my head back, arching my spine. As my back bowed off the bed, he pulled my breast into his mouth, licking and sucking. "I can't wait . . ."

"Now," he roared. "Come now."

I felt him releasing inside me as I fell apart, my vision going black, every color flashing behind my eyelids. My whole body convulsed as the ripples of pleasure shook me.

The weight of his body pressed me into the bed, and I wrapped my arms around his neck. A rough scrape of his stubble burned as he moved from my neck to my face. With a reverential kiss, he brushed the hair off my cheek.

Staring into his face, I tried to memorize the glow of sweat on his hair and the languid smile that played on his full lips.

Cedar flopped back onto the bed, his arms askew beside his head. "Why haven't we been doing this for years?"

"We could have."

Words escaped my empty, lust-tainted head before I could think about them.

"We should have."

As he closed his eyes, he had a dopey expression. It made me want to smash him with a pillow, then kiss him senseless.

The midnight chill was seeping into the room, cooling my sweaty body.

Pulling the blanket over my shoulders, I let my lids flutter shut. "It's okay, Cedar. I know what kind of girl I was back then. There was no promised between us, and I've never been the girl the boys go wild for."

My statement wasn't for pity or attention. It was a fact.

I sat up, my feet resting on the cold wood floor, grounding myself. "Then, those boys are idiots."

Behind me, I heard Cedar rolled over to his side.

Inspecting the swirls of wood, knots, and grain, I tried to keep my tone casual. "You were one of those boys."

"My original statement stands. I was an idiot."

"Were? Past tense?" I teased.

As he growled at me, he swiped at me with his hand to pull me to him. His skin was warmer than mine, and I immediately heated. He laced his arm around my middle, his cheek resting against my side.

"I think it's well established. I was as dumb of a teenage boy as you can imagine."

His eyes fluttered shut, his thumb rubbing against my stomach lazily.

I stared down at him. In the light of the midnight lamps, his unshaven whiskers glimmered gold. I ran a finger over the scar on his eyebrow, tracing the smooth edge.

This is dangerous, Devin.

"How many tattoos do you have, anyway?"

"Seventeen."

"Looks like more than seventeen." After trailing his fingers down my arm, he stopped at every bird marked along my forearm. Over the Viking ax and the multicolored ivy until he reached my nape. Tracing the lines etched into my tender skin, he paused. "What's this one?"

"It's kanji for springtime radiance. Haruki." I paused as I thought of the delicate lines. "My mom has one, too. We got it together on my dad's birthday after . . ." Still, after eight years of him being gone, the words clotted in my chest. "After."

My voice cracked. It had been a long time since I gave it space in my heart to grieve him, but the pain never really went away.

"He was a great guy. I bet you miss him."

"Every day." I gulped, blinking away the wetness threatening to spill over.

When you lose someone you love, a piece of you will always be stuck back there with them, with the delicate spot in my chest where I was eighteen, full of innocence and hope for the future. It was stripped away the day I found out he had passed.

I would never be that girl again. There were so many days when I wondered who I would have been if my dad had lived. Maybe I'd have picked a different major, going into business the way he and my Jiji did. Or I would have come home more often. Maybe Cedar and I could have been more than regret and anguish on a porch. Maybe.

Losing my father and the subsequent distress of Cedar and Alivia rekindling would always be inextricably linked.

As much as I wanted to fall into Cedar, to confess the depths inside me, I couldn't trust him. I hadn't in years.

Instead, I pulled my hair away from my neck, pointing at the four little marks behind my ear. "These, I got for my friends, Summer, Autumn, and Wren."

His fingers traced over the mark on my inner forearm. "And this one? The heart?"

I smiled ruefully, thankful for the change in topic. "That's a planchette, like from a Ouija board? You know, to summon the spirits and all that."

"And have you?" he asked, a grin flickering.

"Not today."

His fingers danced over my hip, past my cherry blossom on my pubic bone, to the lettering on my upper thigh. "TITSOAK?"

This was by far my most absurd tattoo, one I got as a dare after a night of drinking and a movie marathon. "A quote from a movie. It's silly, not deep."

He traced each spindly letter before drawing a path from the outside of my thigh to between my legs.

I parted my knees.

Lips found lips and then he was over me again, his fingers opening me up for him. This time, there was no talk, only mouths and tongues—and then he was inside me.

With every thrust, I was breaking my own heart. As I climaxed, I couldn't fight the ominous sensation of our clock running out. Soon enough, he would move on, and all I was allowing myself was more to miss.

Spent, I closed my eyes as Cedar walked the three steps to the switch on the wall. As the light went out, I ran a hand over my face, imprinting the sights of the night on my mind. This is what he looked like after sex, slick hair and a warm gaze. A complacent smile and strong arms.

This is the man I've always loved and, in a few days, we'd be over.

Thirteen

Cedar

A FAR-OFF WHINING NOISE woke me at nine. Beside me, Devin's face was smooshed into a floral print pillow. The bedding set was one Edith brought with her into the marriage.

I tried not to think too hard about having sex in my mom's bed. We'd wash the sheets, of course, but something about it felt very juvenile.

Sometime today, I need to reach out to the listing agent about that rental in town.

Would Devin like the house? Never had I wanted someone to live with me, but I could already picture Devin there. There was even a small outbuilding in the backyard where the light was perfect for her morning painting. I could wire up a space heater for her. It could be her own studio.

Sure, she talked about leaving, but that was before. Surely, after everything between us over the years, she would stay.

Leaning over, I pressed a soft kiss to Devin's bare shoulder. Her skin was silky beneath my lips, and I fought the urge to kiss lower.

Flannel and rubber boots on, I walked across the yard to the chicken coop. Phoebe and Barbara approached immediately, squawking and fluffing their wings.

I knew their names, of course, but I couldn't help but play dumb to get that beautiful flush of indignation rising in Devin's eyes.

On the top of the henhouse, Josh cast me an imperious look and let out an obnoxious call. Scattering the feed over the ground, I kept one eye on the asshole rooster.

His bite from the other day still left my finger sore. Nasty jerk.

On the other side of the yard, Caleb and his crew were finishing with the downed tree. I wasn't sure what time they had showed up, but they were packing their tools into the large white chipper truck. The polite thing to do would've been to walk over and greet them, but I didn't want Caleb and his smarmy attitude to ruin my good mood.

I opened the gate so the chickens could move around the yard better and I could get into the roosting nest for the eggs. After a few tense exchanges between me and Barbara, I was able to collect three eggs. As I turned back to head to the house, I found Caleb on the other side of the coop, a disgruntled Josh flapping his wings and stretching his neck at Caleb's feet.

Maybe the little jerk wasn't so bad.

"Can you come grab him? He's freaking me out."

"Are you really afraid of a chicken, man?"

"I don't like birds, okay? They're tiny dinosaurs and have soulless eyes."

Scooping Josh up, I fought back my gasp when the little shit pecked at my healing cut. Traitor.

"What's up?"

I wasn't exactly projecting masculinity by standing there in an egg apron with a rooster in my arms, but what could one do?

His gaze not leaving Josh, he spoke slowly. "We're all finished up on the bridge. You guys shouldn't have any issues crossing it. I checked, and there doesn't seem to be any structural damage to the culvert."

Well, damn. I couldn't be annoyed by that.

"Normally, I'd wouldn't start service until the bill was paid, but seeing as you're almost family, I waited." He rocked back on his heels, the toes of his workingman's boots scuffed up from hard labor. "Are you able to pay, or should I wait for—"

There was no way in hell I was letting Devin go out with Caleb. Not after the night we shared.

"I'll grab my wallet."

After I paid a smug Caleb, I drove to the store from the house to get hazelnut creamer for her coffee. It was an odd feeling driving after so many days of being stranded.

On the way back from the store, I made a quick turn, stopping in front of the Brevik Gallery. The owner was a friend of Edith's and had been to the house a few times. Before I could tell myself it was a fool's errand, I walked inside to the older woman behind the back counter who had a large laptop open in front of her.

Her dark eyes crinkled up in a smile that brightened her face. Despite it being years since I last saw her, she looked the same. If it wasn't for her all-gray hair, I would have sworn she was under forty.

"Cedar Eden, that you? My goodness, you've grown."

"Hi, Mrs. Hirsch."

"Catalina, please. You're too old to be talking with that missus stuff." Closing her laptop, she set her dark-brown hand on her chin. "What can I help you with, young man?"

"This might be an odd request, but could you help me track down a painting?"

Her warm gaze brightened as I showed her the picture on my phone. She didn't comment on the painting, but I saw a flicker of a grin on her lips. "That, my boy, I might be able to do."

Wisps of steam floated over the coffee as I set it down on the bedside table beside her dark-rimmed glasses. From her spot in bed, Devin lowered her phone to her side and pulled herself up to sit.

"Hi."

Her voice was tentative, her gaze darting from the coffee to my face and back.

Taking my spot beside her, I handed her the steamy mug.

Over the rim, she watched me with her brows pulled together.

"Good morning."

"Is it still? I almost never sleep in like that." She took a small sip, raised a brow, and blinked a few times, then took another sip. "Is this hazelnut creamer?"

"Yeah, your favorite, right? I ran to the store this morning."

"To get me creamer?"

Shrugging, I took a sip of my own coffee. "Among other things."

The side table was too small for two mugs, so I set my almost-empty coffee cup on the floor. Late morning light was filtering into the room, white-gray and chilly. The ruckus of birdsong outside our window was the only sound as she studied me.

She was rarely without her glasses, and somehow, she looked younger without them, her green eyes no longer magnified by the thick lenses but still framed with those impossibly lush black lashes. A small line over the bridge of her nose where her skin was a shade lighter.

"Why don't you wear contacts?"

She pursed her lips, one brow pulled down, as her gaze narrowed. "Why should I? To look prettier for you? That's a little archaic, isn't it?"

Throwing my hands up, I shook my head. "Hey, I didn't say that. I like your glasses. It's only that I don't know a lot of women who wear them every day."

Her frown lessened, but she still crossed her arms. "I could give you all sorts of answers about thwarting beauty standards and societal expectations, but to be honest, I'm cheap. These glasses cost me the same as a three-month supply of contacts, and they last far longer. I'll wear my contacts for special occasions, but I don't really like them."

"I like you in glasses. I always have."

She took another sip of her coffee, a darkness falling over her face. After setting the mug down, she laced her fingers together, her words soft into her lap. "Don't say always."

Frowning, I leaned forward, tipping her chin up to look at me. "Why?"

Her mouth opened, then shut as she shook her head out of my grip.

"Why, Devin?"

Clamping her lips together, her gaze was on the wall behind me. Breathing slowly through her nose, she shook her head again.

"I know whatever this thing is that's between us you don't want it to be permanent. I know you're leaving soon, but I really like you."

Her gaze softened, eyes flickering to mine. An immense conflict brewed in her expression.

"Don't say things you don't mean, Cedar. Don't make me want more if you can't give it."

"I'm not promising you anything," I reminded her. "And I'm not asking for anything more than you're willing to give."

Breathy, she turned her face to me. "I know that."

"I want you." My fingers were on her wrist, moving up her arm to the crook of her elbow. "I'm going to kiss you now."

"I hate that you're doing this to me, Cedar," she gasped.

"You want me. I know you do," I murmured into her throat, the slick salty taste against my tongue.

"I do, but . . ."

I sighed as my teeth nipped her collarbone. "Talk to me, Dev. Tell me. Tell me what it is, and I'll give it to you."

Her nails dragged along my nape slowly, thick lashes fluttering open. Our breath mingling, her green eyes bore into mine. Little flecks of gold and emerald took me in.

"I want to draw you."

I considered telling her I saw the painting she made of us but decided against it. How she would take this information, I couldn't be sure.

"Okay."

She pulled on a robe and then was gone, leaving me alone. The light footsteps sounded in the house and then she was back in the bedroom, a sketchbook and pencil in hand.

"Are you going to draw me like a French girl?" I asked, rolling to my side.

She studied me before tilting her head to the side. "You mean nude? Not this time."

"But you have, right?"

Why I was even asking this question, I didn't know. She was an adult woman—of course she had seen naked men. Still, I didn't like the idea.

"Of course, the form is one of the first I studied while in school. It's not sexual." She set her sketchbook and pencil on a chair beside the bed and examined me with a shrewd expression. "I want you on your side, facing me."

I complied with her instructions, silent as she assessed me.

"Here, let me." She kneeled, her hand on my cheek as she tilted my head, fingers moving across my skin with the slowest torment.

A small line formed between her brows as she flattened the collar of my shirt.

With my free hand, I brushed a lock of hair that fell out of her ponytail, and she pulled away, a terse turndown of her mouth.

"Stay still. You're my subject. You can't move. Now, chin down—a little more—and eyes closed."

"You look like a stern librarian with the glasses and that expression."

"Great, so dowdy and unfuckable."

"Definitely not. You look like you're about to boss me around, and you know what?" I leaned forward, my voice lowering. "I'm kind of into it."

A blush bloomed over her cheeks, a coy smile she quickly hid away playing on her lips. "Stop moving. You're going to mess up my concentration. And close your eyes."

A few minutes went by. The weight of her assessing gaze on me made every inch of my skin feel tight.

"It's never been sexual, seeing a naked body?" I asked, unable to contain myself.

"Not professionally, no. In school, we were all there for the same reason. You break each part down initially, clinically even. It's not a naked man or woman, it's an elbow and the shadows or the angle of the throat against the perspective. I'm sure it's the same as your work. You focus on the part that needs treatment."

"True." I could hear the scratching of a pencil. "What part are you drawing now?" I asked, cracking one eye open.

"Your shoulder. Now, close those eyes."

"You have great shoulders. Have I told you that? I love kissing down your trapezoid, where your clavicle meets the sternocleidomastoid. Then plunging down into your pectoral muscles that hold up those . . ."

The scratch of the pencil stopped, and I cracked one eye to see her narrowed gaze on me. "You're showing off."

A grin quirked up.

"Maybe."

"Close your eyes and *stop smiling*. You're going to mess up the vision."

The room was nearly silent after that, only the sound of the wind in the trees, birdsong, and the soft rasp of her fingers moving over the paper.

"What—" Her gulp was audible, even from my spot on the bed. She coughed, then found her voice. "What other parts do you like?"

"Your obliques. Your deltoids, your gluteus medius, leading directly to that luscious gluteus maximus."

The sketch book hit the side of her chair.

"That is not what it's called."

"I promise you it is. That beautiful plump ass of yours."

"Leave it to you to make the medical terms sound sexy."

"I aim to please."

"I still say it sounds like a made-up cartoon name. I'm sure I learned that at some point but forgot it. Summer would know that kind of stuff—she had the oddest cache of odd facts she hoards. Never play against her and her fiancé on trivia night. They will decimate you."

"Got it."

Resuming the sketch, she grumbled something I couldn't quite hear. Minutes later, the pencil stopped moving, and I felt her above me.

"Okay, I'm done."

Still laying on the bed, I stuck a hand out. "Can I see?"

Wordlessly, she handed me the book.

The lines and shadows were rough, but she had depicted me in a way that made a part of my heart soar and the other part plummet. Something in the smudges and strokes she captured me was a different version of myself. There was a vulnerability in the drawing. There was love. Was this how she saw me?

"It's amazing, Dev."

"It's rough, and I need to do better shading on the jawline, but—"

Wrapping my arms around her middle, I pulled her down on top of me. I couldn't tell her what this drawing meant to me. But I could show her.

Rolling her over on her back, I pushed the robe off her shoulder, my mouth skimming over her soft skin. This time was just as needy as the night before.

My shirt was thrown to one corner of the room, my sweatpants another. With her robe open, I nipped and licked my way down her body, coming to a stop between her legs. The taste of her from the night before was still on my tongue, and I parted her with one hand, slipping a finger inside. Her moan of pleasure and the tightening of her hands in my hair let me know I was hitting the spot she needed. With one hand, I covered her breast, rolling her nipple between my fingers as she rode my other.

"Enough of that." She pulled my face up for a kiss before rolling me onto my back. Straddling me, she rubbed her slickness over my hard cock.

The groan I let out was ragged as she teased me. With one hand braced on my chest, she rose, sliding me inside her with the other hand. With this angle and the view I had of her tits bouncing above me, I wouldn't last long.

My fingers dug into her ass as we moved in sync. She pulled my face up to her breasts as she rode me harder. Swirling my tongue around her nipple, she gasped as she hooked her legs around my waist.

I was so deep inside her as we moved together, and I felt the tensing of her body, the hitch in her breath, and the stuttered cry as she got closer.

Already, I knew her signs, and already, I wanted to hear them again.

Her nails scraped against my upper back as she fell apart around me, her pussy squeezing me in a vise grip until all I could do was empty inside her. There was no pulling out, no separating us.

As we both came down, we fell sideways on the bed, me still inside her. Her lids shut, she traced a hand over my bare shoulder.

As her eyes fluttered open, a look of pain hit me in the chest.

"Cedar, what are we doing?"

I fought back the sensation that I was getting too close. What she wanted—and, hell, what I wanted—I wasn't sure. But all I knew was that whatever my future had in store, she was a part of it.

Brushing her hair off her forehead, I smiled. "Being together."

Conflict warred on her face. "But—"

"We'll figure it out."

She didn't ask for more, tucking her chin into my neck as I pulled her closer.

Despite having the best night of sleep I had in ages, despite it only being eleven in the morning, I drifted off, my arm wrapped around her waist and Devin's cheek resting on my chest.

Hours after, a hearty helping of a vegetable soup and two orgasms later, we were seated on the small couch, watching the first episode of a British dramedy.

With my head in her lap, she ran her fingers through my hair as the woman on the screen was stealing a sculpture from her stepmother.

On the coffee table, Devin's phone buzzed loudly, shimmying across the wooden surface. Caleb's name flashed across the screen before she grabbed it and answered.

Gulping down the irritation, I waited as she made small talk before the words I had been dreading came out.

"Yeah, tonight still works."

She couldn't possibly think she could still go out with Caleb after everything we shared in the past twenty-four hours.

That's when I snatched the phone. "She isn't going to dinner with you, Caleb. Not tonight. Not ever."

Silence hung on the other end for so long I thought I might have hung up on him in my impatience to get the phone.

"Nothing going between you two, huh?" Caleb chuckled.

Beside me, Devin was reaching over, trying to yank the phone, but I got up.

"Things change."

"Give my phone back," Devin hissed, grabbing for my arm.

Sidestepping her, I kept the phone to my ear. "And don't call her again." Before Caleb could get another word, I hung up on him.

Arms crossed, Devin cast me a withering glare. "What the hell. You had no right."

"No? You really think you can go out with him after we slept together? I won't allow it."

"Allow it? *Allow it?*" She sputtered out. "Who do you think you are to tell me what to do?"

Stepping to her, I buried my hands in her hair, holding onto her nape to bring her face up. "I'm the man you spent the night with. The one that made you come."

"That doesn't give you the right."

With a narrowed focus, I leaned down closer, my mouth inches from hers. "You really want to go out with him? Look me dead in the face and tell me he makes you feel the way I do."

Her eyes darted away as she grasped her elbows, her jaw set.

"Tell me you want him to kiss you." The shaky exhale told me everything I needed to know. Hand still in her hair, I pulled her closer to me. "That when you think about getting fucked, it's his face you see."

After several painstaking moments, her gaze flashed to mine with an expression of surrender. "You know it's not."

Those words were all I needed.

When her phone rang again after our consecutive orgasms, I had to strangle the urge to silence it.

What if it was Caleb?

Fortunately, I didn't need to embarrass myself, as her friend Summer was inviting her out to the brewery again to see Autumn tend the bar for the first time.

For a Wednesday night, the place was thick with people, about half holding steins with the brewery logo emblazoned with the words *Mug Club Member* and a number between one and a hundred.

Beside me, Devin smoothed over her floral print T-shirt with *All oopsies, no daisies* printed over the chest, tucked into her ripped black jeans. A purple lock of her hair fell from her high bun.

My hand itched with the impulse to wrap that hair around my finger and bring her closer. Of course, I couldn't do anything of the sort. We were in public. Together.

When Devin invited me with her, I agreed right away, but as we were walking into the brewery, where one of her closest friend's worked, I was experiencing misgivings.

Was this a date? We had already slept together, more than a handful of times, and a first date seemed redundant. But meeting her friends, being together here, was *something*.

Behind the tall wooden bar, a row of taps behind her, Autumn was pulling a drink. With her auburn hair up in two pigtails, she wore bright yellow overalls and a clashing green T-shirt.

When she saw Devin, a wide smile broke over her face. She got us our drinks, and when Devin tried to put down her card, I waved her off, giving Autumn mine first.

As we turned to face the small room, I saw Summer waving us over. The smile on her face falling as she saw me alongside Devin.

As we approached, Devin squeezed my arm. "Don't let Summer scare you, okay?"

"She can't scare me—"

Devin waved at me. "Summer, you remember Cedar from school, right?"

Summer's shrewd blue eyes narrowed, not matching the small smile playing on her lips. "Of course, Cedar Eden, homecoming king."

In her barbed tone, the words sounded like an expletive.

"How have you been, Summer?"

"Fine." She cocked a brow as if she was waiting on me to call her bluff.

The tall man beside her was leaning over the table, an amber beer in one hand, his gaze darting between me and Summer as if it were a tennis match. A gleeful expression played on his face. "Aren't you going to introduce me, Sunshine?"

"Cedar, Van. Van, this is Cedar Eden. He's a shithead who doesn't know a good thing when he has it."

Van frowned at me, his gray eyes darkening.

"Summer," Devin admonished. "Stop it. Play nice."

Over the rim of her drink, Summer hummed noncommittally. In sync, we sipped from our beers.

Devin coughed. "Ugh, gross, IPA. I told Autumn the Dunkel." With one hand on my forearm, she leaned in closer. "I'll be right back. Play nice."

This was pointed at Summer, who tossed her blonde hair over her shoulder dismissively.

Devin didn't get three steps away before Summer set her drink down and hissed over the table. "So, what's the deal? You fucking her around again? Making her think you're single when you have a girlfriend?"

"No, I—"

"What, think because you guys are staying in the same place you can get laid and then you're going to leave her sad again?"

"Again, I never—"

"I never liked you. In school, around town. You were always full of your-self. Never took anything seriously, including my best friend's feelings."

"That's not how it happened—"

"Listen closely to me. I don't care about whatever excuse you have for hurting Devin years ago. I don't want to hear it. Dev's a big girl, and I trust her to take care of herself. But the second she calls me with as much as a hitch in her breath, I will decimate you. Are we clear?"

I didn't know Summer well, as she was a few years younger than me, but something told me this was not a woman who lied about ruining a man's life.

"She's not exaggerating. The last guy who pissed her off is still in prison," Van quipped before taking a long slug of beer. "Long may he rot."

Hands up, I leaned away from her. "I get it. Message received."

She scowled at me, shaking her head. "Good."

Devin returned, holding a fresh drink. "Sorry about that. Autumn is still learning. What did I miss?"

To her credit, Summer put on the most innocent expression. "Cedar was telling us about his job. Sounds fascinating."

Two beers, three packets of locally roasted peanuts, and a hearty portion of food-truck pancit and chicken adobo later, Van was regaling us with a story about a recent work conference he had in Scottsdale.

"—And the best birria tacos I've ever had. This place looked like a total dump from the outside, but, damn, I can still taste that food."

"You'll have to check it out when you get down there, Dev." I motioned to Van with my beer, my focus on Devin beside me.

"Do you have a work thing down there, too?" Summer asked.

"Um, no." Devin's gaze snapped from me to Summer, her words uncertain. "I was thinking about maybe moving to Arizona."

Summer stared at Devin, her mouth hanging open. "Sorry? I must have heard you wrong. I know there is no way my best friend of a decade decided to move to Arizona without telling me." She said Arizona with such disbelief it might as well have been the Swiss Alps. "What about your job?"

Lips pursing together, Devin traced a finger over the rim of her half-full beer glass. "I kind of got laid off."

"You what?" Summer said loudly. "And you didn't tell me?"

"I didn't want you to worry. You always try to take care of me, and you don't need to do that."

"That's not true—"

"Tommy Fischer? Remember that?"

"I maintain that he jumped into that creek on his own."

"Really?" Devin crooked a brow, a smirk crinkling her green eyes. "With his backpack on, in early March?"

"He deserved it."

"I'm an adult, Sum, and it knew if I told you, you'd rush in and try to fix everything, whether or not I wanted it."

"I would never—"

Beside her, Van snorted.

The venomous look Summer shot him could have melted rubber off a tire.

"It's fine. I'll be fine."

Summer's churlish gaze slipped from Devin to me. "And what about you? You're not going to chime in here and tell her she's making a mistake?"

"She's perfectly capable of making her own choices. She's bright and lovely and talented. Whether it be here or in Arizona, I believe in her."

With an eye roll, Summer mimed barfing. "Gross. That was adorable."

"No matter where she is, she'll do well. Do I want her to stay? Of course

I do. I'd love for her to stay in town, but she can paint anywhere and—"

"And you're painting again?" Summer asked, incredulous. "Why didn't you tell me?"

"It's not a big thing, just a little side hustle I've been working on."

"What are you talking about?" I asked. "Your paintings are incredible. Even that drawing from this morning, it only took you a few minutes, and it was better than anything I could have spent days on."

Across the table, Summer huffed, but her eyes softened as she glanced from me to Devin and back to me, as if she were seeing something new.

It was petty, but I still shot her a self-satisfied smirk, my arm over the back of Devin's chair.

Still fishing around in her purse, Devin glanced up at me as I opened the door to my SUV. Though my vehicle wasn't lifted much, it was still taller than she was used to. Her hand was soft and small in mine as I helped her jump down. The ground was mushy, moss and clover under our feet, as I led her into the woods.

The waning half-moon peeped out behind a wall of heavy clouds, stars dim in the sky. Navigating by memory, we made our way through the overgrown forest until reaching the base of the tree house.

Even though it was cold and dark, I took the first steps on the ladder, sliding the unlocked trapdoor open with a loud bang.

Devin followed me in.

With a cell phone as our only source of light, I moved into the small space. I was glad I stopped by earlier, sweeping away the dead leaves, spiderwebs, and pine needles. I left a few old blankets in the corner.

Devin took the same spot she took the last time we were up here, curling her knees to her chest.

"I'm going to miss this spot."

Her words were rueful as she ran a finger over the knotted wood floor.

Her words blasted away my romantic plans of seduction in the tree house. She had always planned on leaving, talked about what she would do in Arizona, about her friend who was giving her a couch to crash on, about the companies she had researched who were looking for graphic artists.

"Not to sound like Summer, but are you really moving to Arizona?"

She was quiet for a long time, the heavy breathing of someone who was thinking.

Outside the tree house, an owl hooted, and the wind shook its burgeoning leaves against the clear corrugated roofing.

"Are you asking me to stay?"

Leaving was always her plan. What kind of guy would I be to ask her to stay? I had nothing to offer her. I didn't know how I felt. She deserved better than me.

"I wouldn't ask that of you."

Yes, yes, stay with me. Let's figure this out.

When I didn't respond, she nodded. "I need to go to Arizona. A fresh start. No bad memories of my failures there."

"It hasn't all been bad. You have friends here, your family. Me."

"I don't have you. Not really." Her eyes filled with tears, an inexplicable sadness threatening to flood over. Her words were soft. "I'm a stupid girl."

"No, you're not. You're one of the smartest girls I know."

She shook her head, teardrops sliding down her cheeks. "Not with you. I've always been stupid with you. You make me stupid and reckless." She drew in a deep breath. "When we were doing whatever it was we were doing as kids, I thought I loved you. I was crazy, over the moon, in love with you."

I knew, of course, I did. But to hear those stark words so matter of fact, so brave, I knew it was more than was due.

"That was years ago . . ."

"No, Cedar, you stop. It's my turn to talk."

Her voice was stronger, steel barbs silencing me.

I leaned back from her vitriol.

"A part of me has always loved you. But I never knew you. You never allowed me—or really anyone—to know you. Always hiding behind this facade of cool guy, funny guy, easy going. Everyone's friend. But you never let people in, even when they open to you, even when they try everything to love you."

"It's been less than a week since we reconnected—"

"And I loved you for too long, Cedar. I gave you a part of me I've never shared with someone else. I have spent years being in these half relationships, these one-night stands and flings with men who I will never care about. Because no one could ever compare to the way you made me feel." Her gaze grew weary. "Make me feel."

My breath shuddered in my body, her words washing over me.

"Cedar, I can love you forever, but if this isn't real, I cannot continue to be in this space anymore. I cannot hold you, kiss you, and feel you to be pushed away. Every time I we are together, I love you more, but I know you don't love me. I cannot get closer to you to only have you break my heart again."

I laid a hand on her cheek. "You know, I never wanted to hurt you, Dev."

"But that's not the same as love," she whispered.

To say anything but *I love you too* in that moment wouldn't be enough. There was no way I would be able to lie to Devin.

"It's not. You're right."

In the low moonlight, I saw the tracks on her face, tears that she hadn't wiped away yet.

I had never earned Devin, and to touch her when she had bared herself to me was selfish and wrong. But still, I couldn't turn away, couldn't leave her alone. As a kid, I had done the wrong thing and not gone after Devin.

There was no going back to those days, but she was with me.

So, I reached for her. Even if it was wrong, even if we'd both be hurt in the end. My hand cupped her cheek, brushing away the errant tears with the pad of my thumb. "Stay with me tonight?"

She wouldn't tell me no. The darkest, most possessive part of me relished in knowing I had Devin.

"Just tonight?"

"Maybe tonight is all that matters."

My mouth found hers, a frenzy of lips and teeth. Both our shirts stayed on, my pants pulled down to my ankles, and her jeans were tossed to the corner. There was no foreplay as she climbed onto my lap, her legs wrapping around me, and I was inside her.

A sense of urgency thrust with each motion. It all felt reminiscent of high school hookups, the fear of being caught, of never knowing what would happen minutes later, of what the other really felt.

Only I knew how she felt. She had given herself over to me time and time again, and still, I held back. For what? This week had meant more to me than years with any other women.

Deep inside, something was shifting within me. This was more than sex, more than these frantic moments on a treehouse floor.

This was Devin, the closest I would ever find to righteousness. If only I could be as brave as her to accept it.

Fourteen

Devin

THE COOL GRAY LIGHT of the dawn woke me before Cedar. As he rolled over, there was a crease from the pillow running over his left cheek. As was my normal wake-up routine, I grabbed my phone from the bedside table. Autumn's affirmation was the first one I saw. *I am open to the messages the universe has for me today.*

After double-tapping the message to add a heart, I then switched to my favorite social media app. With the volume turned off, I watched as a handsome man dance to a popular song, promoting his new television show on a streaming service. As I did with the thirty previous videos of this man doing this identical dance, I liked the post, then scrolled onto to a woman making peanut butter pasta and then a dog wearing a pickle costume.

Mindlessly, my finger moved over the screen as Cedar snored softly beside me. The easy comfort of having his firm body pressed into mine as I woke was surprising. It had been a long time since I woke with a man in my bed and even longer since I wanted that man to stay.

Cedar was always my exception, but there was no way I could know if I was his. Not without baring myself worse than I already had. I didn't want to look too deep into his actions from the night before, defending my autonomy to Summer. For praising my art.

She's bright and lovely and talented.

The way eighteen-year-old Devin would have swooned at those words. But I couldn't be that girl, not anymore.

No matter how much I wanted to believe, they meant more. Cedar never said forever. In fact, even when he was praising me, there was the way he talked of me leaving, as if it was a foregone conclusion.

Even if I was the one who suggested it.

And then the tree house.

Clicking the side button on my phone, I groaned, my eyes squinching shut.

I told him I loved him. What a stupid fool I was to say those words, knowing he didn't feel the same. I couldn't expose myself more.

Why must I be the brave one? Why must I be the one to take the risk of heartache, when Cedar's track record with wanting me was spotty at best? No, I needed to protect myself. If he wanted this to be more serious, it had to be him. I had given up too much already. I couldn't allow that last vestige of my pride to go away.

His arm slid over my waist, pulling me down lower onto the bed and to his side. Face buried in my neck, his breath was hot against my skin. As he shifted, his groin nestled against my leg, growing harder. His nose swiped at my collarbone. Still groggy from sleep, his hand drifted between my thighs.

I could deem the night before, the drunken confession, and the subsequent sex on the tree house floor as elusive moments. But morning sex was different. Morning sex was in the light, raw and slow and always carried more meaning.

Meaning Cedar refused to give me.

Boundaries—I had to have them, right? His fingers moved over me, parting my legs. I could've held off, could've told him we need to talk before we go any further—only his mouth on my neck felt so good. And the way his thumb pressed just right against my clit was sending sparks through my body.

After. You can talk after.

Flat on my back, his body slid down mine, the covers pushed off us and onto the floor. His tongue traced my belly button, my hip bone, that little freckle where my mound and my pelvis met.

"I just woke up. I haven't showered and—"

"That's exactly how I like you." His words were a warm caress on my inner thigh. "Open your legs. Let me taste where you need me most."

Bringing my knees up, I dug my hands into his hair as his tongue swiped through my folds. My hips rose against his face, and he took that opportunity to grab my ass, his fingers digging deeper into my soft flesh as his mouth sucked and licked.

He hummed against me, his tongue swirling around my clit, before pulling it into his mouth.

My thighs tightened on each side of his head as he delved deeper, his mouth fucking me harder. My breathing staggered, my cries punctuated with staccato gasps. The climax came on quick, my brain a buzz of white noise and a burst of orange-and-red light behind my eyelids.

Still, his tongue kept working, his grip on my ass tight enough to leave bruises. White light washed over me as I collapsed onto the pillow.

Moving over me, he wiped his face on the sheet before taking my mouth for a searing kiss.

"I need all of you," I murmured, taking a handful of his ass and pulling his hard cock against my core.

As he slid inside me, I was primed for another orgasm. His strokes were slow, hitting where it was most tender. Lips still on mine, he kissed me as he moved in and out.

I could taste myself on him, my climax, and the joy of seeing me fall apart in his arms.

With his pace set, he rose on one elbow, while the other hand cupped my chin. His fingers splayed over my cheek and held my face still.

"Look at me. I want to see your face as you come all over my cock."

With those words, I was undone. Sound and light and nothingness enveloped us, the slickness of our bodies and the hard stare of his blue eyes into mine as I fell apart in his arms.

With a shuttering sigh, he followed, his body heavy as he collapsed on me. My hands were in his hair, and he rested his chin between my neck and shoulder.

Drawing lazy, slow circles on his nape, I pictured what I never allowed myself before. More mornings like this. Nights of going out together and the surety that he was mine.

Against my skin, he hummed that familiar tune, the one that had been plaguing me all week.

Cupping my cheek, he leaned in close. "I want to talk about last night—I do. But I need to shower first. I think I still have some pine needles in my hair."

Pressing my lips together to stifle the grin, I nodded. "Maybe we could go into town, get some groceries for dinner tonight."

It wasn't the promise of forever, but it was another night together. Another chance for us. Maybe this time, we could be more. Maybe I didn't need to run to Arizona. What I needed was beside me, his stubbled cheek resting against my collarbone.

His blue eyes lit up before he pressed a soft, allaying kiss to my lips. "I'd like that."

The old pipes creaked as Cedar started his shower.

Turning back to my canvas, I wrapped the carefully measured bubble wrap and brown paper around the painting up for shipping.

A knock sounded on the front door. From my vantage point in the loft, I could see the top of a blonde woman's head. With the canvas in my arms, I climbed one-handed down the ladder, my foot slipped on the last rung.

It was this portend that told me whoever was at the door wouldn't be someone good for me. But I had already made enough noise. I couldn't pretend not to see her.

Nudging Kinny aside with one foot, I pulled open the door.

She was taller than me, with long blonde Utah curls and glossy pale pink lips. Oversized tortoiseshell sunglasses were perched on her long straight nose. Instinctively, I knew she was the sort who never washed her rice or put the shopping cart back.

In another world, she could have passed for Alivia's sister. It was déjà vu seeing this woman on the porch, as if I was catapulted back to that terrible day so many years before. Only I was the one inside.

"Hi. Can I help you?" I asked, wiping the dust from the packing paper on my black leggings.

The woman removed her sunglasses, tawny eyes scanning my dirty leggings, messy bun, and glasses, then down to my shirt, with its green cartoon ogre and the words, *Not today, I'm swamped.*

"Is Cedar here?"

"He's in the shower. I can—"

"How do you know he's in the shower?" she snapped, pushing past me. With a quick glance around the living room, one corner of her mouth curled up, she murmured, "Still a dump in here."

The door was left open, and Kinny started waddling toward it, so I had to scoop her up. Holding the fluffy oval of fur, I slammed the door, watching this woman as she perused the small living room.

"You can't just come in. I don't know you."

"And I don't know you."

"I'm Devin. I'm house-sitting from Goldie and Edith—"

Kinny squirmed in my arms, and I set her back down, where she padded the few steps back to her oversized pillow.

"But Cedar is here, too? Why would you house-sit for his mom when he's here?"

Arms crossed, my blood started pounding in my ears. Something was wrong. Very, very, very wrong.

"That's none of your business."

"It is my business when I come to see Cedar to find some random woman in my fiancé's mom's home."

A fog descended over my head, muffling all other sounds as her words reverberated.

"Sorry—" My voice sounded so weak, even to myself. "What did you say?"

My voice came out shrill.

She scoffed. "I'm Tainslee Roberts. Cedar's fiancée."

"No, no, no." Backing up, my calves hit the ottoman, tripping me, and I landed with *oaf* on my butt.

I hadn't realized I was speaking out loud until the fifth 'no' came out.

At my feet, Kinny whimpered, her little paws coming up to rest on my knees.

"What is your deal?" She crossed her arms against her pristine cream silk top.

"I—" Swallowing again, I pushed myself up, moving past her. "I'll get Cedar."

The bathroom door was left ajar, and with one push of my hand, it swung open.

"Cedar."

He ducked around the shower curtain to look at me. The water made his hair look shades darker. A humor filled glimmer lit up his face.

"Come join me." He wiggled his brows.

In another life as another girl, I would have.

"No, someone is here for you."

"Who is it?"

"Your fiancée."

"Who—" As he glanced behind me, I registered Tainslee had followed me up the stairs and into the bathroom. Color drained from his face. "Devin. This isn't what it looks like."

I let out a low, humorless chuckle. "Your fiancée is waiting." As I pushed past Tainslee, she had to jump out of the way.

I heard Cedar shuffling around in the bathroom, yelling for me to wait, but I kept walking downstairs.

Settling into the couch, I pulled my knees up to my chest, the dirge of hurt building up behind my ribs.

I could hear the murmurs of Cedar talking to his fiancée.

Fiancée.

We had spent the past week together. We had slept together and shared stories of our lives since we last saw each other.

As they raised their voices, I could hear little bits and pieces.

"You can't just show up—called first—"

"Don't tell me what to do."

"You don't need to worry about her, Tains—"

Those were the last words I needed.

Grabbing my purse off the back of the kitchen stool, I made my way to the door, then stopped to grab that hoodie from the coat rack.

It was petty and weak, but I couldn't find it in me to care how it would appear to others.

I wanted to keep that hoodie that smelled so much like him. I wanted to hurt him just a little and to remember this sensation one last time, when my intuition told me this was a mistake, and like the fool I always was for Cedar, I ignored it.

After wedging the canvas into the passenger seat, I spared a glance at the house once more before climbing into the driver's side.

It was foreign putting my hands on the steering wheel after almost a week of not driving. As I put the car into reverse, a small drop of dried blood on the middle console caught my eye, from when Cedar had sliced his arm.

As the wooden slats of the culvert bridge clacked under my car, the outline of Cedar and Tainslee in the upstairs bedroom appeared in my rearview mirror. As the house grew smaller in the distance, I turned to the left and onto the road.

Almost one decade later, I was still running from a wound only Cedar could have caused.

Fifteen

Cedar

Tainslee, as always, was punctual. She was always at events exactly on time. She prided herself on her time management skills. Never one to show up too early, but she had, never in the years we dated, allowed herself to be late. And in typical Tainslee fashion, she had picked the perfect time to implode whatever was happening between Devin and I.

My head was still sticking out of the chilling shower. "Do you mind?" I glared at Tainslee, who didn't move from the bathroom's doorway.

"What? Giving you privacy? I've seen it all."

"That was before. We're not together anymore and—"

"About that. Who is the skank who answered the door?" Tainslee asked. "You cheating on me?"

I didn't want to talk about Devin with Tainslee. "That's impossible, Tains. Since we broke up a month ago."

Seeing she wasn't going to leave, I grabbed the closest thing I could find—my mother's or Edith's bathrobe—and shrugged on the pink-and-green-striped covering.

She followed me into the bedroom, her glare darting from the unmade bed, with two district impressions of each pillow and Devin's open suitcase on the top of the pine dresser.

"Why is her stuff in here with yours? Why aren't you in your old room?"

The one and only time I brought her here was for my mom's birthday the previous summer. Despite my mom and Edith being more than welcoming and offering their room to us, Tainslee insisted we get a hotel room at the expensive Freedom Bay Resort.

"Because a tree branch shattered the window. Someone is coming out tomorrow to fix it, but until then, I'm staying where it's dry and warm."

"With her." She sniffed. "That's what I wanted to talk to you about, before that girl . . ."

As always, Tainslee was perfectly put together, the golden curls framing her face, the brown eyes narrowing shrewdly at my words. For so long, I had adored that about her, but all I wanted was Devin's messy buns and paint-stained fingers.

"There's nothing to talk about. We broke up a month ago." Stepping over Devin's jeans from the night before, I walked to the dresser to pull underwear out of my duffel bag. Facing away from her, since that was apparently the only privacy I'd get, I pulled on my underwear and jeans under the robe. "You can't just show up here unannounced and expect me to talk. You could have called first."

"I called. You wouldn't answer. I have every right to—"

"You have no right. We aren't together any longer."

Pulling the shirt over my head, I could hear the telltale signs of Tainslee huffing when I didn't give her the answer she liked.

A year ago, I saw her acting this way as passionate and respected that she was a girl who held herself and others to a high standard. But this felt snobby. While Devin wasn't nearly as sophisticated as Tainslee, I liked her authenticity. She knew what kind of woman she was, and most importantly, she knew what kind of man I was.

Devin would never ask me to quit a job I loved to go into corporate investment—or whatever Tainslee's father did. I never could understand his job.

"Oh, so, what, you're just moving on with some random while I'm still broken up over us? What does she have that I don't? Huh, Cedar? Do you think she's prettier? Or smarter? I don't get it."

"It's not about her. You don't need to worry about her, Tainslee. She had no role in us breaking up. That was my decision. We both knew we wanted different things in life. What was the point of dragging us out?"

"I loved you. We could have been good if only you would have put in a little extra work."

"You mean change my entire personality? Throw away almost a decade of schooling to work for your dad? Buy you an engagement ring I'd be paying off years to come and settling for a life half lived?"

"Well, yeah. Lots of people do it. You would have been fine. Because I love you."

It was all so desperately familiar, the way she would only pull out those words when she wanted something from me. The hollowness in her tone juxtaposed with the vulnerable way Devin spoke the night before.

"You don't love me. You love what you think I could be with your shaping. But that's not me." I swallowed, sitting on the edge of the bed.

Devin cared about me in a way Tainslee never did, saw through my bullshit and still cared. The difference in how I felt after a few days with Devin compared to the years with Tainslee was stark.

"And where do you get off telling Devin that you were my fiancée? We were never engaged."

Arms crossed against her chest, she snorted. "Devin, what kind of name is *Devin*? You still haven't told me who she is."

"She's no one," I snapped before Tainslee could upset me further.

"Doesn't sound like no one if she's answering your door first thing in the morning."

Leaning over the edge of the bed, I separated a pair of socks. "You don't have to worry about her."

"I'm trying to look out for you, Cedar. You know that's all I care about. Now that you've had your little sabbatical, you can come home, and I think we can work things out between us. I know I was being impatient with the whole ring thing, but there's no need to end our relationship over timeline issues." Tears brimmed in her lash extensions, and she swiped them away with a well-aimed flick of her manicured nail. "I love you so much. We can work this out. I know it."

With the second sock tossed at my side, I lowered my voice, trying and failing to keep my tone calm. "There's nothing to work out. There is no relationship. You and I are not compatible. Please, for your own sake, let this go. I know it's hard for you to accept defeat. But this, you and I? It's a lost cause. I don't care if you want to tell everyone that you dumped me. Tell them whatever you need to come out on top. But please, stop."

With this, her tears dried up, her tone vicious.

"You're an asshole." She could see crying wasn't going to work on me any longer, having always been resourceful. "You were never good enough for me, anyway."

"Okay. Whatever it takes to get you out of this house."

Turning on her tall booted heels, she flounced out of the room with a well-aimed "Fuck you and your little ho."

I hoped Devin didn't hear that last remark when Tainslee walked past her.

Walked past her.

Oh, shit. Devin. There was no way Devin didn't hear part of this conversation. I was going to need to do some major damage control.

Following Tainslee, I shuddered to a stop at the foot of the stairs, where she was stomping through the open front door and to the Mercedes her father had bought her the year before.

From her cushion on the floor, Kinny glared up at me.

There was no need to look around.

Devin was gone.

The absence of her was all over. Her warmth, the vanilla, and faint turpentine scent of her hands was gone.

Hoping I was wrong, I stood on the front porch. An empty oval of fresh pine leaves and branches marked where her car had been sitting, the churned-up tire tracks on a soft lawn.

Slowly lowering myself to the wet step, I slid my hand under my chin to study the space. Beside me, a mushroom was growing out of the wooden step, yellow-orange and spongy on the damp surface. Flicking it, I watched as it dented but didn't fall off.

Dented. Is that what I do to people?

For years, I told myself I was a good man, that I did the honorable thing. But deep down, I knew this was wrong because I would never deserve Devin, especially after what happened today.

Regret is a funny thing. Growing up, I made a habit out of not regretting things.

Goldie imparted the wisdom of taking mistakes and turning them into learning experiences. Of not repeating them. I prided myself on being honest with others and to own up to my wrongs.

When I shot my BD gun through the window of Mrs. Gruin's kitchen window, I knocked on her door and confessed. The time Edith caught me smoking pot in junior year, I admitted it. When Tainslee dropped hints about engagement rings and I realized I could never see myself marrying her, I did what I thought was the honorable thing and ended it.

I had spent years and time and effort and my pride in being an honest person. Someone trustworthy. In all my days, I had few doubts about that.

Devin shattered everything I knew about myself and what I wanted. With Devin, I was sure of something: I never was with any other woman.

How would I explain this to Devin?

Sixteen

Devin

FOR A PLACE AS familiar as Ridgewood, it didn't take long for me to realize I had no clue where to go. I had my friends, sure, but as supportive as they would be, I couldn't handle the unspoken *I knew he would hurt you* Summer would feel. Not to mention the threat of bodily harm she would no doubt be plotting, the sympathy from Autumn, and the jokes from Wren. It would make it real.

Never had I any issues with dishing about my half-baked boyfriends and one-night stands. But Cedar was different. This was all too raw.

They always had the best intentions, but there was no getting around the mess I had created for myself. I knew he was bad news for me and knew it the moment I saw him standing in the living room that nothing about the way I felt for him had changed.

No, my feelings were—if anything—stronger than when I was a moony-eyed teenager. Looking at him through this lens of maturity, I could see the flaws in him, in *us*, but still, I loved him.

It was a wide-eyed love, not through the rose-colored glasses of a girl who didn't know herself but a woman who had tried it all and knew this was the best she would ever feel. And that made the pain of it all the worse.

Because if I guessed no man could make me feel this way before, now I knew for certain.

But there was no getting around what his fiancée—girlfriend, ex, whatever she was—had exposed.

In the bubble of being stranded in that home, I could pretend Cedar and I were meant to be together. That we had a future. But just as easily as we had fallen together, someone else was able to rip us apart.

After a few minutes of drying my tears and rereading Autumn's affirmations, I was able to get the painting sent off to my client. I was lucky enough there were only two people in line ahead of me.

An older dark-skinned woman with graying hair stood ahead of me in line.

After checking out, she was in the lobby beside the PO boxes. As I got to the exit, she called out, "Are you Devin Haruki?"

One hand on the door, I turned to face her. "Yes?"

A wide smile broke over the woman's face. "I thought that was you. I was just looking at your website an hour ago. I'm Catalina Hirsch. I own the Brevik Gallery downtown."

As she extended her hand, I took it slowly, a crease forming between my brows. "Hi."

"I'm a good friend of Marigold and Edith's."

At the emotion of Cedar's family, a pang shot through my chest, but I pasted on what I hoped was a convincing smile.

"Wonderful."

With my hand still firmly clasped in hers, she pulled me closer. "I'd love to see a few of your pieces in the gallery. It's very compelling stuff. You should email me."

"Oh, I-I don't really paint like that anymore."

The last time my work was hung in a gallery was a few months after my graduation years before. Only two pieces had sold, and I had no luck getting into any others. That was when I cut my losses and took the job at Green Glow Organic Juices.

"No? What's this stuff you've been selling online, then? Doesn't look like nothing."

"That's just me messing around. It's not—"

"It's lovely, and I want it." She patted my hand. "Email me." Somehow, she slipped a business card in my hands before I could register what was happening and then she was out the door, the metal clanging against the doorstop, chilly air whipping my ankles.

Back in my car, I shoved the business card alongside my frozen yogurt punch card and gift card for a department store with fifty-two cents on it.

My phone buzzed with a picture of Wren in a tight dress, her dark curls wet and thick socks on her feet, a small caramel-colored wiry haired dog lying on her back, feet in the air.

Wren: Adrian is taking me out to dinner tomorrow night at this really nice place, but now I feel like my clothes are all garbage. Does this make my boobs look squished? I feel like it's a uni-boob situation but maybe I'm over thinking it

Autumn: slight uni-boob but like regency romance cleavage type, so it's cool. Is your dog dead?

Wren: No, she's fine. Maizie sleeps like that. What shoes should I wear? Boots, heels?

Autumn: I'm guessing you don't want to hear that Birkenstock's go with everything

Wren: no and no. Summer? Dev? Help a girl out here

The conversation was all so familiar and comforting until Autumn dropped that little bomb.

I hesitated. I could keep it in, but the truth would come out soon enough, and I couldn't handle any more cute comments about me and Cedar.

Before I said it, I wasn't sure it was the right landing place, but it was the one place that always felt like home. As supportive as my mom tried to be, I always felt like a guest in her new house.

I was so not fine.

A moment later, the text I was dreading came, not because she didn't care but because the shame of knowing she was right was too blatant.

Summer: I call bullshit. Do we need to have lunch? Drinks? Do I need to find my Taser?

Devin: no Taser, maybe a drink later. I can walk over to the brewery after I clean myself up. I'm sure Baba still has all my clothes from high school hanging up. I won't be cute, but it will work

Wren: you're always cute. Do I need to drive over? Is this all-hands-on deck situation?

Before I could tell her no and that the two-hour drive from Icicle Creek was too far, she sent a follow-up.

Wren: I'm getting in the car now. I can crash with you at your grandparent's, right? I'll have to leave tomorrow by eleven in time for my date night, but that will give me seventeen hours if I don't get stuck in bridge traffic

Autumn: see everyone at six, I'm off then. And you have to pay for your drinks, I got in trouble for not charging someone the other day

Summer: Boys buy you drinks, not the other way around

Autumn: but I don't drink

Wren: why are you working at a brewery again?

Allowing the sweet bickering of best friends to chime as notifications in my purse, I drove out of the post office parking lot, making my way to my grandparents' house.

Just as I thought, my grandma still had some of my old clothes hanging up in what she always called my bedroom, even though I hadn't stayed overnight for over a year.

She took the old Ridgewood High Jazz Choir shirt from my junior year out of my hands, with its paint splatters on the hem and a bleach stain on the right arm, then replaced it with her favorite black high-low dress with lace sleeves. "What about this one?"

"It's a little—"

I couldn't say what I wanted, that it was something I only wore when she was around, thus why it was left at her house.

I opened the dresser to find wads of my old colorful socks from when I insisted on wearing mismatched pairs every day, thinking it was quirky. Well, I had worse things to be embarrassed about that day than neon pink socks with donuts printed on them.

"You looked beautiful in this. You never know when these things come back into style. I wish I would have kept that safety pin skirt I made myself back in '68. I was a real peach in it, let me tell you."

Fashionable was the last thing on my mind, but I took the dress, vowing to replace it in the closet after she left.

Baba bustled around the room, fluffing pillows and smoothing the duvet. "Well, you change, and I'll get a little snack going. Brownies and tea?"

"That sounds great." I flopped back on the bed, the old pink-and-blue-striped duvet the same thick softness as all those nights I spent here as a child.

When I was ten, they took me to Nordstrom in Seattle and let me pick out my own bed set. Even though I had cousins on my mom's side, I was the only one on my father's, and Baba and Jiji always let me know how much they adored me. The ribbed material felt safe under my fingers.

"Unless you'd like special brownies."

Pulling up on my elbow, I furrowed my brows. "Special in what way?"

"Marijuana, of course."

When would this day give me a break?

I blinked at her. "Baba! You can't be serious?"

She flapped a hand at me. "I'm seventy-three. You think I don't know what pot brownies are? What generation do you think made it popular? It's been legal here for years. Helps with my arthritis and your grandfather's sleep. He doesn't need melatonin anymore."

There was no processing that information.

Rubbing a hand over my face, I squinched my brows together. "Regular is fine, great. Regular is great."

I hadn't drunk in front of my grandparents until a few months after turning twenty-one. There was no way I was tripping with my grandmother.

She patted my legs. Even though my eyes were closed, I could feel her smirking.

Waiting until she closed the door to leave me alone, I lay flat on my back. In the quiet of the room, I could hear the whoosh of cars driving down Fjord Drive. Slowly, as they always did at the corner, to take in the unadulterated view of Freedom Bay and the Olympic Mountains to the west.

I still had four hours before I was expected at the brewery to debrief with my friends.

Here, in this room, I was taken back to my youth. The tears shed on this bed, the gossip whispered during sleepovers, and the confidences shared while I sat cross-legged in a circle on the floor.

As much as this room felt like home, it also made me feel like a child again. The same child who loved Cedar from afar for so many years, the one who got to kiss him for a few glorious weeks, and the girl who shattered on the doorstep.

Here I was back again. In the same room, with the same ravaged heart.

Arms splayed out, I stared up at the ceiling light that looked like a boob. Inside the glass was a few dead moths behind the frosted white surface.

Fundamentally, something shifted in me the moment I heard those words from Tainslee.

Fiancée, *fiancée*? Could it be true? Was he engaged this whole time? Nothing about the way he acted over the past week betrayed he was involved with someone else, but how could I truly know any better if he was? The only genuine experience I had with Cedar was trusting him and then finding him with another woman weeks later.

And could Tainslee look any more like Alivia? He certainly had a type: tall, blonde, statuesque, and classic. Nothing like me.

Pulling my purple hair over my face, I pinched the ends, playing with the soft brush against my fingers.

Maybe I should have heard him out. Maybe there was more to the story. But deep down, a sense of foreboding rose. The same as years before, he never promised me anything. How I felt was in my head, and he kept his feelings close to the vest.

Yeah, he wanted me, but sex isn't love. Homemade pasta dinners and joking about his mom's asshole rooster isn't love. Even if Tainslee never showed up, he wouldn't ask me to stay. When I would hint, he would change the subject. I was familiar enough with the markings of someone unserious to know when I was being played.

Even if there was more, how could I trust him after this? I barely trusted myself. If he wanted to talk with me and explain, I would listen, but could I swallow whatever excuses he had and not give away my dignity? I had already given him too much.

No matter what, I would always wonder when he would be done with me. When would another blonde bombshell land on the doorstep and take him away? There was no trust between us. I couldn't trust that he cared, and I couldn't trust that he'd stay.

To love in that liminal space might have been okay years before, but I couldn't allow it again. I might have had to live my life without half my heart, but it was better than a whole heart broken.

Seventeen

Cedar

BEHIND THE WHEEL OF my Blazer, I sat on the bridge for far too long, trying to decide where I could track Devin down.

Her mom had moved closer to town after Mr. Haruki passed, but I wasn't sure where. Honestly, I couldn't picture Devin going to see her mom first. More than likely, she would go see her friends. Autumn seemed like she could be helpful, but Summer would try to murder me before I could get a word out. Best to start with Autumn.

On top of all this, my calls went straight to voicemail after a ring and a half, so I knew she was silencing them herself.

Taking a chance that she was working at the brewery, I made my way to Front Street.

With the sun breaking through the clouds, the downtown was busy with tourists lining up at the bakery for a doughboy, and the antique shop put out their wares on the streets. Parking was at a premium, but I was able to squeeze into a spot about a block from the brewery.

Despite the sun, it was still in the mid-fifties, and all the heat lamps were blazing as I made my way across the patio.

Autumn was leaning over a table, a large plastic tub in one arm, wiping the polished, unevenly hewn wood with the other.

Two men were sitting at the bar on the far end, mugs of amber beer in their hands, their focus glued to a cooking show.

Tossing the dirty rag in the tub, Autumn turned on her Birkenstock clogs and stuttered to a stop as she saw me. "Oh, you're here."

So, Devin must have already told her what happened—or what she thought happened, at least.

As much as I would be working against her friend's poor opinion of me, at least I didn't have to explain why Devin wasn't answering my calls.

"Do you know where she is?"

Autumn furrowed an auburn brow, her blue eyes narrowing. "I don't know if I should tell you."

"Please, I know she heard some of the things my ex-girlfriend said, but I need her to hear me out."

"Don't tell him shit, Autumn," a voice identical to Autumn's called from behind me.

Somehow, even though I couldn't see her, I knew it was Summer.

"Everyone deserves a second chance." Autumn set the tub down on the back counter. "We don't know the full story."

"He already had a second chance, and all he deserves is a kick in the ass." Summer settled on a high stool.

She was dressed more professionally this time, in a white button-down and black slacks, yet her vicious sneer remained the same.

Putting my hands up, I pleaded, "I know I fucked up with Devin, but doesn't she deserve the truth from me instead of jumping to the wrong conclusion that I would let my ex-girlfriend be rude to her?"

"Is that what you think happened?" Summer raised an imperious brow. "Wow, men are such fucking idiots."

The guys in the back corner shouted and glared at her, but she paid them no heed.

"What does she think happened?"

Summer pursed her lips, glaring at me. When she finally opened her mouth, it was with a loud dramatic pop.

"I told you if you were fucking around on my best friend, I would hurt you."

"I'm not fucking around on her."

"So, your fiancée showing up, that's totally normal?"

"She's not my fiancée." Shaking my head, I pushed off from the bar, about to leave. "I shouldn't have to explain this to you."

"You better do more than explain." Summer tucked her hair behind her ear, a gleam of pleasure in her face at seeing me squirm. "You better figure out how to grovel—and big-time—if you want Devin to hear a single word come out of our mouths about Devin."

"I won't grovel to you, Summer. All I want is to tell her the truth. Tainslee will never be my fiancée, girlfriend, or anything else. We broke up a month ago. She took it harder than I expected to accept, but that is over. Now what I need is to talk to Devin."

Autumn's expression softened at my words.

"I believe you. She's at—"

"Don't," Summer barked. "You're far too trusting, Autumn."

"And you're too cynical," Autumn shot back. "Her grandparent's, the big white house at the bend on Fjord Drive with the pink azaleas. You can't miss it."

"Thanks, Autumn." I turned to walk away, but Summer caught my arm, her nails digging into my skin.

"Don't make me regret not castrating you. I don't fuck around when it comes to my friends."

Gulping hard, I nodded. "You care about her a great deal. So do I."

Releasing me, she nodded—the best response I could get, all things considered. "Prove it."

The house was bigger than it looked from the street, and as I walked up the artfully arranged stone pathway, I considered turning back. But that wouldn't do.

An older man with wire-rimmed glasses answered the door, silver streaking his thick black hair. His straight dark brows and large hooded eyes were the same as Devin's.

"Mr. Haruki? Sorry to bother you. I'm looking for Devin?"

I couldn't remember the last time I went to the door and had to talk to a parent figure like this. Junior year of high school? Maybe even sophomore year.

Mr. Haruki's dark glare penetrated me. "You must be Cedar."

"Did Devin tell—"

"Devin didn't say a word. I know people." He turned around, walking back into his house, but left the door open, an opportunity to follow. He stopped a few feet from an open doorway and turned on his heels, his finger raised. "And I'm a powerful man in this town. When I say I know people, *I know people.* You understand me, sonny?"

"Ye—" I coughed into my fist. *What is with the threats today?* "Yes, sir."

As he clapped me on the back, I stumbled. Despite him being about a half a foot shorter than me, he packed a punch. "Good talk."

Devin was sitting on a white floral print couch, her legs tucked up to her chin, her phone in one hand. Her glasses were slipping down her nose, and her hair was in the same messy bun.

The sleeves of my sweatshirt were falling over her wrists, but seeing her wearing it made a spark of hope ignite in me.

When I walked in, her green eyes widened, and she pushed her glasses back up her nose. Opening her mouth, then closing it, she seemed to be at a loss for words.

"Your grandpa seems to think I'm the devil."

"Oh, that. He gets his gossip from Summer."

A lump formed in my chest.

Great, the absolute worst person to advocate for me, that castration comment still clinking around in my brain. Why in the world would a sexagenarian and a twenty something woman be gossiping? The pair seemed unlikely.

"Really?"

"Oh yeah, Van works for Jiji. Plus, Jiji and Baba are like grandparents to all four of us girls growing up. Wren's parents were—whatever—Summer's dad was always working. Autumn, well, she liked the snacks, I guess? So, they still stop by, even when I'm not around."

From the corner of the room, I saw Mr. Haruki pass, slowing to glare at me. Two fingers in a V pointed at his eyeballs, gesturing, *I'm watching you.*

"How did you find me?"

"Autumn," I hesitated, deciding it was better to play nice. "And Summer."

"Really?" she raised a skeptical brow. "And Summer?"

"She didn't tackle me to the floor when Autumn told me, so I'll take that as resigned acceptance."

"Pretty much."

I took a seat on the other end of the long couch, my hands on my knees. There was the sense I was being called down to the principal's office and needed to be on my best behavior.

"I'm sorry if you heard any of the terrible things Tainslee said."

"That she said?" Devin repeated, as if the words were foreign. "The one thing that stuck out to me was the fiancée part."

So, what Summer mentioned was true. That made sense if, despite everything I was feeling, Devin thought I had a secret fiancée and would want to run off.

"She's not my fiancée. She's my ex. We broke up a month ago."

"I heard what you said to her. Sound carries in that house. You, of all people, should know that."

"I told you she is not my fiancée. We broke up a month ago. I moved away to make a fresh start. She knows that. She was messing with you or me. Honestly, she played so many mind games it's hard to tell who was the intended target."

"I don't give a damn about her. I have spent too long growing and becoming a better person for you to relegate me to the back seat again like a dirty little secret."

"You're not a dirty little secret. I just didn't want to talk about you to my crazy ex-girlfriend."

Devin scrubbed a hand over her cheek, the face that, only hours before, I had held in my palms and kissed so tenderly. Her once-warm cheeks were so warm under my fingers. Now her expression was an icy wall.

"I heard what you told her. *Devin is no one. You don't have to worry about her.*"

Wrinkling my brow, I thought back to what Devin heard.

Yeah, when you take out those snippets, it sounded rude, but that wasn't what I meant.

" Lainslee doesn't need to know who you are."

Devin widened her eyes, her mouth hanging open. "Do you hear yourself?"

"Yes?" I offered. "It's true. She lives thousands of miles away. The chance of you two meeting was slim. I didn't see the point of talking about you with my ex-girlfriend."

"You don't see the point?"

Stark but without venom, her words were laced with a sadness I could never argue against.

Realizing my words were doing the opposite of what I intended, I back-tracked. Normally, I could smooth talk my way through these situations, but with Devin, I was a stumbling mess.

"I don't see the point in Tainslee knowing anything about my life. Since she's no longer in it."

Her face softened, but her eyes were careful. Leaning in closer, I pulled her hand from the death grip she had on her own leg and studied her while lacing my fingers between hers.

She stared at our hands, her face mournful. "So, she's not your fiancée."

"No. She's not. We were never engaged. I don't know why she said that. There is no way I would do that to her or you. I would never sleep with a beautiful, charismatic vegetarian who has no idea how to start a fire in a wood stove . . ."

"I can start a fire!"

"I would never do that if I was in a relationship with someone else. I respect you too much, and even though I don't want to be with her again, I respect Tainslee too much."

She studied me, her expression impassive before saying the words I so desperately needed to hear. "You say she's not your fiancée, I believe you."

Devin

"You say she's not your fiancée, I believe you. But—"

A large rush of air erupted from his mouth as he squeezed my palm. His other hand in his hair, he sighed heavily, shoulders dropping. "Okay, good, good. So, that's cleared up."

"No, it's really not." I sank deeper into the couch, pulling away from his grip, to rest my shaking hands in my lap. "It's not even about what you told her or didn't tell her. I don't care about your ex-girlfriend. This is about how you make me feel. The fucked-up way you mess with my head. How I spent years telling myself that you couldn't be exactly what I wanted to have you come back and be more. And still." I swallowed hard, the words choking me. "You know, when I was eighteen, I thought that if I was only thinner, blonder, and prettier, then maybe, just maybe"—I put my hands up in front of me as if to push the words away—"just maybe you would like me. And then you kissed me, and for a moment, for one moment, I thought maybe you could like me for who I was, without all that."

"I did, I do. I did like you—"

"I don't need to be taller or thinner for you to love me. I am a good person, Cedar." Slapping my chest, I willed myself not to cry. "I have a whole life that has nothing to do with you. I am worth everything, not the scraps you can give."

"I know you are, Devin, I know you are. Just give me a chance to explain."

With a shake of my head, pieces of purple hair fell out of my messy topknot. I willed my voice to be firm, to not betray how thin my resolution was. "No, no more chances. This is a lesson for me for the last time with you. You don't get me like this. It will never matter how much I try to wish and hope for more. I can't change you. It doesn't matter if what we have was wonderful. I can't turn a selfish boy into a good man."

"I am a good man. I want to be better for you."

His voice pitched up, a note of panic lacing it.

From the other side of the couch, I wrapped my arms around my knees. My words spoken to my yellow Lunchables socks. "As much of a relief as it was to hear that she isn't your fiancée, that you weren't using me as some rebound *yet again* or worse. The fact remains it was far easier to believe her than you. I don't trust you, Cedar."

He rocked back as if he had been punched.

Saying the words made them all the more real. I couldn't trust him, and I couldn't trust myself not to falter back into the safety of hope with him. If I didn't get these words out now, I might never. And then I'd still be that girl in the in-between, still wondering and wishing but never having the guts to ask for what I wanted.

"I don't trust you to be honest, and I don't trust you with my feelings. You knew I've loved you for years, and you give me nothing. You haven't done a single thing to prove to me that what we shared these past few days was more than some silly fling. I was too naïve at eighteen to know the difference, but I'm older now. I can't be with a man I don't trust. So, fiancée or not, I'm done."

In a smooth motion, he was out of his seat and kneeling before me. His blue eyes boring into mine as he reached forward, taking my hands off their grip on my legs. "Devin, don't do this. If Tainslee hadn't shown up, I would have—"

"What? Asked me to stay? Professed your love for me?"

Even as I said those words, a pang entered me at the hope for those things, no matter how futile.

"Maybe you didn't give me a chance to explain."

"Why would I? What have you ever done to deserve one? Break my heart at eighteen, weeks after my dad died? Not give me a single thought over the years until I am literally naked in front of you? It took her showing up on the doorstep for me to come to my senses, but I'm here."

Rocking back on his heels, he dropped my hands as if they were scalding. His fists balled up in his hair, he sucked in air and let out noisily, as if he was having trouble processing my words.

My grandparents' large clock stood in the corner, ticking loudly. Outside the window, birds tittered in my grandmother's rhododendron bush, and cars whooshed by, slowing at the corner the way many cars did.

He shook his head over and over until he was able to speak. "I don't love her. I love you."

I huffed out irritably. "What?"

"Yeah, I love you."

His fingers came up to cup my cheek, his warm gaze light on me.

Those were the words I had waited years for, the declaration I had always told myself would soothe this hole in my chest for good.

Yet hearing them in response to finding another woman in our space, I realized it wasn't enough.

I could love Cedar forever, but there was always going to be this chasm of pain inside for years I had spent needing him and not being acknowledged.

His words were empty, a balm for a wound he created.

I couldn't stop the derisive snort that erupted. It was all too much.

"You love me? No, you don't. Those are just words to you."

"What?" He blinked at me, shock coloring his face as he took in my rebuff.

"You don't know what it means to love someone. It's a bandage, so I won't see all the hurt you've caused me. I deserve better." I pulled his hand off my cheek, pushing it back at him.

"You do, and I think a part of me has always—"

My voice raised, I shook my head. "Don't say always. Don't use words you can't understand. You talk about love as if it's a cure all, but it's not, Cedar. I have loved you for years—a decade, really—and even I know that love isn't enough."

"But it's different with us. More."

Traitor tears were threatening to expose how painful this was for me.

Swallowing hard, I had to look away, focusing on the large Yasumasa Morimura painting on the wall. "You're right, I am different. Because I see through you, see through all this good guy facade to hide what's inside you, and that is pure selfishness. You want everyone else to adore you, to want you, to love you. But you won't do what's needed to care for someone else. You say you love me, so I'll forget. So, I'll say it back. Those words aren't for me, not really."

"But I do love you. I know I do."

I squared my shoulders, rising. "Then, prove it. Not with words. I don't want to hear those words again until you can back it up."

"But I don't know how to do that."

Pursing my lips, I fought back the tears. "I've waited a long time to hear those words. I can wait longer to feel them."

Cedar sat back on his heels, his hands falling to his thighs, his blue eyes darkening with the knowledge that I meant what I said.

Mustering all the strength possible, I spoke low and slow. "I think you should leave."

The last time I felt my chest splinter like this, I had run away, stumbled over roots with bleary, salty-teared eyes. This time, I was able to watch as he walked away, my vision clear and the same knife sharply slicing that scar in two.

When his footsteps were too far for me to hear and the door clicked after him, I allowed myself one last steely gaze around the room before bursting into new tears.

Somehow, I was able to dry my eyes enough to get changed for the brewery. Without my armor of a graphic tee, I felt exposed in the plain green blouse and dark jeans my grandmother insisted I should borrow. It wasn't how old-fashioned the outfit was, only the formality.

But she was being so helpful, and I had used up all my fight with the conversation with Cedar earlier. What did it matter what I wore?

When I walked into the brewery, the three girls were already seated, their gazes roaming over my outfit.

"Look at you, all fancy for us," Wren said, pushing her dark curls off her face.

Settling onto a stool, I frowned at her. "They're Baba's. She told me I couldn't go out wearing a tear spattered Shrek T-shirt and old leggings."

Rightfully, Summer sniffed.

"I think you look amazing, Dev," Autumn said, a wide smile breaking over her face as she pulled me to her side for one of her warm hugs. "You always looked so nice in green."

"Thanks, Aut." I leaned into her hug, allowing the familiar scent of sage and earth to envelop me.

Accepting a beer from Wren, I drank it down to the middle of the horned Viking helmet logo. No one commented, but I saw the furtive glances exchanged between all three.

I had the sneaking suspicion they had all arrived early and strategized on how best to help me.

Motioning at their full drinks, I commented, "That one your second?"

"Maybe?" Wren grimaced, then let out a big huff of air. "Okay, yes. We weren't sure what the best plan of attack was to help you, and we needed to be a united front." At this, she shot a sharp look at Summer.

Her hands up in surrender, she scoffed. "I told you. I'm not breaking the law tonight. All body parts will stay attached." Bringing her beer up to her mouth, she mumbled into her Hefeweizen, "Even if he deserves it."

"So, what do you want?" Autumn asked, her hand wrapped around her bottle of orange-vanilla soda. "To vent? To curse his name? I know some great rituals to cleanse the negative energy."

"No setting anything on fire," Wren warned.

As well intentioned as Autumn could be, her proclivity for fire-based rituals had gotten us in a few sticky spots.

"That was one time! And we dowsed it with water before it spread too far."

"Yeah, only took your mom's favorite curtains with it, right?"

Crossing her arms, she gave all of us her closest approximation of a disdainful look. She looked like she was trying and failing to be Summer.

"Oh, wipe that look off your face. Only one of us is allowed to get angry wrinkles, and it's not you," Summer chided.

Before the cousins could start bickering, I interrupted. "No need for a fire spell or for cutting things off. Tonight, I want to have a drink with my best girls and not think about why men can make us so dumb."

With that, even Summer agreed, a toast going up around the table, and we soon finished what was my first drink and their second. Soon, we got another round and then another. Then we were tripping down Front Street and into the colorful alleyway and into the Casa Sol Mexican restaurant.

Seated at a booth in the back, we finished two baskets of chips and salsa before we even got our food.

Putting her fork down from her half eaten chile verde, Autumn leaned in closer. "So, what are you going to do now?"

"Same thing I was planning on doing before I saw him again. Go down to Phoenix and stay with Becca."

"You can't really be leaving town over a *guy*," Summer said "guy" so disdainfully it might as well have been a gallon of shit.

"It's not because of him. I wanted to do this before I saw Cedar again."

"And yet you would have stayed for him," Summer said.

"Yeah, I would have, partially, maybe. I have those job interviews lined up." That wasn't strictly speaking, true. But I had a few places that emailed me to apply. "And a place to crash until I find an apartment. I was always planning on leaving. Now I just have one more reason."

Resting my chin on my palm, I took in my friends. Took in the way Wren drove hours to get to me from Icicle Creek to tell me to follow my heart. Summer's ferocious defense of me, whether I asked for it. And Autumn, sweet, positive-thinking Autumn, who encouraged me that everything would work out for the greater good if I only allow myself to receive it.

I would miss them. But this town held little for me anymore.

"I get wanting a fresh start. Why do you think I moved to Icicle Creek?" Wren wiped at the condensation ring from her guava agua fresca on the table with her red sweater sleeve.

"That's different." Summer sat back, arms crossed. "You aren't four states away."

"It's only three if you go down through California." I sipped my lemonade.

"Is that supposed to make me feel better?" Summer huffed.

"No, but I know how you love being the pedantic one so—" I shrugged, a green pepper still on my fork from my vegetable enchiladas.

With her finger pointed at me in outrage, Summer narrowed her eyes. "Don't rationalize with me in my hour of need."

"Your hour of need? Ms. So In Love With Her Hot Boyfriend And Killing It At Her Career."

"Without one of my best friends, yes. My hour of need."

"Yeah, Devin, I know you just dumped the only guy you've ever really been into, but won't you think of poor Summer?" Wren said with a wry smile before bursting into laughter.

"Yeah, not everything is about you, Devin." Summer cracked a smile at her own dramatics and then, for the first time of the night, even I was laughing.

Nineteen

Cedar

AND THEN SHE WAS gone. I took the easy way out; I let her go. Just as I should have done almost a decade before, I failed to go after her.

Growing up, I told myself I didn't like women who played games and vowed I wouldn't chase a woman. But Devin was different. She never asked me to chase her. What we had was the farthest thing from a game. She didn't leave me to get my attention or to get back at me for hurting her the way that my exes might have but because I deserved it. Because I hurt her in a way I wasn't sure how to repair.

Her words kept coming back to me.

I've waited a long time to hear those words. I can wait longer to feel them.

I felt like a spoiled, petulant child when I thought back on that last exchange. Devin was worth so much more than that, and I aimed to be the one to give it to her. If only I could figure out the best way to show her.

It had been five weeks. In that time, I had started my new job; I moved into the rented bungalow in Ridgewood Place, the candy-colored homes that dotted the downtown area—the kind that had ridiculous HOA policies, like not allowing you to park your car in your driveway and what color flowers you can plant in your garden.

On a walk around the neighborhood, I met Pepper, a beautiful golden retriever, and her owners, Fitz and Lina, a younger couple who got married a few months before in a New Year's wedding.

On Thursday nights, I met my mom and Edith at Casa Sol for dinner. Clover came home for Spring Break with a new girlfriend, Taylor. On the surface, I was adjusting well to being back home.

Catalina at the gallery let me know she found the painting. It was currently privately owned, but if I was interested, she could get me in touch with the owner.

Despite Devin being gone, despite everything that had happened, I desperately wanted it.

It was a shallow sensation. Every night, I would lie in my bed and know, deep in my chest, there was no getting around it. Devin belonged beside me.

Without thinking about how foolish it would be, I cleaned out the back shed, adding in insulation and shelves for supplies. I refinished the floor with an easy-to-clean linoleum and built a desk on one side.

I avoided Freedom Bay Brewery, even though I knew I could likely find her there. As much as I needed her back, I still didn't have my answer to how I could prove to her I was dedicated to her alone, to "show her," as she demanded.

I crumbled a little more than a month in, showing up and hoping that if Devin saw me, she wouldn't run the other way. Instead, I found a nearly empty barroom with Autumn behind the counter. This turned out to be the entry I needed. Autumn was terrible at secrets. Over the hours, I was able to find out all sorts of things about Devin.

She was in Arizona, staying with some friends, and had an interview the next day at some place called Sonora Valley Marketing.

Devin hated the water and loved the agave margaritas. She went to a bar with live parrots and was talking about joining her old roommate Becca in a few months for a float down the Salt River.

She went on a date.

That one was a knockout punch to my celiac plexus, right to the chest. A date? Of course she would. Any man would be lucky to have her.

I thought of the way Caleb's eyes watched her as she walked back into the house. The way her mouth turned up more to the left when she smiled. The tiny impressions of her glasses on the bridge of her nose. Her purple strands falling out of her messy buns. Her paint-flecked hands as she drew.

"She said it didn't go well," Autumn said, then bit her lip in her telltale *I said too much again* expression.

"Really?" I didn't try to hide how much I thrilled at the news. "What was the matter with him? Did he hurt her?"

"No, nothing like that." Autumn ran a rag over the cherrywood table, then paused, her auburn brows furrowing as she scratched at a dried coaster. "What's the point of giving them coasters if they don't use them, right?"

She smiled at me, and I had to fight back the rise of impatience at her subject change.

"Then, what was the issue?"

Getting the bit of dried cardboard off the table, she grinned to herself. "Oh, you know, he just wasn't—" Her eyes darted up to meet mine, and she swallowed hard. Straightening up, she shoved the scraps of the old coaster in the pocket of her orange overalls.

"He wasn't what?" I asked, hoping, praying, pleading what I wanted to hear would be true.

"Nothing. No one. It doesn't matter."

Redness crept up her neck and into her cheeks, her face blazing scarlet. Her freckles stood out orange against the redness.

"You're a terrible liar."

"Yeah, I'm aware," she snapped in the rudest tone I had ever heard from her, which was barely less than pleasant. "Can you just forget I said that?"

"Are you really asking me that?" I leaned in closer. "Tell me she's moving on, Autumn. Say I've got no chance with her again."

"You should let her go. It might be what's best for her, moving on and all."

Autumn's voice was shaky.

"I love her. You're one of her best friends, I trust you. Say I've got no shot, say I've ruined my chance and I'll—" I wouldn't move on—I was too far gone from that, but maybe I could allow Devin to. "I won't ask you again. Tell me the truth."

Tossing the rag into its bucket of cleaning solution, Autumn turned back to me, her lower lip between her teeth. She tugged on one end of her pigtail braid, wrapping it around her finger. Her mouth opened and closed before she slowly said, "What do you want me to say? That she's forgotten you? We both know that will never be true. And yeah, maybe you would be better for her than the mopey girl she's been for weeks. But you really hurt her—like earth-shattering painful, rip-out-your-heart-and-stomped-on-it pain. That girl has always loved you. Ever since we were kids, really. The way she would watch you in high school—she used to make us all go to your games, even though she didn't know a thing about soccer. And then you strung her along that summer, only to ditch her for your ex-girlfriend." Straightening, she squared her shoulders and narrowed her eyes. "If I was Summer, I'd tell you it seems like now that she's somewhere new, she can start over, and you think you can call her up? You haven't been serious about a single thing in your life, and now you think you deserve my best friend."

"But you're not Summer, so what would Autumn say?"

"I'd say"—she pursed her lips, making a little bubbling noise, then clucked her tongue—"if you really want her back, you better show her she's worth fighting for. And you're not going to do that standing in the brewery a thousand miles away."

Twenty

Devin

THE DAY AFTER MY confrontation with Cedar, Baba went back for my things, bringing them into the spare room I should have been using.

Before this mess, before I knew what it meant to really love Cedar and to learn that I loved myself more, the weakness in me was begging me to throw myself over him, to take his words, and to settle for good enough, truthful enough.

But I owed myself more.

When my mom returned from her trip, she tried to have me move in with her, but the spare room she was offering to clean out for me was where she kept her weight rack and Pilates machine.

The job search went faster than I expected, where a few firms in the Phoenix area offered me interviews. My top choice was a small marketing firm. The base pay was less than I made in Seattle, but with the cost of living in Arizona being slightly lower, it almost evened out.

My first phone interview went well, and I was asked to send in my portfolio as well as come down for a second interview. If hired, they would even give me a small relocation bonus. Not enough to cover any decent moving costs but maybe for the hotel rooms on the way.

Becca told me I could crash on her couch the week of the interview and use that time to look around the area to find a good apartment.

Baba and Jiji were firmly against the idea of me moving away, but once they saw I was resolute, they backed off.

For over a month, I tried to get things back on track with my life. Job searching and apartment hunting and weekly dinners with the girls. I baked brownies with Jiji and helped Baba in the yard, cleaning up the weeds. My mom and I walked around the track at the high school, where she filled me in on the latest gossip from the local rotary club meeting.

A month in, when a cute guy who frequented the brewery, Arturo, asked if he could buy my beer, I knew I wasn't ready and that it would be a mistake. He was nice and surprisingly funny for a guy who spent his days on computers, but his eyes were brown, and his hair was dark, and he didn't have that little scar on his hairline.

He wasn't Cedar.

Still, when he asked me out for dinner, I accepted. Using the adage that "to get over someone you need to get under another," I wanted to forget Cedar.

I was using him—I know. But spending my nights at my grandparents' house, eating cheese and crackers and rewatching episodes of the same fantasy show wasn't going to make things easier in my new life.

He picked a nice Italian place, much fancier than I was expecting for a first date. Walking in and seeing all the candlelit tables, the dim lights, the couples together reminded me all too well of the long days and nights I spent with Cedar in the dark of his mom's house. Once we were escorted to our table, I excused myself to the bathroom.

In the gold-flecked reflection of the mirror, I studied myself. Under the cold faucet, I dipped my fingers in the cool water, hoping it could bring me back down to earth. To this beautiful restaurant, with a handsome guy who was interested in me.

The contact in my left eye irritated me, and I rubbed on my tear duct with a nail, afraid to disrupt the lens.

The contacts and the plain gray dress with no pattern wasn't me. I wasn't this woman. What the hell was I doing here?

A toilet flushed behind me, a leggy blonde coming out of the stall. Her sky-high gold heels clicked as she made her way to the sink beside me. She fixed her voluminous golden waves in the mirror before walking away.

I flexed my toes in my flat leather sandals. They were my nicest shoes, but I felt dowdy in them.

At least I wash my hands.

Sliding into my seat, I was about to open my menu when Art leaned across the table.

"I hope you don't mind, but I ordered us a bottle of wine. Do you like reds?"

A flutter of annoyance rose. Yes, I did, but to order it while I was gone? To not have my opinion matter?

The server approached us, two glass stems between his fingers. He turned the wine so we could see the label: the painted couple entwined in a tarot card style—the Lovers. It was the same wine Cedar and I shared during our pasta dinner. The same night he told me he wanted me.

If I kiss you, I won't stop. I want to consume you, and there won't be enough of you for any other man.

If only I had stopped there. If only I had left, maybe then these tears wouldn't be threatening to spill over my cheeks and ruin my gray muslin dress.

Maybe, maybe, maybe. The way I never wanted him to say always. Because on the day I saw Cedar again, the day the comb broke in my hair, I knew everything would change.

As I blubbered into my white cloth napkin, Art and the sommelier exchanged nervous glances. There would be no fancy Italian dinner, no date.

Art dropped me off at my grandparents', the door barely closing before it was in drive. It was just as well.

I wasn't ready for a cute IT man or any other person. It was foolish to think I could move on, that anything could be the same.

The late spring turned to summer, and the sun broke through the clouds. As the temperature tipped over sixty degrees, the shorts came out, revealing heavy cream-colored legs that hadn't gotten vitamin D in six months. For days, a peeling nose and pink forearms of a sunburn assailed me.

Was I better for my week with Cedar?

As the weather warmed and the promise of desert living loomed, it was easy to think those rain-soaked nights were a mistake. A mixture of being stuck together, of old flames from our younger days and pheromones.

But then I would see his picture featured in the community Facebook welcoming him as the newest member of the staff at Ridgewood Physical Therapy.

One night, while out at the bar, a man came in with a guitar for an open-mic night.

I sat in the back, nursing my drink, as the familiar first notes of the song played. It was the song Cedar always sang under his breath. Transfixed, I listened to the lyrics of regret and losing the person you love.

Pain bloomed over me, and I had to hide my tears in a scratchy cocktail napkin as I left my half-full drink on the table.

I left for Phoenix the next day. My grandmother insisted on driving me to the airport, even though I told her I was fine with taking the light rail.

Standing below the Alaska Airlines placard, she pressed a slip of paper into my hand with her credit card information on it and extracted a vow that if anything odd happened, to get the first flight back to SeaTac.

Despite my living in Seattle for years, Baba was scared Phoenix was more than I could handle.

Walking out of Sky Harbor Airport, I found the sky dark with clouds and then rain erupted. In wonder, I watched as the water floated on top of the brittle ground, flowed over the streets, and bent the spindly plants growing under windows. Back home, rain would soak into the ground, softening everything.

This place was harshly solid in a way I wasn't used to and so brown. In that moment, I yearned for the plush ground beneath my feet, the give of moss under my boots, and the thick trunks of the forest surrounding the houses. The stickiness of sap and pine needles stuck to my hands as I climbed the ladder into the treehouse and Cedar's eyes as he watched me across the damp, leaf-strewn floor.

I missed him.

When I got in Becca's RAV4, we headed down the street from her apartment to a bar with live parrots in cages around us and two-for-one margaritas. Becca's boyfriend started flirting with me after his third tequila soda.

The next day, Becca drove me around town, looking at apartments, and I found a studio in Mesa off the 101 loop ten minutes away from the marketing firm.

The place was cramped, but there was a pool and a bar and grill half a block away. I was already making plans in my head. Once a week, I would get a drink with Becca, sans Chaz.

Autumn's older brother, Oliver, lived in the area too, in Peoria, and maybe I could get to see him and his wife Janie, so I wouldn't be completely alone.

It was fine. I was fine. Totally normal.

No, I couldn't even tell myself that.

Despite what I assured my friends, I was running away. I knew it; they knew it.

Five days into visiting Phoenix, I knew I had made a mistake. The weather was beautiful, sunny every day, and the dry heat everyone joked about felt nice on my skin. The late spring warmth was welcome after months of a damp chill that never really leaves you. For the first time in half a year, I could feel my toes. But it wasn't home.

But if I stayed in that town, I would have caved for Cedar. There was the willpower I had for everything else and then there was what he did to me. Made me foolish, made me wanton, and worst of all, made me forget how easily I could be hurt by him.

If in the days after I asked him to leave he would have come back, I didn't trust myself enough not to fall back into him. He knew me in a way no one else did. No one ever made me feel that way, and since, I was left alone. There was the one who got away and then the one you never should have held in the first place.

Twenty-one

Cedar

THE FIRST THING I noticed when I got into Sky Harbor Airport was the dry chill of the air conditioning. The air had a bitter, clinical taste that was different from the soggy sweetness of SeaTac.

I knew where Devin worked, looked up the address online while I was on the tarmac, but didn't know where her apartment was.

As desperate as I was to see her, I couldn't show up at her work interview, right? Instead, I checked into a hotel near the freeway, hoping my destination would be easy to find. Most roads in the area were laid out in grid-like fashion, unlike the streets of Seattle, which were like a bowl of spaghetti thrown at the wall.

After dropping off my duffel bag, I headed down to the hotel bar, hoping to figure out my next move. The inside of the hotel looked identical to all other hotels, clinical pastels and mirrors, slippery-looking vinyl cushioned couches, and a coffee bar with single-serve creamers beside off-brand tea bags.

Belly up at the bar, I sipped my beer, my focus on the baseball game. Beside me, an older couple were cozied up, their head tucked into each other, giggling over their drinks. A group of twenty-something-year-olds sat on the other end, joking about the round of golf they finished, white outlines of sunglasses glowing against the pink skin of their faces.

The Diamondback game halted as it switched to the news, and everyone groaned.

I glanced at the screen to see the "breaking news" headline. The din around me got louder and louder as the words flashed on the screen. "Phoenix area blaze claims lives of many."

"Quiet!" I yelled at the crowd. "Someone turn up the news."

On the screen, a beautiful woman with long, flowing dark hair sat behind a desk. "Good evening, I'm Susan Bassini from KPTO Phoenix. We have breaking news of a blaze that has, so far, ravaged thousands of acres of land, destroyed millions of dollars of property, and claimed the lives of twenty-three people. For more information, we'll go to our field reporter, Stella Aldona. Stella, what can you tell us?"

The view shifted to a newscaster standing before a burned-out building, her blonde hair not moving as the palm trees in the background bowed to the wind.

"Good evening, Susan. Reports from the Maricopa County Fire Commissioner say that the fire was likely started on the second floor of the building, possibly from faulty wiring. These buildings here, The Senita Business Park, seem to be the epicenter for the fire. The occupants include the financial firm, T.B. Chester, the marketing agency, Sonora Valley Marketing Inc., and the Law Offices of Ryder, Park, and Green. We have now confirmed there are fatalities, but how many are yet to be identified. The names of the deceased have not been identified publicly yet, but some bystanders we spoke to say the number may be as high as twenty. The high number of victims led many to ask what safety measures failed on this property and who is to blame. From Phoenix KPTO, I'm Stella Aldona. Back to the studio."

I stared at the burned-out building, the charred sign behind the reporter, the looping "S" on Sonora Valley Marketing's sign singed black.

With a twenty left on the counter beside my half-empty beer, I was in the parking lot in less than thirty seconds. The unfamiliar key fob for my rental car, thick in my hand as I tried to unlock the doors, accidentally set off the alarm before I could wrench the door open. It took seven tries to type in the business name into my GPS, my fingers slipping over the touchscreen keyboard.

By the time I reached the area, the sky was dark with dirty smoke, and the street I needed was blocked off. My rental was car left in a nearby strip mall, in front of a small restaurant advertising their menudo special for the day.

Along the barrier, a clump of people huddled, some on their phones and getting videos of the fire, others talking with the two officers who stood on the other side.

Shouldering my way to the front of the group, I scanned the parking lot a block away, where the bulk of the people were congregated.

Across the street, flames were lighting up the top level of the building, windows blown out by the heat. White trucks were packed into the parking lot, with the water hoses dowsing the ground around the businesses.

To my right, an officer was arguing with an older woman who was asking to cross the barrier to see if her daughter Sarita was among those who got out.

The officer was young, with a patchy dark mustache over his thin lips and acne scars on his cheeks. "Ma'am, I promise, the firefighters are working to clear the scene as quickly as possible. If you just wait here, I can find out—"

"No, aparta, chico. Let me go to her."

"Señora, por favor." Sweat beaded on his temple. "Don't make me call for more officers to keep you here."

"At least can you check if she's there?" the woman pleaded. "Mi hija, my baby."

A muscle ticked in the man's jaw, but he glanced over his shoulder at the crowd, then spoke low into his radio.

"I'll be right back. Everyone stays behind the barrier. This is for your safety," he bellowed.

Once he was far enough away not to see me and when the other officer looked away, I ducked under the yellow tape and ran to the crowd. In the distance, an officer was crouching near a young woman with an oxygen mask in the back of an ambulance. He motioned to the horde behind the yellow tape as the woman cried.

Scanning the group, I was overwhelmed by the magnitude of pain and fear surrounding me. The lucky ones were sooty and bruised, the less fortunate on oxygen beside the ambulances. There was the one being loaded into trucks, the sirens flipping on as the door slammed shut. And then there were the still ones, five lined up in a row on the edge of the parking lot.

Could one of those be Devin?

Until I saw those bodies, I hadn't thought of that conclusion. Because it couldn't be. In no world could Devin be gone. I never got the chance to prove myself to her, to show her that there was no future for me without her by my side.

Then two women stood, parting the scene, and there she was.

At the edge of the crowd, she sat on the curb, wearing what was likely an ashen white button-down. Her knees were bloody and blackened, and her dark hair was all I could see, the purple highlights obscured by the ash.

It was Devin, and she was alive.

Twenty-two

Devin

THE COMB BREAKING IN my hair should have been my first sign I was making a mistake. All my life, Jiji told me it was a sign of misfortune. Never one to tempt fate, I normally listened to him, but this was my second interview for this job and couldn't afford to call out over an ancient Japanese superstition.

So, I ignored my instincts and set off for the marketing agency. The group chat with the girls was blowing up with odd requests for my plans of the day, far more detailed than we usually were with one another.

Pulling on the hem of my borrowed plain black skirt, I was glad I dressed up. Summer had insisted I borrow one of her many unofficial black-and-white uniforms as the manager at the hotel. The buttons stretched against my boobs, and the skirt was tight against my thick thighs.

I would have marks on my stomach where the waistband was cutting in. Why didn't I buy my own clothes before I left? My gut rolled with nerves and with the disappointing lunch from a nearby Thai restaurant—really, whoever told them ketchup was a good enough substitution for tamarind in Pad Thai is a monster.

At the juice start-up, we all wore whatever we wanted as long as we got the work done. My favorite *Serious Goose* shirt felt very businesslike, with the goose wearing a necktie, but a look around the lobby told me that wasn't enough.

People were dressed considerably more professionally than I was expecting, so I was glad I left the graphic tees in my suitcase.

A small window in the back showed a darkening sky, turning a suspicious dingy color.

An older woman with gray hair swept in a sleek chignon approached with her hand out. I stood on shaky-heeled feet. The pumps were my mother's, something she used for company events, not my style.

Her hand was warm and dry, and for a second, before I took it, I hoped mine wasn't sweaty.

She gave it three pumps, her smile not wavering. "Devin, Della Buell, it's so good to put a real face to your name. Follow me back, and we'll—what the heck?"

People crowded past Della, pushing to the small window behind the receptionist. Della frowned as she glanced at the group's increasing size.

Shoulder to shoulder, they stood, looking at the opaque sky beyond. As more filled the small room, the skyline beyond the window burnished into a dusty orange. Years of traveling across the Cascades in late summer told me everything I needed to know about that sky.

The air inside the lobby got hazy, thickening before our eyes. The office was at the back of the building, far from the front door. Someone opened the door to the hallway that connected the businesses, and smoke rolled in, a dark spell of danger.

Something was on fire. A few workers from an office upstairs trickled past, clutching their laptops, purses, and files. The smoke thickened into muddy air, obscuring our vision.

"Everyone out," bellowed Della, her graying hair sweaty on her forehead.

Grabbing my purse, I followed the trickle of workers.

What was only a clear hallway fifteen minutes before had been obscured. The stairs to the left of us were completely concealed by rolling acrid smoke, and as we rushed, bumping and slamming down the long hallway to the only real exit, screams echoed from above us. There was a good chance no one from the top floor could find their way down the stairs through the smoke.

Behind my glasses, my eyes burned. I tripped over something on the floor, falling onto my knees. Around me, people crashed into one another, fumbling hands and kicking feet, as they struggled to reach the front door.

Why was there only one narrow exit for this building?

On my knees, I scrambled for purchase, trying to stand, but the people around me had me trapped. Whenever I pushed myself up, someone would be at my back or stepping on my leg. My glasses slipped off my face and onto the floor, where they were crunched under a brown leather Oxford.

As I wrapped my fingers around the glasses, my pinky was stepped on by a woman's navy pump. The plastic frames were cracked over the left lens, and the temple piece was askew as I slid it back over my face.

I was getting pressed into the wall, and the smoke was thickening. Even if my glasses weren't fatalistically bent, I couldn't have seen the light of the exit anymore.

Was this how I would go? Lungs filled with smoke, broken glasses, all while wearing a boring blouse? There was so much I still wanted to do.

What would my mother think? She already lost her husband, and now me? Baba and Jiji would be devastated. My friends, I thought back to the previous year when Summer was attacked by her ex-boyfriend. How scared we had all been at the idea of losing her to such a senseless act. Yet, here I was, in an equally senseless position.

Smoke coated my throat, and I stuck my face into my blouse, trying in vain to breathe cleaner air. My mind went to my father in his final moments.

Did he know he was going to die? Was he as scared as I was?

And Cedar. All my anger for him seemed so silly in that moment. He said he loved me. I could see it in his eyes and feel it in the way he held me, yet I ran away, too scared to be hurt by him again. I'd give anything to go back to that day and to tell him to break a million times over if I could only have one last moment in his arms.

A hand grabbed me by the armpit, and as I was pulled up, I recognized my rescuer as the receptionist behind the desk who got me a cup of coffee while I waited for Della.

Her grip was tight on my forearm, but I didn't care. Together, we made our way to the beacon of light at the end of the hall as the building creaked around us. The air outside was the sweetest I had ever tasted.

It couldn't have been more than a few minutes from when the first sign of smoke started to when I got out, but it felt like ages.

Once outside, I collapsed onto the concrete, rocks cutting into my bare knees. Pulling in large gulps of clean enough air, I coughed and spit and blinked.

Beside me, the receptionist sat, her head between her knees. Black soot and tear tracks marred her face, and I'm sure I looked the same.

From inside the building, an alarm blared, minutes too late to alert anyone.

"Come on. We have to keep moving," I demanded, pulling my rescuer up from where she collapsed.

My arm was around her waist as we walked across the parking lot to the edge.

Through my cracked glasses, a fire flared. A line of flames climbed the hill that abutted the building, scorching the yellow flowering brittlebush that grew sparse on the reddish ground.

By the time we all congregated in the parking lot of the Fazoli's across the street, the building was surrounded.

Sirens wailed as we watched the protective uniformed clad firefighters get out of their white-and-red truck.

I had only been at this business for a few minutes, so there was no sentimentality in the place, but seeing the building engulfed in flames was terrifying. The fire licked at the cars parked in special spots closest to the doors.

As most of the firefighters battled the blaze behind the building, dowsing the ground to stop the flames from spreading to the desert land beyond, a few others approached our crowd, asking if anyone was left in there and requesting a full account of the staff.

A firefighter emerged from the building, carrying a limp body. As more were carried out, the severity of the fire struck me.

Glancing around through bleary eyes, I searched for the people who were standing in the lobby when the sky began to turn, like the portly, balding man who told the receptionist a joke about a Frenchman wearing sandals. Or the middle-aged woman with frizzy blond hair and a neon pink tee shirt. A younger girl with the shaggy hair dressed in all black. The guy with the septum piercing. No sign of them.

How many others are in that building?

I hadn't realized I was crying until my neck was damp from the dripping tears. Only minutes after the fire department showed up, the first news crews pulled in, helmet-haired reporters and a camera crew.

The reporter first approached the firefighter in uniform, taking notes and nodding, before she gave him a veneered smile and walked closer to us.

I hoped she wouldn't try to interview me.

Only feet away, the reporter shuffled back and forth on the sidewalk, glancing back to the burning building, before stopping and asking the camera woman, "Is this good?"

Someone wearing a polo with KPTO embroidered on the chest gave her a thumbs-up. Arms wrapped around my middle, I watched as they counted down, and the reporter spoke into her microphone.

I couldn't catch the whole one-minute report over the sound drowned out by the spray of water, people chattering and yelling, and an ambulance siren.

My butt firmly planted on the curb, I watched as the flames turned to black smoke, to gray, then white as the fire died. Once the fire was contained, we could see the shell of a building riddled with broken windows and a crumbling roof.

I pulled my phone out of my pocket to find the screen cracked and gouged out of the corner. It wouldn't turn on, no matter how many times I pressed the power button. My hands were black and red, soot caked into cuts all over my palms. My knees were no better.

As the paramedics came around, they triaged the worst cases of smoke inhalation and burns. When three ambulances would leave, a few more would show up to be taken to the hospital. After thirty minutes, I was treated on scene for minor smoke inhalation as well as my cuts and bruises. Across the lot, my rescuer, Sarita, had on an oxygen mask. She had inhaled far more than me, pulling me out of the smoke.

From a distance, I saw a crowd forming a block away, people doing looky-loos at the smoldering building. The street had been blocked off using yellow hazard tape, and police were directing people to stand behind it.

We were essentially trapped in this fast-food parking lot. A few people were motioning toward our group, and I could hear the faint sounds of yelling and curses. How long had it been since the fire started? Twenty minutes? Forty?

The late spring sun was blistering on my skin, and I longed for the sogginess of the Pacific Northwest. Screwing my eyes shut, I tried to visualize the way Autumn always talked about. A mossy blanket under my feet, the chill of the Pacific air blowing in from British Columbia. The whisper of cedar boughs against each other as the wind picked up. Darkness falling as you walk deeper and deeper into the forest.

No, that was a real darkness falling over me—a shadow.

"Devin?"

I blinked up at him. He blotted out the low burning sun, a halo around his head as he stared down at me. Even though he was in shadow, I could have drawn those features from memory, the sandy hair, the blue eyes I knew better than my own, that scar on his temple. Maybe I did need oxygen and that the smoke inhalation was causing me to hallucinate.

Before I could choke out the single name, I was swept up in his arms, his firm body wrapping around me.

No, this was real. Cedar was here.

He was holding me, and I was safe. Racking sobs shuddered through me as I melted into him. At that moment, I didn't care to know why or how he had found me. All that mattered was he was there.

My body shaking, I tried to calm myself. My throat burned too much to say anything, but the tears flushed out the smoke in my eyes.

I tried to pull away to look at him, but his grip was too strong around my waist. After a few deep, painful breaths, I calmed, feeling safe.

When I realized we were still shaking, it took me another minute in his embrace to realize it was Cedar who was shaking. His shoulders moving, and the low guttural sob that was escaping wasn't mine but his.

He was crying. He was here, and he was crying.

"I thought . . . I was so scared . . . I never . . . it was—" His words rambled over me, never finishing. When he pulled away, putting me down on the ground, his hands roamed over my face, smearing the soot and tears away.

"Okay," I croaked, the one-word scorching as it emerged.

"Have you been seen? Do you need to go to the hospital?" He inspected me, his gaze moving over my hair and to my throat and hands.

Behind us, a police officer approached, a scowl on his serious face. "Sir, I told you to stand behind the barricade until we can get everyone accounted for."

Cedar's arms around me. He glanced at the cop. "I'm sorry, sir, but I love this woman, and I had to know she's safe."

"Save your grand gestures for another day. I have a job to do," the officer barked.

It must have been our tear-stained cheeks or the overwhelming job ahead of all the first responders at the scene, but the officer then shook his head and walked away.

"I don't—"

My voice was hoarse, and those two words clawed their way out. Swallowing down the pain, I opened my mouth to ask more, but Cedar shook his head, pulling me into his chest.

"Don't. You can ask me whatever you need to afterward."

All the emotions of the day were falling over me. The interview, the fire, and almost dying, then seeing Cedar there, thousands of miles from his home.

In that moment, I couldn't bring myself to composure and allowed it all to crash around me. Deep in his embrace, I tucked my sooty cheek into his chest and cried.

Once I was cleared to leave, Cedar ushered me to his rental car. At some point, I would need to return and get mine, but it would be hours before the scene was free of ambulances and fire trucks.

As I climbed in, he leaned over and buckled my seatbelt for me, careful not to brush against the bruises and scrapes.

Even though he had never been to the area, he got back on the highway, took an exit five miles away, then pulled into a generic hotel in a touristy downtown area.

As we walked through the lobby, other guests gawked at my singed clothes, my sooty, tear-streaked face, and my utterly disheveled appearance, but I was too tired to care.

In the elevator, he pressed the button for the fourth floor and then the ground shifted beneath us. From the car to the lobby to the room, Cedar's hand in mine. In his other, he carried my purse despite my protests, saying, "You have one good hand, and I'm holding onto that one."

Tossing my bag on the bed, he waved his hand at the bland room. "Here it is." Grabbing a bottle of water from the minibar, he handed it to me. "Drink up. I'll run you a shower."

"Eight dollars," I rasped.

I tried to give the water back, but Cedar shook his head. "No, Autumn told me you hate how the water down here tastes. Do you think I care about the minibar charge right now? Drink gallons of it if it will make you better."

Not about to argue, I ripped open a small packet of hard candies nestled between a chocolate bar and salt-and-vinegar chips. As he ran the water in the bathroom, I plopped down on the edge of the bed, the water and cherry candy melting sweet on my tongue.

Toeing off my shoes, I glanced around. His bag was the same one he had at his mother's, the leather and canvas Filson brand duffle.

That's when all the questions I had raced in. What was he doing here? How did he find me so quickly? What was he here for? And did I hear him right when he said he loved me?

Sure, he said that before, but this was different, wasn't it? Him being here, saying those words. Could he mean them the way I always dreamed of?

"The shower's ready." He clutched my hands as he led me into the steam-filled bathroom.

Since he arrived in that parking lot, he had been tending to me. How far would he take it?

The shower was massive, clear glass blocking off half the space, and a bench on the other side was tucked into the corner.

"Okay, well, towels are there." He motioned to the counter. "And I don't know what kind of soap and stuff they have in those containers on the wall, but they smelled good, so hopefully, they're nice." He hesitated, looking around the bathroom as if there was more to explain. "I bet you want some privacy, so I'll leave you to—"

Swallowing hard, I prepared myself for the burn of the word. "Stay."

Twenty-three

Cedar

NEVER HAD A WORD sounded so sweet. It was raspy, and I could tell by the pinch between her brows that it pained her to say and still there had never been a word that meant so much.

I couldn't be sure Devin would forgive me, that, after all this, she could take me back, but in this moment, blackened by ash and dirt, it was enough.

With sooty fingers, she touched the bottom button of her white top, blood and ash smeared over it. Wincing, she grabbed the hem of her shirt, pulling it away from stomach but stopped with a loud huff of air.

Stepping forward, I eased each button open, parts sticking to the dried blood on her skin. Sliding the open shirt off her shoulders, I took care to not brush against the bruises A purpling mark on her ribs was blooming, and I swallowed hard at the sight.

"Who did this to you?" A muscle ticked in my jaw as I ran a finger over the sight, not quite touching it.

Devin shrugged, her throat too raw to speak.

With a shake of my head and vowing that if I ever found the person who caused it, I would make them pay, I flung the soiled shirt to the bathroom floor.

Kneeling, I unzipped her skirt on the side, sliding it down over her hips and legs.

In any other situation, slowly undressing Devin would have been a sensual dream, but it wasn't the time to let my dick get any ideas. It was about cleaning Devin up, mending her wounds, taking care of her until she felt better, and repenting.

Devin stood there, watching me with an inscrutable gaze.

Hesitating at her bra, I looked up at her green eyes, and she gave me a quick nod, turning around so I could unsnap the clasp. She didn't hide her body from me, and with her underwear joining the rest of her clothes, she stood before me.

Bruises, soot, and scratches marred her skin, but she was still the most beautiful woman I had ever seen.

As she stepped under the warm water, she tipped her face into the stream, its pressure washing away the top layer of debris.

Her hand outstretched, she motioned to me. "Come."

I didn't know what would happen after this if she would stay with me. But I wasn't about to refuse one last time with her naked. Even if it was about cleaning her up. Just to touch her again was plenty.

My clothes were in a heap beside hers and then I was behind her, squirting soap into my hands. Careful not to press too hard, I ran my palms over her skin, washing away the soot. The water at our feet was a murky gray as it swirled around the drain.

As I scrubbed away the filth of her experience, her jaw ticked as soap ran over the deep scrapes on her palms and knees, but she didn't flinch away. The bruise on her ribs was blooming into her tattoos, a myriad of pain. Once the worst of it was off, I kneeled at her feet, rinsing the soap away.

While these marks weren't made intentionally, that crowds push and trample in emergencies and there was no way she would have made it out of that blaze completely unscathed, the sight of her marred flesh set my teeth on edge. She had been hurt. Someone had done this to her, whether it be the other workers trying to get out or whoever was responsible for the fire in the first place.

I could have lost her.

Her ankle in my hand, I realized I was gripping it harder than I meant, my fingers digging into the soft skin.

Devin's fingers tightened on my shoulder, and using her fingers under my chin, she tipped up my head. Even though we were under the water and there was no way she could have seen the difference, she knew I was crying.

I wasn't a crier. I didn't cry when Alivia dumped me in college or when I tore my LCL during a big game at college. But knowing how close she had been to being one of those still bodies on the pavement was destroying me.

On my knees, I wrapped my arms around her bare middle, her soft stomach cushioning my cheek. Short, hard nails scraped against my scalp as we rocked. The tiles hard under me, but I couldn't let her go.

"I was so scared. I saw the news, and I rushed over to find you and then—"

My words were tremulous, falling over us and down the drain like soot.

Her hands moved over my hair, the hard rasp that let me know she was still here.

"I'm so sorry, Dev. I was coming for you before the—" I swallowed. "Whatever it takes, let me prove this to you, give the big speech and—"

"I want speech," she croaked, condensing her words. "But no."

No? Was this a no like she didn't want me this way? Had I missed my shot with her? Was being in the shower together about her comfort and nothing else? My arms dropped from around her waist.

Standing on quivering legs, I backed up the two steps from her, the back of my knees hitting the bench in the corner. "Okay, whatever you want, I can leave you alone."

"No." She shook her head, worrying her lower lip with her teeth and put out a hand motioning between us. "Us, for real?"

Her three-word question drew a smile to my face. "Yes, for real. I know you kept telling me not to say always, and I get why. I understand. But I have to say it now. For real, and for always."

Her response was a smile, the corners of her green eyes crinkling. "'Kay."

Then she was kissing me, her lips finding mine. Our bodies slick together.

Careful not to put my hands on her bruised sides, they slid down her body to cup her ass. Backing her into the wall and away from the shower spray, I delved between her legs, finding her hot and waiting.

She ground herself against my hand, a moan escaping her lips that I cut off with a kiss. Sliding two fingers inside her, I circled her clit with my thumb. One leg hitched up around me, her foot on the bench, opening herself to me.

My already hard cock grew heavy with need. Never had I wanted to plunge inside her more. But this couldn't be about me.

Again, I was kneeling at her feet, my mouth on her center, sucking on her clit, my fingers deeper inside her.

I was spending a lot of time on my knees for this woman, and it would surely hurt like hell in a few hours, but nothing would make me leave the taste of her sweet cunt.

Gripping my hair, she fucked my face, pressing me harder to her. The little whimpers and gasps I had spent the last month trying to recall echoed around the steamy room. Her nails dug in deeper to my nape as she fluttered around my fingers, her body shuttering at her release.

I kept licking and sucking, her strong thighs tightening around my head. She came on my tongue, the musk of her exploding in my mouth and took it greedily. Then her grip relaxed, and she leaned against the cold tiles of the shower.

Sitting back on my haunches, I stared up at her, the water still streaming down her body. Her eyes fluttered open, and she grinned at me, one hand beckoning me to stand. This kiss was languid, the motions of a woman satisfied. Her hand reached between us, wrapping around my rock-hard cock. After pumping her fist down the length of it, she searched lower, her hand cupping my tight balls while running her middle finger over the sensitive spot beyond that. No one had touched me there before.

"Fuck," I hissed. My eyes rolled back into my head, and I groaned, pushing into her grip.

A little noise like a triumphant chuckle sounded, and I knew she was enjoying the power she had over me. If she kept that up, I would come from this hand job alone, something I hadn't done in over a decade.

Alarm bells were ringing in my head. I was pushing her to do more than she was ready because she should've been resting.

Pulling away, I gave her my most stern look. "We don't have to. You're hurt and—"

"Don't care." She pushed me down on the bench and turned around, her luscious ass in front of me.

With her legs on each side of mine, she lowered herself over me, my cock sliding into her wet center. Through the steam, I could see us moving in the mirror's reflection, joined, as she mounted me. The sight of her riding me, the crease between her brows, and the parting of her lips as she went faster. My hands gripped the unmarked skin of her hips as she ground herself over me.

With one hand, she guided me to touch her clit and with the other to her breast. She was calling the shots here as she leaned against my chest, rising and falling on my cock.

It took all I had not to explode into her, but I needed her to come again, to feel everything I hadn't said in the past month in my touch.

Her head tilted back, and our mouths found each other as her pussy clenched around me. The kiss muffled her cries as she shattered above me and then I was coming, filling her up.

Her body sagged against mine, and I wrapped an arm around her waist to keep her upright. Once we both caught our breath, she ran a finger down my cheek, her eyes drifting closed.

"Bed."

It was the middle of the day, and I wasn't sure if I would be able to sleep after the events of the morning, but I helped her to her feet and then turned off the shower. As I took my time with the towel, she stood still as I got every inch of her skin dry, a coy smile playing on her lips.

As she drifted off to sleep under the crisp white hotel blanket, I made a vow. No matter what happened next, I wouldn't give up on us. I may not know the future, but I knew who I would spend it with.

Twenty-four

Devin

THE SUN WAS LOW in the sky when I woke. I barely remembered lying down under the clean bleached blankets, but it must have been hours since I was out.

Beside me, Cedar slept, his soft lips parted and a pillow crease on his cheek. His hand was resting territorially over my hip, and his feet were wedged between mine.

Had this day really happened? The failed interview, the fire, and Cedar showing up. Not quite a rescue by my savior, nonetheless. What was he doing here? Did he come for me?

For too long, I put my hopes into this man, and my desecrated heart told me it was foolish to do it again, but logically what other reason would there be? He had nothing in this place. Nothing but me.

I had hoped blindly for this man for years, wishing for things that I never thought could be. But he was here. He was mine, if only for today. My harsh words were coming back to me. Yes, at that moment, I didn't trust him but also didn't allow him a chance to explain. I allowed my fears of losing him to get in the way of the chance to love him. For him to love me.

And as he held me under the blackening sky so close to that fire, I felt nothing but love. Nothing but a sense that, with him, I would be alright. If I was foolish before, for believing in him, I would be even more foolish to allow him to go.

Cedar had never lied to me. Never gave me false promises. So, when he told me he loved me, it was real. Deep down, I always knew that. There was no world where he would say what I needed to get what he wanted. And certainly, he wouldn't travel thousands of miles away for less than complete love.

Beside me, he stirred, his face nestled into the crook of my neck.

My palms stung from the scrapes, but I couldn't let that stop me from running my fingers over his bare shoulders. He might break my heart again. This could all end in devastation, but I was going to savor these moments. What the future held, I couldn't know, but two things I was sure of: that fire was a sign moving was not a good idea. Even if I had to move into my mom's house and sleep beside her pilates machine, I needed to be home.

And second, there was no getting over Cedar Eden. What we would be after today, I couldn't say. But I knew more than I ever had before, that no one would ever compare. I didn't want anyone to try. If he wanted to, I would offer myself up to him for the taking. Maybe that made me weak, perhaps made me a fool. But loving Cedar was worth it if he felt the same.

The thought of a future with Cedar had me drawing in air, the sensation rough against my throat.

One blue eye opened, lighting on my face, and the grin he gave me was enough to take my ragged breath away.

"You stayed."

Nodding, I cupped his cheek with my hand, my fingers resting on that scar on his temple, the divot rough against my skin.

My stomach rumbled, a reminder that it had been hours since the lack-luster Pad Thai. Hours since everything had changed.

"I should feed you. I don't know if this place had room service but—"

"I can feed myself, you know?"

Smoothing my hair from my temple, he leaned closer, his forehead against mine. "But you shouldn't have to. I want to feed you and wash away the soot and be here. And I know you don't need me, but maybe you still want me."

Maybe? *Maybe?*

As if my love for him had never wavered. As if there could be anyone else that compared. Even when I wanted to curse his name, even when the sting of feeling second best compared to the leggy blondes of his past haunted me, I still wanted him.

Loving him was foolish and vulnerable. But I could never stop the feeling.

"You don't belong down here so far away from your friends, from your family, from—" He swallowed hard, his blue eyes downcast.

"Finish your sentence," I murmured, needing the words desperately. Needing him bared to me.

Hope filled my chest, and for the first time, I rejected the impulse to tamp it down and allowed it to expand, to create visions of what could be.

"You belong with me. It's taken me far too long to realize it, and I will spend all my days proving it to you—" He huffed, burying his face in my chest, his day-old stubble rough against my breasts as he shook his head. When he raised himself on one elbow, it was with a resolute glint in his gaze. "I had this big plan. I was going to show up with a bouquet and take you out for a nice dinner and—"

"I don't need that." It still hurt to talk, but it was getting easier. "You're here, for me?"

His eyes softened.

"Of course, I am. I wanted to go to you the minute you kicked me out of your grandparent's house but also—" He swallowed hard, glancing away. "I had some reflection I need to do. Growing up. You were right about me.

You always saw what no one else did. I needed to do the work to deserve you. I'm sure I have a long way to go—and who knows, maybe I never will. But at least I feel like I know how to try. You make me want to be better. Every single day, I will get up and try for you. For us. I want to make you vegetarian pasta every night and collect eggs from asshole chickens for your breakfast. To sit for your paintings, and to be the first person at what I know will be many gallery installations. I want to teach you how to make a fire and to let you teach me how to make those pancakes. Every night, I want those paint-flecked fingers on me and every morning I want to wake up to you blinking blindly at me until you find your glasses. Please say you'll let me."

I opened my mouth to answer, unsure of the right thing to say. Swallowing hard, I ran my fingers through his messy hair as he kept talking.

"Loving you happened so swiftly I hardly knew I was there until it was too late. I can't take it back, I won't. It's like there is everyone else and then—" He cupped my cheek, his thumb tracing my lower lip. "And then there's you, and I think I've always known that you were special, that, to me, you were perfect, but it scared me. It's so intense I can't be real, it can't stay. Could it? But then it never went away. From that night at the bonfire, you took that terrible fruity beer out of my hand, and your eyes were so big, and I was overcome. Because it was messy and complicated and isn't it so much easier to be with someone who never challenges me, never expects me to be better for myself? But that sensation of holding you, it remains. I've always loved you, even if I was too scared to admit it."

My voice was rough, from the tears trickling down my cheeks and the smoke damage, but no matter how it burned, I was getting the words out. "I tried. For so long, I wanted to forget, to not love you the way I do. But I can't. No matter how hard I try, the years and the bad dates and the world spinning away, how much I love you has never changed."

His answer was a soft kiss, a tender nibble of my lower lip as he rolled on top of me. His hands careful not to brush against the bruises. As his lips moved over my body, a low hum I couldn't make out until his mouth was over mine had me realizing he was whispering the same words into my skin.

"I love you, I love you, I love you."

We never made it to dinner that night.

Epilogue

Late fall in Ridgewood meant one thing, the damp oppressive rain, as always. The row of pumpkins on the three steps of our rented home in Ridgewood Place glowed with battery-operated candles. My first attempt at carving was deemed "unsightly" by the homeowner's association of the neighborhood. Why anyone would have an issue with various horror movie villains depicted in intricate detail, I couldn't be sure, but we gave those to Van and Summer for their house on the outskirts of town. The HOA had already fined us when I painted a scene featuring the woods and our treehouse on the garage door. Apparently, the shade Swiss Coffee was the most creative I could get if I didn't like ultra-white.

Cedar had signed a year lease, which we wouldn't be renewing. We were already on the hunt for a new place. Once I returned to town, I technically lived at my mom's house for three months before she told me—since I was never actually there—that I might as well move in with Cedar.

I got a new job at a department store chain, working as a graphic designer and brand manager. The job was mostly remote, so I only needed to go into the office in Seattle twice a month. The job afforded me with an employee discount for their high-end clothes and flexibility to still have some extra time for my growing side work as a painter.

In the months since we moved back, I had created three paintings and was in talks with Catalina Hirsch to have them exhibited at the gallery. It wasn't a fancy place in Seattle, but it was a start.

Scalpel in hand, I carved out the quarter wave of my replica of a pop art painting. I took some creative liberties with the depth, as pumpkin skin wasn't my usual medium.

From my place in the kitchen, I heard the door opening and called out, "I had to give away the Freddy Krueger pumpkin because that bitch, Lois, told me it's 'not fitting with the propriety and decorum our neighborhood upholds.'"

No answer aside from a low bang followed by a curse.

"Cedar? Is that you?" I wanted to think that my survival skills had gone up a notch since that day I tried to confront him straight from the bath, but I wasn't that much better. Knife in hand and pumpkin guts sticking to my wrist, I walked around the corner to find Cedar wrestling with an oversized canvas in the hallway.

"What are you doing?" I asked, watching him as he pivoted the frame.

Stopping, his eyes met mine, a furrow between his brows. He glanced from me to behind him, a shifty expression on his face. "What are you doing home, I thought Baba needed your help with errands today?"

My grandma had fallen and fractured her leg five weeks before while trying to hang a harvest wheat decoration on the outside of her home. I had been going over every few days to help around the house and keep her company while she was laid up.

"Jiji forgot to tell me she had a checkup today; she might get a walking boot put on." Setting the paring knife down, I wiped my hands on my apron. "What you got there?"

"This was supposed to be a surprise for when you got home from Baba and Jiji's. You weren't supposed to see it until I had it hung up." On his forearm, his new tattoo stood out dark against his sun-tanned arm. Though

I had never drawn a tattoo for someone else, he insisted that any ink he had on his skin must be created by me. The treehouse inside a cherry tree, the pink blossoms blooming over the roof.

In the months since Cedar came to get me from Phoenix, my grandparents' opinion of him had changed. Though Cedar had more than proved his mettle, Jiji was reluctant to forgive him. They finally bonded over the Fourth of July party, when Cedar set up the entire pickleball court for the guests, something Jiji struggled with in years past.

Despite Summer's frosty attitude toward him, her fiancé, Van, had taken to him right away, bonding over the love of the Sounders and Seahawks. They were even planning to go to a game in late November. Autumn, of course, liked everyone, and Wren told me if I was happy, she was happy.

Quirking a grin, I stood my ground. "So, what do you want me to do, cover my eyes like a little kid until you get it past me?"

"That's a good idea. Close your eyes and stand in the—" He paused as he rearranged the canvas. "In the kitchen with your eyes closed. Don't come out until I tell you."

"Ced, this is ridiculous."

His blue eyes narrowed in on mine before he rested the canvas half in the door frame. His hands on my shoulders, he turned me away from the hall and marched me back into the kitchen.

"You're being silly."

"I'm being romantic." Placing me behind the counter, he handed me a glass of wine, which I took with sticky fingers—I really needed to wash my hands. "Devin Hanae, don't you dare come out until I say so."

Leaving me with a quick kiss to the nose, he went back into the hallway where bangs, more curses, and the suspicious sound of screeching echoed.

Ten minutes later, I had cleaner hands and finished my wine, when Cedar came back to collect me.

His fingers covered my eyes as he walked behind me, guiding me into our bedroom. "Are you ready?"

"You know I am."

Free from my blindfold, I blinked across the room at the oversized canvas adorning the wall above our bed. Greens and browns embellished an explosion of ferns around the entwined couple. Us.

Not only was it us but the painting I made for my senior presentation. Years before, I had sold it off for fifty dollars to some random man at the college. I never thought I'd see it again. Hadn't thought about it much, in fact.

In the time since, I had drawn and painted Cedar and I countless times. This wasn't even my best work. The line work was uneven, the perception atrocious, and I was clearly going for a fauvism when I should have stuck to a more impressionist style.

"I don't—how did you—"

I couldn't decide what to look at, Cedar or the painting.

"Catalina. I asked her if she could track it down."

"I hope you didn't pay too much for it. I think I sold it for fifty bucks."

"Don't worry aboutt hat."He flapped his hand at my comment. "I had to have it. Since I saw it. Catalina's been working on getting it for months."

"Months, but how did you even know about this thing?"

So, he told me the story of looking it up online, of tracking down the painting, of how the only place that portrait belonged was in our room. Of what it symbolized to him.

"It was a part of you, of us. This painting doesn't belong in some random man's foyer. It belongs to me. Just like you do."

Meeting in the middle, my hands found his waist, and his lips were on mine. Walking back into the bed, he fell on top of me. Fingers and teeth, my legs wrapped around his waist. We came together, with our new painting hanging high above us as proof that we were always meant to be.

In the kitchen, beside the abandoned half carved pumpkin, my phone was lighting up with a new message in our group thread. I wouldn't see the words until the morning.

> *Autumn: two lines mean positive, right?*

Acknowledgements

The early version of this story was created mid pandemic, the original title being Lover for the Edge of the World. It took me an entire rockstar romance series, a holiday novella, and my baby novel, Reckless Liar to get this story completed. I'm so thankful for all the people who helped on the way.

Cassidy Connors for all things chicken collecting, for proofreading, and for being the first one to laugh at my asshole's named Josh joke.

To my safeplace girls, Laura, Amanda, Shannon, Megan, Carmen, and Renee. Thank you for being exactly who I need in friends and for pointing out that I can't have the word "tits" on my cover.

To Super Deluxe for writing one of the most underrated regret songs ever, *"Year's Ago"*. You can find grainy copies on YouTube and as a PNW millennial growing up on 107.7 it was everything.

To the local coffee shops whose help me out of my slumps, Caffe Cocina, Hot Shots, Latte on Your Way and Over the Moon Roasters.

To the Cherry Blossoms at the University of Washington for existing.

To Megumi for help with Japanese translations and answering all my questions. Heidi for all things medical, Kat Waag for the tree service expertise and for being nothing like Caleb. Kate McWilliams for sharing how much a corgi weighs, M.J. Marino for suggesting Erupting Spring as a title, Greta Rose West for giving me this title. All mistakes are mine.

As always, my kids for interrupting me with talk of e-bikes and

Minecraft. My husband Rusty for building me an office to write, and loving my dreams as much as I do.

About the Author

Linnea March is a contemporary romance author who writes steamy stories about self-confident women and the rugged men who love them. She lives somewhere in the wilds of the Pacific Northwest with her husband, their two boys, and a plump dog. After fifteen years of teaching early childhood education, she put down the googly eyes and picked up a pen. When not writing, she can be found reading her way through an ever-growing pile of books while drinking copious amounts of coffee. She proudly refuses to use umbrellas.

Also by Linnea March

Prevalent Notion Series
Faultless Notion
Treacherous Notion
Ruinous Notion

Seasons of Us
Wren's Winter
Villainous Summer
Second Chance Spring

Other Titles
Reckless Liar
The One You Chose